f-Holes of
MELANCHOLIA

A Novel

by

Laurel Mae Hislop

MANNA MARK

f-holes

Where
the music
escapes

Published in Canada by Manna Mark Books

Vancouver, British Columbia

Library and Archives Canada Cataloguing in Publication

Hislop, Laurel Mae, 1953-

Chitchat / Laurel Mae Hislop

A Novel

ISBN 978-0-9938237-2-5

Table of Contents

To the memory of Etta May Hislop

Prologue

I was born in 1905, the year of Bloody Sunday in St. Petersburg when Papa was thirty years old. He said I was a gift during turbulent times, but I don't recall much turbulence when we lived there, only some disturbing impressions from that year we left our home. I do my best to push the dark memories out of my mind. It's better to remember happy times.

Life in Russia was full of music and concerts and dinner parties with important people. Papa and I had our music and that mattered most. People flocked to our home after I was called to play at the Metropol at ten years of age. 'Katya Pavlova Sadilov is a child prodigy,' they said. But I didn't feel like a wonder child until I mastered my first Paganini piece at thirteen. His music was my measure of success, and remained so even later when we emigrated to Canada and the concert halls were a fading memory.

Some say Niccolò Paganini was double-jointed. He could contort his arms, bend his elbows backward, spread his fingers along the neck of the violin, position the instrument behind his back, writhe across the stage, and play with a mastery no musician could match.

I often dreamed of Paganini, not only in my sleep, but also as I played. At times he stood next to me, but on occasion his spirit slipped into me and urged, "Katya, like this, Katya." Then my bones floated beneath my skin. My fingers transformed into long-knuckled tentacles and it was Paganini who raised my arm and swept the bow across the strings. The notes that followed were not of this world.

CHAPTER ONE

Opportunity

WE started out at first light and by midmorning we could see Papa's house. It was early March and the pond behind the barn was still frozen enough to bear the weight of horse and sleigh. The runners sprayed sparks of snow in a stream on either side of us. Ice cracked under Gust's hooves and George hollered, "Giddap." He half stood and whapped the reins. Clouds of white escaped his mouth.

I saw the surface of the pond crack open, my husband and I and the sleigh plunging into the icy water, the noise of the world hushed. My husband's coat billowed out and away from his body, his scarf drawn up as a hangman's noose and he drifted away, farther and farther until I could no longer see his nose or mouth or the red of his scarf.

It was only one of my apparitions, an accident unlikely to transpire.

I'd not had many such visions since coming to Canada. In Russia, the year we left, they'd been frequent. That was in 1918 and I was fourteen years old. I'd seen thin children melting into the pavement, mangled bodies on the steps of the Winter Palace, and in Palace Square a row of flesh and bone ice statues with faces twisted and tortured in pain. But, the cloud vision was the one that scared me most. It wasn't only visual, but corporeal, dust churning and sucking up the air, a foul smelling froth of dirt making it impossible to breathe or see.

I've kept the visions to myself since childhood. Mama called them morbid thoughts when I tried to describe them, but she hadn't understood. They are not thoughts I will to happen. They're full-colour, all-consuming visions that take over my mind.

Still, until the runners of the sleigh slid onto firm ground I fisted my hands to my chest. I needn't have. My husband brought us safely to Papa's house. Little did I know, how this visit would spark events to change my life.

Mama and Papa ran out to greet us, hugging me and shaking George's hand. They were excited, chattering away in Russian until they noticed George gazing off at the barn and they switched to English.

"I've made up the bed. Your old room." Mama said.

George stepped forward then. "We shouldn't stay overnight.

The livestock."

"The animals will be fine for one night, George." I frowned at him. "Besides, even if we leave now, it'll be dark before we're half-way home." We had to stay over if we were to have any sort of visit. Our farm was a formidable distance away. We'd only just arrived, and my husband was already planning our departure.

George shifted from one foot to the other. "Well, I don't know."

"It is settled then. You'll stay." Papa gave George a comrade's slap on the arm.

My husband looked at the ground. Around others, especially Papa, his face tightened, as if a shoe pinched. Thankfully, he considered himself a man of God. I convinced him he could not, in good conscience, miss a Sunday service when we were only a stone's throw away from the church.

Later that afternoon I cradled my violin and wandered the parlour back and forth. You could barely see the top of Papa's bureau for books. Many were stacked and others lined up, supported by iron bookends engraved with Alexander the Great taming his horse, Bucephalus.

In this room, if I closed my eyes, I saw the vast chambers of the St. Petersburg gallery with its statues and paintings and art. For years the drawings of Paganini had been stencilled into my mind. He'd been a thin man with a bent frame and dark hair that rolled along his spine, as long and as ebony as mine. I told

George that when I stood in front of a mirror, it was often Paganini who stared back.

George knew nothing of Paganini.

He'd said, "Sometimes you worry me. Your imagination is too vivid for your own good." Truth told, I often worried over how little imagination my husband had.

I paced back and forth amongst Papa's jumble heap of books. Only one wall was bare, the space reserved for a piano Papa had been saving for since we'd arrived in Canada seven years ago.

"Owners of land," Papa had declared the day we drove up to the rickety clapboard house on the outskirts of Sylvite, Saskatchewan. On first sight of the property Mama covered her eyes. "This is wilderness. How will we survive?"

That winter she sewed curtains, crocheted coverings for the rustic furniture, and hooked rugs of red and purple fabric. It was 1919, and we had such hope. The Great War had come to an end. Russia was still in chaos, but we had escaped harm. We wanted to love this new life.

Violin lifted to my shoulder, I played the *Caprice No 13*. It wasn't one of Paganini's most difficult arrangements, but my hands vibrated. Few pieces challenged me as Paganini's did, but many fiddlers completely avoided his work. I'd been renowned for my dexterity as early as the age of eight. "Fingers like dancing spiders," Master Auer used to say.

When I finished the song, I sat at the gate-leg table in the far corner of the room and leafed through sheet music looking for something different to play. Mama was in the kitchen and I hummed along with the sounds of clicking jars and the bubbling noises from the canner. The aroma of cabbage and vinegar wet the air.

Papa burst in waving an envelope.

"Good, you're here, Katya." He grinned at me and bellowed, "Olga, come to the parlour. I have news."

Mama piped back. "I have news too. Twelve jars of your best sauerkraut squash ready to seal."

"Come in, woman. The jars can wait."

Mama appeared in the doorway, wiped her hands on her apron, a shiny flush on her round cheeks.

"Remember my friend Gustav?" Papa held a letter up by its corner and jiggled it.

"The piccolo player from St. Petersburg?" Mama asked.

"Yes, yes. He is in Edmonton now. I wrote to him."

"You have been writing to him for years." Mama pressed the back of her hand against her forehead.

"I know, but I told him about Katya."

"That's nice," Mama said. "You tell your friends about your daughter."

"No, no I informed him of her talent."

"That's nice." Mama nodded. "You brag about your daughter."

"I may have to get out a stick, Olga." Papa wagged a finger at her.

I laughed.

"Gustav has an orchestra," Papa said, "in Edmonton. He requires a violinist for a performance at the end of May. They call it Northern Lights Transposed. A good name, eh? He has asked for Katya to play."

I thought, at first, I heard him wrong. An orchestra and me playing?

"They will pay her?" Mama crossed her arms over her ample bosom.

"No, this is a charity, to help young musicians with the gift."

"And where will we find the money?" Mama's eyebrows lifted to a V.

"The money. The money. Is that all you think of, woman?"

"And what of George? Do you think he'll want his new wife running away to play in an orchestra?"

"If George has sense, he will be happy."

"Where is George?" Mama asked.

I reached up for the letter. "He rode to town for a roll of wire to repair something on the sleigh."

"He is back now, outside fixing the runner." Papa grinned, raised the envelope over my head, just out of reach. I tugged at his sleeve and he dropped it in my hand.

It was common paper, not textured as letters from Russia were. I tore the document out of its covering and scanned the words, the trumpets and cellos of the Russian alphabet emblazoned on the page. "Papa, is it true? An orchestra? And I can play?"

"Yes, a complete orchestra." Papa smiled as if he'd eaten a *pelmeni*. Imitating a conductor, he raised his index fingers, closed his eyes, tilted his head back, and swayed to an imaginary tune. Then he stopped, stepped forward, put a hand on each of my shoulders, and pulled me into a hug. "I will speak to your husband."

"No, you'd best let me do it," I said. "Once we get there tomorrow or on the way home. I'll ask him then."

There was nothing in George's manner toward Papa that anyone could criticise, but if the matter required persuasion... It might even be better to wait until we were pressed up against each other under the covers, in our bed.

"That is the way it should be." Mama's plump fingers rolled into fists on her hips. "Do not open your mouth, Vasha. This decision is for George and Katya."

Papa walked around the entire afternoon like a magpie with his beak tied shut. At supper he winked at me when he passed the sausage and again when he passed the *voreniki*. Mama kept a leery eye on him.

Sunday morning George rose early as usual, shuffled around and went outside. Nestled into the same down quilt I'd had as a girl, a dream slipped into me.

I stood high on top of a mountain in a flowing dress, a pale colour, lake ice touched by the sun. The air was frost. My fingertips were blue. The lip of ground I balanced on was only a few inches wide and in all directions a sheer drop. Overhead, a crow flew. It made no noise, but I saw its shadow descend and felt a wing sing by my ear. The sun hung frozen in the sky. A shuffling and the chink of pebbles resounded loud. I peeked, and spied a distant figure climbing up a mountain path. The crow swept by my face again, and my foot skidded, but I remained calm. The bird flew off—became a dot on the distant view. The man grew close. It was Niccolò Paganini, truly him. A marble staircase emerged, and I stepped onto it. He reached out, took my hands and silver motes of sizzling snow whirled around us.

I slipped out of bed and tiptoed along the hall to Mama and Papa's room.

"Mama, wake up." I knelt beside the bed and touched her shoulder.

Papa's space along the wall was empty. Light seeped into the room.

"Mmmm." She rolled away from me and pulled the covers tight to her neck.

"It's freezing, Mama. Can I get in?" I pressed the middle of her back.

"It is still dark." She moved over enough to let me squeeze in beside her. She was voluptuous and warm with her own delicate fragrance of lilac and laundry soap.

"I've had an incredible romantic dream, but frightful too."

"Umm, yes, a dream." Mama's slipped one hand out from the covers and patted my head.

I locked my fingers behind my neck. "I have to tell you, Mama, before I forget."

"Yes. Dreams melt away in the light."

"Remember that awful storm on the ship, on our way to Canada? It was scary like that." From my view through the porthole, enormous waves had reared up, bloodthirsty monsters of the sea. I'd been sure the boat would flip.

When I finished recounting my dream she rolled closer. "You are ice." She hugged me. For a moment we were back in her feather bed in St. Petersburg, snow flying outside the windowpane, snug in her cosy room. The Revolution was unheard of. Bolsheviks did not march the streets and watch your every move. Life was safe and warm.

Later that morning in the kitchen, after the dream faded and before we left for church, Mama set two baking pans out on tea towels, brought the four corners up on each side, and tied handle knots.

"Two coffeecakes?" Papa sat at the table, coddling his cup as if he had no intention of moving an inch.

"Yes, I had the raisins for two."

"The other women do not bring so much." Papa shook his head.

"Will you carry them?" Mama wiped a few crumbs off the table and tossed them in the sink.

As soon as she turned, Papa made a sad clown face. He grabbed the back of the chair beside him and feigned hoisting himself up with a grunt. I stifled a guffaw. If it were up to Papa or me, we would not bother with the church in town, but it was Mama's only opportunity for social discourse. I often wondered, though, why she even made an attempt for that stall of miserable cows who berthed the pews at the Sylvite United Church.

"I can bring the cakes." George picked them up before Papa was on his feet.

"You look nice, Mama," I said. She wore her good coat with the sable collar and fur hat to match. Her purse dangled on her arm as if setting off to the Opera. My mama had more class in her toenail clippings than any woman within a hundred-mile radius of Sylvite.

"We will be late." She pushed ahead and out the door to the waiting sleigh.

It was a four-passenger bob-sleigh and had been in my husband's family for years. It had torn leather seats and horsehair stuffing, pushing through the cracks as if trying to find a place in the world. Harnessed up and ready to go, Gust pawed the snow. Sleigh bells pealed a cheery tune as we set out.

When we stopped across the street from the church Reverend Manning was not outside on the top step as usual, but Mrs. Stanley was there, blathering to Mrs. Kite and Spinster Freeman from the Ladies League. George jumped down to tie up the horse.

"I wonder what her lecture is today," I said to Papa as George helped Mama out of the sleigh. "How immigrants and Roman Catholics are ruining the country, no doubt."

Mrs. Stanley turned, looked right through us, touched the arms of the women and led them into the church. I skidded on a patch of ice and George steadied me. Mama pulled on Papa's arm to hurry him across the yard. For a man with such long legs, Papa could dawdle. But what a handsome gentleman he was. White hair waved behind his ears and he always used wax to turn up the edges of his inky moustache. Papa's good suit fit as it did the day the tailor fitted him in St. Petersburg.

The warm air of the church was suffocating after our ride. I unwound my scarf and let my coat slip off my shoulders. Mama must have been hot too, but she left hers buttoned up tight. George placed the coffeecakes on the long table in the foyer and we entered the chapel. The pews overflowed with women in hats and bald men stuffed into ill-fitting suits. A baby wailed.

Mrs. Stanley occupied her stall like a nasty little terrier. She turned, saw Mama and Papa approach and shifted over to block the unoccupied space beside her. George and I squeezed into an empty spot near the rear, next to two fidgeting boys who kicked at each other. Mama and Papa found seats up front. I barely heard a word of the Reverend's sermon and hardly noticed the hymns. I was too busy conjuring an image of Mrs. Stanley trapped in a dank, dark well as I leered down from above.

After the service the horrid woman held court in the centre of the foyer, holding up her cake as if it had won first prize at the fall fair. Stout Mrs. Wilson shuffled in and said, "Oh, Mrs. Stanley, what a wonderful cake." It was a gaudy white thing decorated with swirls of icing and shavings of chocolate.

"It's a Seven Egg Cake from Ladies Home Journal." She walked to the food display. Balancing the cake in one hand she moved the other baking around to make room for her monstrosity in a central spot.

Another image possessed me, a delightful vision, but I had to act fast. I steered through the crowd toward the table and Mrs. Stanley. I stopped right next to the wicked old hen. I leapt and cried, "A mouse!" Throwing my hands in the air, I lurched sideways and hurtled my whole body at her.

The cake wobbled on her hand. She reached with the other hand to steady it, lost her balance, and she and her creation collided with the floor. White icing splattered the walls, the floor, the ceiling, and Reverend Manning's dark robe.

I brought one palm to my chest. "I'm sorry. Mice scare me half to death." Pausing for a moment, I surveyed the spectacle, swallowed a lump of laughter and then scurried to the side door. I couldn't resist the urge to glance back.

"You. You…" Mrs. Stanley hissed. Skirt askew, she struggled onto her knees, one lovely blob of Seven Egg Cake stuck in her hair just above her ear. Reverend Manning offered her his hand.

"Excuse me." I ran along the hall to the washroom, flung the door shut, squatted, and to smother a bubble of giggles, stuffed my sleeve in my mouth. By the time Mama came to find me, I regretted the incident, not because of what I did, but because of Mama. I embarrassed her. She'd had so many friends in St. Petersburg, but here she had only Papa and me.

"Oh, Katya. You should take more care." She looped her arm through mine and pulled me up. "Don't worry. I helped the Reverend clean the mess." She led me out through the side door to where George and Papa waited.

Once home we settled around Mama's table. George faced me with a serious expression. "Did you knock Mrs. Stanley over on purpose, Kat?"

"Katya would never do that intentionally, George." Mama shook her head.

"I saw a mouse. You know how I hate mice." I tried to push the scene out of my mind, but it had been so comical, that gooey mess of icing in that horrible woman's gauzy hair. I looked over at Papa who did not even try to disguise the merriment in his eye.

Papa chuckled. "Mrs. Stanley has taken a humble position in church for the first time in her life."

"The poor woman," Mama said. "Vasha, you should not laugh."

"Poor woman? That evil shrew?"

"We've got a long ride ahead of us." George stood, left a full cup of coffee and headed outside to hitch up Gust.

Mama had packed a basket of food for our trip home. We were to have an outdoor picnic and I couldn't wait to ask George about the concert. I'd never had a winter picnic but imagined it similar to ice fishing, a commonplace scene in the St. Petersburg of my youth. Ice fishing men had dotted the frozen mouth of the Neva at dawn, holes cut in the ice, warming their hands over small cook stoves. Being outdoors with hot food evoked a certain level of ease. How could he say no?

It was brittle cold and Mama lent me her rabbit muff, the one she kept wrapped up in a silk scarf in the cedar chest. I packed our few things, went outside, climbed up in the sleigh, rubbed my hands inside the luxurious lining, peered at the sky and tried to visualise the musicians in Gustav's orchestra. George fussed with the harness and adjusted a jumble of straps that connected the horse to the rigging.

"There, ready." George bent to inspect the runner, grasped a wooden shaft wrapped in layers of wire, and gave it a shake. "It'll hold till we get home." Then he stood and stretched.

My husband was a handsome man despite one unfortunate oddity, eyes that always appeared half-closed. A family trait, someone once told me. People thought he lacked intelligence, but George was smart. Mama had considered him a catch when he'd first called. "A real Canadian," she'd said. "He has feet to the ground and a good farm too, and a house, solid and big. A lucky girl, you are."

At twenty-one my love for physical attributes was considerable. With George's workhorse shoulders and cherub face, I tingled at the sight of him. And he could be kind. He'd placed warm rocks on the floor and I rested my boots on them. As he covered my legs with a heavy quilt, I brushed his lips with my fingertips. He smiled.

Papa approached from the barn. "Cold. The thermometer reads ten below zero." He rubbed his gloves together by his chest. Relieved of his church clothes, he looked very much the countryman. Long furry pads on his hat dangled to his shoulders and red knit socks exploded from his boots.

"Yes," George stomped his feet on the spot. "Should warm up soon though." He waved one arm at the blue sky and then adjusted Gust's halter.

"John Dari thinks we should seed early," Papa said. "But we will need more snow."

"Heard they had quite the storm over at Lloydminster last week, at least five inches, drifts up over the fences." George studied the rudder.

Gust snorted and stomped. I shifted in my seat, rubbing my boots against the rapidly cooling rocks. My feet would be frozen bricks by the time the men finished talking. The old scar under my nose was numb. I pulled one hand out of the muff and rubbed until my lip prickled.

It was half-past eleven before we set out. I looked back at Papa's house as the sleigh whisked us away. The house grew small and Papa's figure diminished to a dark spot on the bleached landscape. A black bird circled in the sky above the farmhouse, trailing us. Oh, how this flat land resembled a white sea stretching to the edge of the world. Behind Papa's farm, the buildings of Sylvite blurred on the horizon.

Nostalgia

Vasili looked over at the photograph on his dresser. Katya stood out, a porcelain doll against the blurred orchestra of the background. She had been small then, but what a presence on stage. And the call for her to play at the Metropol before age eleven—only a handful had been so honoured. She wore the white dress her Mama had sewn with care. Even then, little Katya knew how to hold her violin with perfect form. He hummed as he undressed for bed. Things had not turned out so terrible.

"Is it wise, Vasha?" Olga sat in front of her commode. She raked a brush through grey-streaked hair that flowed to her waist.

"What?"

"Should she go? I'm afraid for her." She twisted her neck around and looked at him with lantern eyes.

He pulled his nightshirt over his head and walked to her, put his hand out and stroked her head. "You should not worry." Olga's hair was not as soft as it once was, but still beautiful. "Gustav promised to look after her."

"That is why I worry. Gustav is a rogue."

"That was many years ago. He is a married man now."

"Your daughter too, is married now. Do you forget?" Olga had a pleasant face, plump cheeks that would never grow lines, but not so pleasant when she frowned.

"It is an opportunity for her." He bent and kissed his wife's forehead. "She will be on stage again as she was years ago. Remember our pride?"

"What used to be is no more, Vasha, and overgrown with grass. Katya has a different life here."

"She still has the music. Do you recognise this song, Olga?" He pulled his wife up into his arms and danced her around the room, bent her backward until her hair brushed the floor. "Hm

Hmm Hm Hmm Hmm Hm… Oh, those dances at the Metropol."

"You will drop me." She clutched his shirt, and he lifted her back to her feet and kissed her cheek.

Olga settled on the edge of the bed. "But, Vasha, the money. What of your piano?"

"I will buy it one day. It can wait."

"Could you not go with her? Take the egg money."

"It would not be enough. And you need it to buy your pretty threads. It is your money." Vasili walked to the dresser and picked up the photograph. "Ah, I would love to see her play with an orchestra again. But no, she will be fine. You must not worry." He placed the picture back on the top of the dresser.

"What if something happens, like before?"

"That was a long time ago. Nothing will happen." But even as he said this, and believed it, his light mood disappeared.

Katya was born in 1905 at the start of the troubles in Russia. The strife continued over the years, but they had escaped, and it was worth every sacrifice living in this country far from danger. Vasili picked up his good leather shoes from the floor beside the wardrobe and inspected them. The shine had faded, and one heel was worn to the ground, but he opened the drawer, and pulled out a tin of mink oil and the shoe rag.

"Come to bed," Olga said. She turned down the comforter and nestled under the covers.

"In a minute. You sleep. I will come soon." He eased onto a

chair by the dresser with the rag in one hand and a shoe in the other. Olga snored softly as he rubbed the black leather.

It was not so bad, this new country, not Russia, but a musician had some opportunities. If only the world was a different place. He longed for an easier life for Olga. Money had never been a concern when Vasili played for the orchestra of the Imperial Theatre. He performed for the most prominent people in the Empire including the Czar and his family. Until recent years, his home country had valued and respected the arts. He cursed the day he had heard the term Bolshevik. He sighed. But here in Canada at least they had a chance. Life was never like crossing a meadow.

Vasili had bought this Saskatchewan land, sight unseen, from a company in Winnipeg the day they'd stepped off the train there. He should have waited, but what did he know of such things? Vasili knew music as his father had before him, and with music his world was rich. He understood nothing of land or farms, but if peasants could prosper here, surely an educated man could do well.

'Near a fair-sized town with a fine house, barn, and cleared land', the land agent had told him and 'only five dollars an acre.' Vasili paid him outright, received the title right then. He, Olga and young Katya reboarded the train to Sylvite with only two hundred dollars left.

That agent neglected to mention several facts. The fine house was a clapboard box wrapped in tarpaper with a sod roof. The barn was a rickety shack leaned over so far a strong wind might topple it. But the most terrible fact he neglected to tell was that 80 acres was not enough land to profit from. What Vasili had also not considered was the necessity to buy livestock, a wagon, a team, and the equipment required to farm grain. Wheat, the land agent declared, was the only crop worth seeding on the Saskatchewan prairie.

A man named John Dari helped them. He spotted them at the station that first day and helped to unload the trunks from the train. Lucky for them, Mr. Dari's farm was a ten-minute walk from the fine house Vasili purchased. The next day John Dari took Vasili to a nearby cattle trader and helped him to choose a cow. Over the next few weeks he advised Vasili on livestock, supplies, and equipment. The roll of bills in Vasili's pocket disappeared within three weeks. With fall upon them it was too late to plant a crop, but a good cow stood in the barn and a pen full of chickens squawked in the back yard. Many new immigrants arrived without a *ruble*. And thanks to Olga's practical nature, delicious smells wafted through the kitchen every day. She had kept them going that first winter, trading her eggs and milk at Walker's store for flour and coal to heat the house.

Vasili thought how quiet and strange evenings were without

Katya as he sat at the kitchen table gripping a small glass of vodka and fiddling with his pipe. The wind that shook the windows most nights was barely a ripple and the rhythmic click of Olga's knitting needles, the only other sound.

"Maybe the postman is sick," Vasili said.

"No, I saw him go to John Dari's house," Olga said.

The rap of her foot against the metal kindling rack exploded like sour notes from a cello.

"Will you stop that?" Vasili pressed his fingers to one ear.

"What?"

"The noise you make with your foot."

"Why don't you go to bed? You are tired."

He got up, dug in the cupboard for a pipe cleaner, sat again, dismantled his pipe, and prodded the stem. "I am not tired." After screwing the pipe back together, he filled the bowl with tobacco. "I wonder what George will say. Do you think he'll refuse to let her go?" Vasili had spoken to George about Katya's old troubles the night of their wedding and now he regretted the warning. Because of this, George may not want her to travel alone.

"Why do you worry," Olga said. "It is up to her husband."

"I am her father."

"You are her father but remember, you gave her away at the wedding ceremony. And do not forget who invited George Brown to this house."

"She wanted to meet him." He swiped a match along the striking edge of the box and held the flame up over his pipe. A trumpet-shaped cloud of smoke billowed up before his face. "I did not think she intended to marry him."

"Now you complain."

"I do not complain. But she must play with Gustav's orchestra. I have promised."

At the house, after the marriage ceremony, Vasili had squeezed George's arm and then patted him on the back. He did not tell him every detail. He only said, "Watch if she doesn't sleep, if she refuses to eat. Do not leave her alone if this happens. She is an artist and melancholy is strong in one so sensitive." George did not need more information on his wedding night. It was best not to dwell on difficulties.

Olga leaned forward in the rocking chair and the wooden rungs creaked. "The world will not end if she stays home with her husband. You should not have promised."

"If George says no, I will take her myself."

The click of knitting needles stopped. Olga raised a needle and pointed it at him. "You will not. You will not interfere."

Olga was right. The Edmonton concert did not matter. What was one small exhibition in the middle of wilderness compared to the Metropol? Vasili closed his eyes and shook his head. "She wastes her gift here. I should not have brought her here. We should have gone to New York."

Olga wiggled the needle at him. "We discussed it then. New York was too dangerous." She let her hands fall to her lap and leaned forward. "You, my husband, have given her the biggest gift, the gift of life."

"And what good is life, without music?"

"She has the music. Those are your words. She has her violin and now she has a husband too."

"A musician needs an audience. You cannot perform for wheat or cows. The people here know nothing of music."

"But she knows, husband. She knows, and that does not change. Nothing can forbid her to live musically. Come now. We should sleep."

Olga dropped her ball of yarn, walked over to him, and ran her fingers through his hair. "We will go upstairs and make our own music, no?"

Vasili rose and followed her. A man was easily led by his woman.

CHAPTER TWO

Waiting

AS George and I drove away from Papa and Mama's that day, acre upon acre of pastures vibrated with white music. The concert nearly slipped my mind.

"Isn't it beautiful, George?"

"What's beautiful?"

"The glitter of the snow. The black fences."

"Yes, it's nice." He leaned sideways and squinted at the runner of the sleigh.

We reached Hollow Belly Lake by midday. A knot of evergreen trees surrounded the lake, a rare sight on the flat expanse of the prairie. We slid to a stop beside a crude shelter made of rough timbers. One wall simply didn't exist, and nobody had bothered to caulk between the logs on the other three. At the far end sat a rusted cook stove.

"It was built by early pioneers, a trapper most likely. It's been here for as long as I can remember." George tied the horse, helped me down, fussed for a minute with the runner and gave it a kick. "It'll hold." He walked to the side of the shack, shook a handful of spruce boughs out of a prickly mound of snow and then retrieved a box from the back of the sleigh. Before long a feisty fire crackled and a can of Mama's *zharkove* bubbled on the old stove.

George led me forward and held my hands above the burner. "Warmer?" His breath billowed white, his long eyelashes so black in the snow light, his sandy hair tipped with frost like swirls of whipped cream. He spooned steaming stew into bowls and passed one to me. Two tree stumps became chairs, and we placed our dishes on a crude table fashioned from planks nailed together.

My bowl brimmed with nut-brown carrots, slippery onions, and dark meat as tender as bread. I took a bite. "The stew is delicious."

"Your Mama is a good cook." George plunged his spoon into his bowl.

"There's a symphony in the quiet here," I said a few minutes later. "Can you hear it? It's as if an orchestra is poised and ready to go—that moment of mighty silence when the music has built in each musician's head and the room resounds with enchantment. The sky, this minute, is an orchestra hall."

He lifted his bowl, cupped it, and devoured his stew like a

wolf. "I don't hear much of anything." He got up and ladled himself another serving.

"Oh George, it's music. It's everywhere and always. And when I play, I wish you could be inside my head. The notes build one on top of the other until they consume me. Sometimes, I could die of ecstasy. Papa says God has sent me a gift, and it's my duty to share that gift with others." My stew was half eaten on the table. I got up and poked the fire, pulled a couple of mugs out of the box, poured two cups of coffee, and passed one to George.

Over my husband's shoulder, at the edge of the clearing, I spied a crow perched on a stump, eyes glittering. I knew it was the same bird. He'd followed us. The foolish thing stretched one wing up over its head and then I heard a muffled voice in the wind, "Get on with it. Get on with it." I shivered and hugged myself.

"Are you still cold, Kat? I've brought whiskey." George pulled a flask out of his pocket and extended it after he'd poured a measure into his cup. "Here, it'll warm you."

"You know, I've never tried whiskey?" I passed my cup forward.

"Might not be a good idea then." He re-corked the container.

"Listen husband, I'm twenty-one years old. I'm not with the Temperance League and Papa has a glass of vodka every night, sometimes two."

"All right." He chuckled and poured a drip of liquor into my coﬀee.

I held my cup out again. "Don't be stingy."

"Okay, you asked for it." He poured until the cup was full to the brim.

"*Na zdorovia!*" I took a big swallow. The coﬀee was tepid, but the whiskey set it on fire. My throat seized. I coughed and spewed a mouthful back into the cup.

"You're not supposed to guzzle, silly girl." George took a long sip, the skin around his eyes crinkled with laughter.

The next taste I took with caution. Within moments a calmness seeped into my belly. I faced my husband, chin high. Now was as good a time as any. "Papa's friend in Edmonton is arranging a concert. He wants me to play."

"He's putting on a concert in Sylvite?" George scratched his head.

"No, Edmonton."

"Then how can you play?"

"I'll go to Edmonton."

"Edmonton?"

"Yes, only for three weeks. Oh, George, the chance to play in front of an audience again. I'm so excited. I can hardly wait."

"You can't go. We have no money for trips."

"Papa will pay for the train and I'll stay with his friend Gustav and his wife. This is such an opportunity. I may never get the chance again and besides, Papa has made up his mind. I must go."

"Kat, I can't go to Edmonton. You know I can't leave the farm."

"You don't have to come. I'll be fine. Papa's friends are respectable people."

"I don't like the idea of you travelling alone."

"Oh, please, please, please. It means so much to me." I threw my arms around him and kissed him, little kisses all over his frozen cheek until he wiggled out of my embrace.

"Well, maybe." He stood.

I stepped forward, put my arms up around his neck, drew his head close, and kissed him full and long.

He placed his hands on my shoulders and held me at arm's length. "But no longer than three weeks. I'll not have you away longer." Leaning forward, he rubbed his chin on the top of my head.

I danced a jig, kicked snow up, grabbed his hand, and kissed it. "Thank you. Thank you. You are the best husband." George pulled his hand away, walked to the stove, picked up the coffeepot, and tipped the last bit of liquid out. It made a black hole in the smooth white drift next to the shelter. He squatted, rubbed our bowls clean with a handful of snow, and gathered everything up to stow in the sleigh. I glanced back over to the tree stump. The crow had disappeared.

It was March and still cold. April seemed so far away.

George and I returned to the farm, the only humans surrounded by cows, chickens, and other barnyard animals. I missed civilisation. Sylvite was no bustling hubbub, but the town had people at least.

The solitude was easier for George. He had never lived anywhere else. At the age of eighteen, his parents both died of the Spanish Influenza. As an only child, he'd inherited the farm and stayed. That pandemic in 1918, the year before we came to Canada, had swept the world. Many people perished in Russia too, but thankfully, my family had been spared.

Three tortuous hours on a desolate road led us home to George's barn, house, and the chicken coop surrounded by stunted bushes and one starving tree. This was my new abode. Most days I could accept this, but a great wasted energy crept into my bones as we pulled up to the house. And that night, when my husband groped for me beneath the covers, I turned my mind to the song I'd practised in my head on the way back.

George didn't mention the Edmonton trip again. I didn't bring it up lest he might rescind his decision. Still, in the coming days, thoughts of the concert kept my spirits up.

The weeks blended one into the next. My husband showed me how to control the temperature of the oven by adding a piece of coal every half-hour, how to soften the leaves of a cabbage and wrap them around a mixture of ground meat and barley. I played scales for him on the violin and explained the importance of exact pressure to create the perfect pitch.

One day after supper, George stood by the window with his coffee and waved me to join him. "See, there's Ethyl." He pointed. "Right on time." The cow ambled across the yard toward the barn, her immense udder swinging with every step.

"Seven years on a farm and you've never milked a cow?"

"I wanted to learn." I turned away from my husband's face because that was stretching the truth. I viewed milking animals as entirely disagreeable. "Father thought our cows produced better if exposed to music."

George gaped at me. He obviously didn't understand, but this wasn't so outlandish. Cattle had ears too, didn't they?

"It was my job to play, Mama's to milk."

"So you played the violin in the barn twice a day?"

I couldn't tell by his tone of voice whether my husband was amused or disgusted.

"They seemed to prefer Beethoven."

"Come on then. You need a lesson." George handed me my coat, and picked up two pails from the shelf by the door, one empty and one full of reddish water.

"Should I bring my violin?"

"Be serious, Kat."

I was serious. Any audience was welcome at that point, even a farm animal. But I left my instrument and followed George. We arrived just as the back end of the beast disappeared into the barn.

"Hello, Girl," George said as we entered the feral-smelling cavern and approached the stall. "She's pure-bred Jersey. One of the finest milk cows in the province, aren't you, Ethyl?" George stroked the animal's head and rubbed behind one ear. The beast nuzzled him.

She didn't appear special. There were no markings on her pale brown hide, and compared to Papa's cow she was rather small.

George bent for a stool that leaned against the wall in the corner. "First you wash her udder with iodine water." He sat on the low stool, placed the bucket of water between his feet, and sponged her bloated udder over and over. I'd never noticed Mama taking so much time when she milked.

"Your father may think music gets the milk flowing, but with Ethyl it's the massage." Then he stood up and motioned me to the stool. The cow twisted its neck and sneered. I squatted, positioned myself, and reached for the udder, which felt like a bloated garden worm.

"Don't pull, Katya. That hurts her. Watch. Like this." He knelt beside me, reached in, grabbed a teat, and squeezed, one finger at a time.

I tried to mimic what he'd done. It didn't work for me. "My hands don't operate that way, George." The cow shifted and twitched. It swatted me with its tail, stinging the corner of my eye.

My fingers knew how to move over the neck of a violin, press the strings, release the music, but they baulked at the teats of a cow. I tried again though. I wanted to please George. A dribble of milk appeared. A few minutes later, with all fingers squeezing and tugging, the pail began to fill.

"That's better, Kat." George patted the top of my head. Then the cow veered, bumped him, and kicked over the half-full pail of milk.

"Stupid cow." I stood and pushed the miserable creature away.

"Damn." George set the pail upright and repositioned it below the udder. "Back to the house with you." He dismissed me with a wave. "I'll finish up."

Soon the snow melted, and the landscape turned mud drab. This prompted George to spend every hour of the day outdoors. He came in after dark each night but spoke little.

One week I skipped the chores that seemed unimportant. I neglected to gather the eggs every single day. The chickens didn't mind. Butter-making was complicated. I'd never quite learned the skill. So, I took the cream George skimmed for that purpose and fed it to the pigs. We ran out of butter.

"You fed fresh cream to the pigs?" His eyes flared with

astonishment and he dropped the empty pail on the counter.

"Can't we use lard?" I asked.

"I won't eat lard on my bread." George stomped out of the house. He didn't return until well after dark.

I tried to practise every day. Gustav had provided sheet music for the *Concerto for Two Violins* and Papa had his neighbour, John Dari, drop it off for me. The pages were in my top drawer and in the morning when George left for the field I retrieved them and pored over the staves and measures. It was vital to know the piece as well as I knew my own hand.

Every day my husband wrote out a list of chores he expected me to do and left the note on my violin case. Most days I crumpled it and threw it into the fire. On those evenings George sat sullen and silent. Sometimes I made an effort. I soldiered along waiting for that feeling Mama used to go on about— gratification for a job well done.

I missed my home. The smell of bleach and laundry soap reminded me of Mama and so the one chore I didn't mind too much was the washing. George devised a contraption for cleaning clothes out of bric-a-brac he'd salvaged from the farmyard. The body of the device was an elongated tin bathtub. He fastened washboards to the sloped ends, fitted the tub with legs from an old rocking chair, and attached a handle. It was ingenious. Once the water and clothes were in, you could sit beside the thing and rock it back and forth. The suds slurried and swirled like the Baltic Sea.

But laundry was hard work. Water had to be hauled and heated, the clothes wrung, and everything pinned on the clothesline to dry. To save time spent on washing, I wore the same dress and underclothes each day.

In St. Petersburg our lives had been so different. We left bags of dirty linen in the foyer where a washerwoman picked them up on Monday. She returned a stack of freshly folded laundry on Tuesday.

I remembered Mama and I bursting into fits of giggles, our first winter here, when our clothes froze stiff on the outside line. She'd brought them in and stood them up to dry on the kitchen chairs, life-size marionettes suspended by invisible strings. They soon crumpled in the warm room leaving pools of water under the chairs.

"Are you ever going to change that dress?" George asked one morning as he fixed his coffee.

"I like this dress." I curtsied at him.

George poured another coffee and set it on the table for me.

"Look at the hem. It's dirty," he said. "And it's stained on the front."

I bent and picked up the hem of the dress. "This isn't so dreadful. You come in from the field looking worse."

"But I change." He scowled. "And while we're on the subject, I'd appreciate more help around here." He gathered the dirty plates off the table, clattered them into the washbasin, and marched out.

He had nerve. All I did was work. I'd not composed a single song since our wedding day. If I managed two hours of practice in a day, it was lucky. I threw my apron on the floor and went to my violin. I played until the sky turned black.

The day finally arrived. I was to leave for Edmonton. Before first light that morning I put on my Sunday dress and the hat Papa said made me look like the *Swan Princess*. George fixed a breakfast of scrambled eggs with chunks of ham. My stomach convulsed at the thought of food. I paced the kitchen until he had eaten his fill. As soon as he finished, I rushed outside, carpetbag in one hand, violin case in the other. As I gazed out over the green-tinged fields with patches of melting snow, it seemed everything and anything was possible. A waft of manure tickled my nostrils. The sky was blue. A smatter of dark clouds stippled the horizon.

"Good, the rain's held off." George flicked the reins as we pulled out of the yard in the wagon.

"Yes, I'm glad." I shifted in the seat. It was impossible to sit still. I lifted my leg up over the floor panel, put it back again, hugged the violin to my chest, and tapped its leather case.

"I'm not sure you should be going." My husband leaned forward and frowned at the road.

"It's only for three weeks."

That crow circled above us. I squinted into the sun until my eyes burned and watched him vanish into the distance. For the rest of the trip I fixed my gaze on the steady rise and fall of the horse's rump. The wagon moved slower than usual. After an eternity, we saw Papa's house ahead and the settlement of Sylvite beyond on the skyline.

Mama and Papa were in the garden when we drove up, Mama on her knees in the dirt with hands buried in the earth, Papa leaned on a shovel. His face lit up as we came close.

"The train leaves in an hour," George said as they rushed toward the wagon while we remained seated.

"I'll ride with you to the station." Papa patted the horse's mane.

"John Dari will be here soon. To help you fix the seeder, remember?" Mama wagged one dirt-coated finger at him.

Papa hung his head for a moment with a sad face, upsetting his usual spark. The lapse was brief. "The concerto, you have mastered it?" Papa mimicked playing an imaginary violin.

"I perform it in my sleep." I grinned and rolled my head back, feigning slumber.

"So long as you do not sleep when you play." He laughed. Then he dug in his pocket, brought out a thin roll of bills, reached up, and pressed them into my husband's hand. "For the ticket. I wish I could come with you."

I longed for Papa as we walked across the platform at the terminal. My husband, gone silent, scrutinised everything in the station yard except the train. He refused to look at me. I resolved he would not spoil this. He could pout if he wanted. I was off to play in an orchestra, a real orchestra. When I climbed the steps into the car, I glanced at his disapproving face and grinned.

"You can still change your mind," he said. "They'll reimburse the ticket."

"I'll be back before you know it." I slipped inside and wandered along the aisle humming a tune. After a quick wave to George through the window I settled myself on a bench, violin case next to me.

The train had few passengers. The engine started out like a *scherzo*, largo slow, but soon the wheels were in tempo and I watched the landscape flicker past: patches of snow, fence, barn, slough, house, hill, trees, pond. We chugged to a stop in Lloydminster and a stream of new travellers came onboard with much babel and bluster. They shuffled in and up the aisle. No one sat near me.

A girl at school once told me it was something in my demeanour that made people keep their distance. "And it's not the scar on your mouth either," she'd said. "You can barely notice that. Sometimes you act spooky, as if you're not in the room." At the time, I didn't understand what she meant, but as the other passengers took seats as far away from me as possible, I considered her comment. Taking a small mirror out of my handbag, I studied my reflection. Perhaps I could practise looking pleasant. A crooked grin bounced back at me, lopsided because of the scar. But my features were not unpleasant, large dark eyes and fair skin, almost as pale as the crooked scar on my upper lip. Papa always declared, 'An imperfection on the face enhances a person's character.' I glanced around the carriage. A woman with a button-up collar at the end of the compartment sat gawking at me. I stared her down.

As the train rolled along and the car lurched and shifted, it led me to recall a hauntingly beautiful piece by Sarasate. I took out my violin and was barely into the prelude when the conductor appeared next to my seat.

"You must put the instrument away, miss. People are trying to rest."

Fitting In

Vasili shivered. It was a clear, bright Sunday, but cold, and the wagon wheels skidded on hard-packed ruts that hadn't melted yet. He glanced at Olga, bundled in her fur coat, peering ahead toward town. "I see no harm if we enjoy a day of rest. Must we visit that tired-out church every single week?"

"Yes." She shifted and tucked the blanket tighter around her legs.

"Why? We rarely attended in St. Petersburg." Vasili

understood the virtue and necessity of prayer, but did it need a temple? If you sought to pray, the chicken coup would work as well.

"Life was different then. Think back to when we had your mother."

Vasili chuckled. "Yes, remember the mischief she created? I can still see her running up the aisle, jumping on the Alter, and flailing her arms as if to welcome the angels. The Nativity of the *Theotokos* had never seen such entertainment."

"You did not find it funny then."

"Ah, that is true. Time paints us a different picture."

Olga's voice took on a wistful tone. "We were busy then with friends and visitors. We went to restaurants, to the Metropol."

Vasili snapped the reins, and the horse snorted out a white spume. He still ached for home sometimes, especially the Metropol, and he realised it was just as bad for Olga. With Katya gone she was alone too much. There was more time to brood, but she put a brave face on a sorry business. He resolved not to complain again. Church was the only place in Sylvite for women to meet, although he suspected they visited one another in their homes. No woman had invited his wife, not once in seven years. And poor Katya, it was even more difficult for her. She had no musical life here. This trip was vital for her, this chance to perform again. The horse stopped at the hitching post next to the Sylvite Memorial United Church.

"I wonder what kind of city Edmonton is?" Vasili helped his wife down from the wagon.

"Look." She pointed to the entrance. "Mrs. Kline. We should speak with her after the service."

"Katya might be rehearsing now," he said, "in a big hall. Gustav wrote they had secured an auditorium near the river. Remember the rehearsal chamber at the Conservatory?"

Olga pulled on his arm. "Hurry, Vasha. The Reverend waits for us."

Reverend Manning's girth filled the doorway. He was a massive man but solid, not fat, with skin so ox-white you could barely make out his priest collar. As they climbed the steps, he extended his hand and Olga shook it. Vasili always felt small near this preacher, even when he wasn't one step below. The minister thumped him on the back, led them up the stairs and into the church.

They slipped into a pew. Reverend Manning made his way to the pulpit, stopping several times, leaning to speak with this person and that person. Old Mrs. Brent lifted a wrinkled chin and beamed at the large man. Vasili shook his head. What lack of ceremony and where were the robes, the candles? Is this a man of God, with his bare head and smooth face?

The Reverend began. *"He shall return no more to his house; neither shall his place know him any more."*

Except for the small stained glass window high above the

pulpit and a metal cross, Vasili would not imagine this room as part of a church. He peered over the heads of the congregation. Mrs. Bradley sat poised in front of the organ, her auburn hair twisted in a conical fashion, jutting up like a spire. Her musical skills were limited, but she rarely made mistakes. Also, the choir had a few decent voices. But it was bad luck that Edward Plumb's grating tone would screech above all others as soon as the songs began.

Vasili reached into a wooden slot of the frontal pew for a hymn book.

"Olga." He leaned over to her ear. "I wonder if they have an Orthodox Church in Edmonton."

"Shh."

He opened the book and set it on his lap. The service, the icons, the melodies, all so different from home but, he reflected, it was not all bad. Soon there would be songs. That part was better than Russia—not chants, but songs. Still, it was not the Metropol. There would be no Tchaikovsky or Rimsky-Korsakov, only simple hymns, but it was music with voices raised in song. Sometimes Vasili worried over how much pleasure it gave him. At one time he would not have sniffed the air with this calibre of music in it.

The Reverend's voice boomed. *"How long wilt thou not depart from me, nor let me alone till I swallow down my spittle?"*

Vasili turned the pages of the hymn book until he came to

Thou Hidden Love of God, tapped his wife on the shoulder, and pointed to the page. "Will she play this today, you think?"

Olga lips formed a straight line, and she stared at the pulpit. Vasili prepared in his mind for the hymn. He hummed quietly as he fit the book's words to lines of written music he could see in his mind. The Reverend gestured, everyone stood, and the organ began. Vasili sang with as much volume as he could muster, his effort to drown out the caterwauling of Mr. Edward Plumb.

After the service, Olga pulled her husband to the foyer where the congregation had packed in for refreshments. Women herded around the food table while the men leaned on walls, except Reverend Manning. He fluttered from one person to another like a huge errant turkey.

"There's Mrs. Kline." Olga pointed to a woman standing alone. Yes, there was no mistaking George and Katya's neighbour, Mary Kline. God had been unkind, Vasili thought, to bestow on a woman the face of a horse.

Olga prodded Vasili's shoulder. "They shun her. They should be charitable now that she is a widow."

"A goose is not a pig's comrade, my wife."

Vasili knew his wife felt sorry for the poor woman. Mrs. Kline did not fit in with the ladies in Sylvite. She came to town for supplies wearing trousers, like a peasant. But the woman was in pathetic circumstances. Her husband had been ill for years and she ran the farm on her own. Vasili doubted most of the women in a knot around Mrs. Stanley appreciated the meaning of hard work the way Mary Kline did. He also hoped Olga would not become involved with this flock of old hens masquerading as pious members of the community. But, perhaps it was for his wife as the music was for him. She did not cry, but she had no friends here. Vasili feared the Mrs. Stanleys' of the world might draw her interest for lack of other diversions.

"Do you know what I heard Mrs. Stanley say?"

"No, what?"

"'That Mrs. Kline is pitiable,' she said, 'just plain pitiable.'"

"Perhaps Mrs. Stanley should learn to extend pity," he said.

Mrs. Kline stood rooted to the centre of the room like a thorn, her black dress smudged with dust, her shoes caked in mud. Near the dainty table, Mrs. Stanley held court with her circle of women as they all sipped tea and nodded. Olga tugged on Vasili's sleeve and led him to where the widow Kline stood.

"It is a pleasure to see you again, Mrs. Kline," Olga said with a slight bow.

"Thank you, Mrs. Sadilov. It can be a chore to get here, but the roads are clear now." Mrs. Kline held out her hand and Vasili could not help notice the dirt under her fingernails. His wife cupped the woman's palm in both of hers and squeezed.

"Yes," Olga said. "It is a big voyage. Our Katya and George have only been to church twice since the wedding day. First the weather interfered and now it is time to plant."

"Yes, I know. George was over last week. Offered to seed my west field. I was of a mind to leave all the fields this year, but I've taken him up on it."

"You have no plan to sell your farm?" Vasili asked.

"Can't decide. Don't know where I'd go. Guess I'll have to think on it."

"It must be lonely for you." Olga reached out and rested her fingers on Mrs. Kline's arm. "You will visit George and Katya? Our daughter will be lonely too. She is too far away from home."

"Katya is in Edmonton now," Vasili said. Our house is lonely too, he thought. "But she returns at the end of the month."

"In Edmonton?"

"She is performing in an orchestra." He couldn't quash the pride in his voice. "With twenty-three musicians. She will play the *Concerto for Two Violins*."

"Yes, she plays fiddle, doesn't she?"

"She plays. She composes music. She has a huge talent." To show her, he threw his arms wide. "She performed Bach and Beethoven at the Metropol before her tenth year. She mastered Paganini at the age of thirteen."

"That's nice." Mrs. Kline turned to face Olga. "Do you think your daughter might want to buy some hens? I've got no need for all those eggs anymore."

Vasili prayed Katya's experience in Edmonton was more restorative than a trip to the Sylvite Memorial United Church.

CHAPTER THREE

Performing

GUSTAV met me at the train station in Edmonton. I didn't remember him from St. Petersburg but picked him out from Papa's description, a thin man with a pointed beard. He stood on the platform next to his wife, Elsie. She had abundant red hair, stood a head taller than her husband with shoulders twice as wide as his.

"Katya. Just like your Papa." He hugged me with more force than you'd expect from so slight a man and kissed me on both cheeks.

Elsie stood pillar straight and inspected me. It was she who picked up my bags and carried them off the platform and down the street.

"Will we go right to rehearsal?" I asked Gustav as we walked behind her.

"No, no, tomorrow we start," he said. "Now we walk to the

house. Elsie has fixed the attic room for you."

The side of the road was frozen, but thankfully not covered in snow. Grooves of hard mud left by wagon wheels had created an uneven surface and so we trod with care. I had not expected a city with grand architecture like St. Petersburg, but I had hoped for more than this backwoods hamlet. There were many streets, but they could have been lanes in Sylvite with the single-storey buildings and dirt paths leading up to front doors. Gustav's house was one of a row of small places on a quiet road overhung with gnarled maple trees.

"Your room. It is up there." Elsie pointed above her head as we stepped into the entranceway.

A steep ladder led to a trap door in the ceiling. I climbed the ladder and pushed up on the door with one hand. It was a cavernous room with a sloped ceiling but homelike, despite the rough open beams and cobwebbed corners. A small mattress, table and chair sat on a faded oriental carpet in the centre of the floor. I sat and unlaced my boots. Elsie's head appeared at the entrance hole. She climbed the ladder, crouched and came into the middle of the room where she could stand up straight.

"You will be comfortable?" she asked.

"Yes, thank you. This is lovely. It's so kind of you."

"I will make you some food," she said.

"No, don't bother. Mama sent *bliny*. I ate them on the train."

"Then you should rest. You must be tired from your journey."

"I am." As soon as she left, I collapsed into bed.

I woke the next morning to the sound of the piccolo. Flat on the mattress, eyes shut, my head twitched in time with the strident but lively notes. There was no worry of eggs in the henhouse, no brawl of a cow, and no lecture on what chores needed to be done. I reached out and patted the violin case beside my bed.

As we climbed the steps to the practice hall the next afternoon, Gustav said, "We have twenty-three musicians." When he opened the door, his voice drowned in the discord. Most of the musicians were busy tuning their instruments, a wonderful din of noise. Only the horn players were idle, perched on a window ledge smoking—clarinet, flute, saxophone, leaned against the wall. A woman, the only other woman in the room, sat at the piano. Sausage fingers rolled scales across the keys with an agility difficult to believe. Her great haunches oozed off the bench.

It was a tiny room compared to the practice chambers I'd known at the Conservatory. The floors were of rough wood. A crooked stovepipe sloped at an angle from the centre of the room to the ceiling.

Gustav curled his arm through mine and led me around. Because of the noise, he was forced to yell and made puppet gestures with each word. "This is Julien Levesque. He plays our

French horn. Good joke, eh? And this is Stenya Letov. He is a little shy but plays the trumpet like an elephant."

I bent to Gustav's ear and whispered as we walked. "I'll never remember all their names." The door banged open, and a burst of wind barrelled through the hall. Everyone turned to look. A man flew in, coattails flapping, a violin case fixed in his hand, a black beret of long wavy hair spilled off to one side.

"Antonio, come. You have overslept again? You rogue." Gustav held out his arms.

"Please master, do not cane me," the man said, and he scooped Gustav up as if he were a child. He laughed as he did it, a merry laugh, like a cantata, more beautiful than any sound I'd ever heard. Gustav's legs dangled in the air and a moment later he landed lightly back on his feet.

"Antonio, this is the violin player I told you of, Katya Sadilov. Katya, our concert-master, Antonio Serov." Gustav waved his arm in a flourish. "A rascal at times, but a genius."

"It is a pleasure." He bowed and lifted my outstretched hand. My fingers sizzled.

Antonio played like a glorious fiend. When his instrument struck its first notes, the orchestra faded and the other musicians in the room blurred. Only he was clear, black hair against pale skin, the rich brown of the violin as he held it next to his cheek, his slim body as if in flight with coattails curled behind him. I was hardly aware of my own violin or the sound it produced.

During a rest, Gustav walked over.

"Your Papa did not exaggerate," he said. "You play as good as a man." He picked up my violin from the chair, turned it over and tapped the back wood. "This is a grand instrument."

"Master Auer gave it to me." I addressed Gustav but could not drag my eyes from the concert-master.

"Ah, yes. The great Master Auer."

"He plays like Niccolò Paganini." I pointed to Antonio who, at that moment, was in front of the horn players gesturing with frenzy.

"Yes, but you know what people say, that Paganini bartered his soul to the Devil before he received his gift."

"Well, if that's the case, the Devil must have a refined soul." I winked at him.

Antonio swivelled and pranced to where we stood. He threw his hands up. "Gustav, what has happened to our horn players? Do they play for a funeral?" Then he turned to me and lowered his eyelids. "I will apologize. It is your first day but, Gustav, did you feed brandy to those sheep last night? I have never heard them play so badly."

"Perhaps it's the lack of brandy," I said. "They play as if in church."

"My God, Gustav, she is right." His face crinkled with humour. "I will bring brandy tomorrow and make them take off the ties that knot their necks. But you must promise me." He leaned down toward me and whispered, "not to tell their wives."

"I have never known what to say to wives," I said.

"She thinks you play like Niccolò Paganini," Gustav said.

"Paganini, hm?" Antonio smiled and stroked his cheek.

"Yes," I said. "In fact, I will call you Niccolò ." If, like Paganini, Antonio had bartered his soul to the devil, it seemed he'd made a good bargain.

"Of course. Call me Niccolò." Antonio grinned and my breathing stopped.

The next day I couldn't help but stare at Antonio during rehearsal. He glanced in my direction many times and smiled twice. I barely remember what songs we played. When we finished for the day he walked over to where Gustav and I stood near the heater in the middle of the room. The belly of the stove was only the size of a cracker barrel but threw enough heat to keep the large hall comfortable. I rubbed my hands above its glowing top.

"It is a good stove," Antonio said. "A fire in the centre of a room is all we need. Like the fire in the middle of a symphony or that red mark on your neck." He reached over, touched my neck, and where his finger met my skin, it seared. I adjusted the collar of my dress and covered my fiddle's love bite.

"Do not be ashamed." Antonio wagged his finger. "It is a mark of passion. You love your instrument."

"I cannot wear a neck cloth," I said. "I need to feel the vibration in the wood."

"Yes, I know." He twisted his head, tugged at the scarf around his neck to reveal an identical mark.

I wasn't wrong about him. He feels the music as I do.

Antonio approached me during a break in rehearsal the following day. His intense gaze caused a shiver, but a hot flush exploded on my cheeks.

"Can you stay tonight, Katya? We should practise the *Concerto for Two Violins*." Grinning, he turned away before I could answer and addressed my guardian, several feet away. "Can I play with her, Gustav?"

"I do not think this is possible, Antonio. Elsie and I must attend a charity dinner tonight. I cannot stay."

"I will take care of her. She is safe with me." Antonio crossed his heart.

I turned and confronted Gustav. "I'm not a child."

Gustav laughed, winked at Antonio, walked over, and thumped him on the back. "You be sure that you do, you scoundrel, or you must answer to her father and her husband. Both men are big and very strong." The smile faded from Antonio's face. He picked up his fiddle. Gustav eased his piccolo into its case, walked out of the hall and closed the door.

The *Concerto* was the reason they'd asked me to come to Edmonton. Over and over I'd practised it. My arm knew the notes as it knew its own marrow, but that evening as I stood beside Antonio it caught amnesia. He reached out and put his hand over mine. My knuckles melted.

"Hold the bow with your fingers like this." He re-adjusted my fingers.

I did not need his help with this, but words of reply bogged deep in my throat. A long strand of hair fell over his cheek when he bent. I raised my face. He leaned closer and his peppery scent made my head whirl. For a moment I thought he would kiss me.

He straightened and took a step back. "Gustav told me how well you play, but not how beautiful you are."

Before I could think of how to reply, with a flourish he scooped up his violin and began a song. The notes ravished me. My arm regained its memory. I thrust the fiddle under my chin, gripped my bow, and matched him stroke for stroke. The instruments led us past the song, beyond the air, outside the earth and universe. When it was over, we collapsed into our chairs.

"Working men think we musicians are lazy and soft." He wiped his forehead with his sleeve. "Have you noticed? This is a country of working men."

"Yes, a country of working women too." I stared at the music sheet open on the stand. "They think me too thin to be of much use, but I don't mind. If my sole purpose was to fight household grime and dust, I'd perish." My fingers twiddled the pegbox of my instrument.

"Gustav treats me as a son. If I had not met him, I would be back in Moscow now. He found employment for me as a teacher of the violin."

"Do you have family in Moscow?"

"I am an orphan, but I was lucky. A man at the orphanage taught music. He paid for me to go to the Moscow Conservatory. When he died, I was restless and came here." He put his fiddle down and unscrewed the bow. "I don't know what I thought it would be like. Before Gustav, I worked ten-hour days throwing bags of grain from cart to railcar for pittance."

"My family is here. My Mama works hard. I wish her days were easier. She had a servant at home. I don't think Papa knew what a struggle life would be in Canada."

"But it is good for you and me." He smiled. "We have the music."

He walked me to Gustav's house. The streets were dark, the air cold, but I felt so warm it might have been a summer day. As we approached the house, Elsie's sturdy frame appeared in the open window. We climbed the few steps to the front door, and it swung open.

"Antonio, you made it," Gustav shouted. "Come in. Come in.

We will have some brandy."

"The last time you asked me in for brandy, we were both late for the morning rehearsal," Antonio said.

"Only the dead think sleep is more important than drink." Gustav took my arm and led me into Elsie's brocade sitting-room. It was a place bursting with pattern, the wallpaper, the sofa, the curtains, even the spittoon in the corner was overlaid with gold-threaded green fabric.

"The *Concerto*, it is perfected?" Gustav seated me and addressed Antonio.

"Every note," Antonio replied.

Elsie poured brandy and offered me a small goblet. I took it and tipped back. The liquid fumed in my throat, smoother than whiskey with a perfumed smell.

"We could use another French horn." Gustav frowned. "But there is no accomplished player within a hundred miles."

"Why not try the boy who rehearsed last month?" Antonio asked.

"No. He has no restraint."

"Julien could work with him. He has enough restraint for every musician in the orchestra."

My mind wandered off, aware only of the rich timbre of his voice, not the topic of conversation. Elsie tapped me on the shoulder and poured another ounce of brandy into my glass.

"I will miss you, Antonio." Gustav pulled on his pointy beard.

I snapped to attention and turned to Antonio. "Do you plan to go away?"

"He is to audition." Gustav gleamed with pride. "For the New York Philharmonic Orchestra, next month, God willing, if we raise enough money." He slapped Antonio on the back and smiled at me.

I could not return his smile. A skinny death had crept inside my bones.

"Your Papa tells me you are not only a brilliant performer but also good with words," Gustav said. "We need words written for our program, something to interest, something with power to open wallets."

That night, upstairs in the attic room, by candlelight, I got out my pen and ink.

The Northern Lights streamed across the sky when Johann Sebastian Bach wrote the 'Concerto for Two Violins' during the Baroque Period. Almost one hundred years later they flared and danced when Niccolò Paganini, an Italian composer, fiddled his way into the hearts of music lovers throughout Europe. He named his violin 'the Canon'. He could capture an audience as no violin player ever before. He performed feats never duplicated. If a string broke, he would play on, fascinating the crowd with his dexterity. Sometimes he broke three strings in the middle of a performance and continued with only a single string, wild and frenzied, but true to the music. It was said, he had bartered his soul to the

Devil. Yet his con amore *passages were rendered with such tenderness, grown men were given over to tears. Now, another hundred years have passed and Concert Master Antonio Serov basks in the lights of the here and now, halfway around the world. Join us at the 'Northern Lights Transposed,' and experience a musical sensation that spans the globe and centuries.*

Gustav loved it. "Antonio, we must call you the Edmonton Paganini," he said at rehearsal the next afternoon.

Antonio took the paper from me. I pinched my arm while he read. After several moments he looked up, raised an eyebrow and tossed the paper on the chair. With his fiddle in one hand, his bow in the other, he flipped the instrument over his head, twisted his other arm behind his back and ran the bow across the strings. A shriek to send a deaf man running for cover, sprang from the f-holes and he laughed.

"You see, the tricks I will perform for you, my lady?" Holding his fiddle in front, he bowed.

Antonio played so fast that afternoon I had trouble keeping pace with him. In the second movement of the *Concerto*, Gustov raised a hand for us to stop.

"Antonio, what is this? You play like a horse trying to escape his own tail."

Later, as we packed our instruments away, Antonio came to me and whispered, "It is you, little flower. You make my blood race and the music comes too fast."

I kept my eyes fixed on my violin, placed it carefully in its case, and loosened the bow. Had I looked up, he would have noticed the ruddy heat of my cheeks.

Gustav joined us, piccolo case in hand. "Antonio, have you heard any more from the Mayor's wife? We have not yet seen her cheque."

Antonio frowned. "We have her pledge."

"Can you visit her again?"

"You go, Gustav."

"No, she will want you. Her eyes melt when she looks at you." Gustav slapped Antonio on the behind and laughed. "She is not so bad to look at too, eh?"

"She is married to the Mayor."

"That old bull. It is no wonder she has an eye for the young stag."

That night, my limbs fought with the mattress. I pushed the covers off, tucked them up, threw them off again, and dug my fingernails into my scalp. Frenetic music scrambled my mind. When it was too much to bear, I got up, climbed down the ladder, and slipped outside.

The moon was a perfect crescent. Tree branches cast eerie shadows on the side of the house. I ducked through the hedge to a secluded patch under the trees.

The night air was cold, but deep inside I burned. A potent spirit overtook my arms and my legs. I danced a *Barynya* on the scuff of frosty lawn, nightdress twirling, leaping, waving my arms up, up, up to the spectacular stars. It was impossible to stop the dance. Glowing flickers rose from the bushes. Seconds later, my fingertips were alight with tiny fairies. I could not say how long I danced with them, but after a while my legs did buckle and I collapsed to the ground. The fairies dispersed in the branches. A cinnamon haze spattered the morning sky. I watched a crow hop off the rail of the fence, bob through the hedge, and out of sight. Skin covered in gooseflesh, I crept into the house and up the ladder to my room.

Back in my room, I tried to invoke an image of George. It had only been two days but I could barely remember his face. A letter to Antonio began to write itself in my mind, but in my head, he'd become Niccolò, not Antonio. I sat at the small desk, picked up a pen, and I'd hardly dipped the ink when words appeared on the sheet.

Dearest Niccolò,

When you glanced over at me on that first day, nodded, and ran your fingers up the neck of your instrument, I trembled. The trumpet player in the back row surely felt vibrations in the floorboards. During rehearsal, I heard only you. It was as if you and I had performed a solo, an aria so enchanting, a nightingale would weep.

K.

Tomorrow, I decided—I would slip him the letter behind closed doors.

We arrived early to the hall the next day. Gustav opened the front door and a full-throated male voice boomed out something that loosely resembled a song.

I put my hands to my ears. "That's awful. Who's in there?"

"Alas, it is Antonio." Gustav chuckled. "Good thing he did not wish to perform the Opera, eh?"

"Well, the tone is feisty." I kept my ears covered.

"I smell coffee and cooking. I wonder what the rogue is up to. Shall we see?" Gustav took my elbow and led me into a large kitchen with long bare counters and a jumble of pots and pans hanging from nails on every wall.

Antonio stood poised before a long cookstove, holding a knife and cutting board, an apron over his suit, his long hair tucked behind his ears. He was slicing rounds off a roll of meat as he sang, shaking each slice off the knife into a frying pan. The pieces crackled and spat as they hit the grease. The air exploded with a tang of garlic. He noticed us and quit the song.

"A treat for you today." Antonio waved the knife like a conductor baton. "*Kotlety* pats, a recipe straight from Russia. Well, almost straight from Russia. My landlady wrote it out for me. Sometimes she pretends she is still there."

True to his word, Antonio had brought brandy. A round bottle sat on the counter beside several cups. He stopped cutting, poured a healthy stream into three cups, added coffee from the stove and passed a mug to Gustav and me. He lifted his in salute. *"Za vashe zdorov'ye!"*

"To your health too." I took a long gulp.

"It is early." Gustav drained his cup.

"It was Katya's idea." Antonio resumed slicing the sausage. "It will loosen their ties."

"Where are the others?" Gustav looked around. "Would it be so hard for them to arrive early?"

We heard the slam of the front door as he said this, and a moment later Stenya Letov and one of the horn players arrived. Stenya's negro lips spread to a wide grin when he noticed the bottle. Brandy was poured. Soon, they were all there crowded around the stove. They laughed, talked, drained mugs of brandied coffee, and devoured sausage and pickles from a platter at the cool end of the stove. This was how I remembered St. Petersburg, the jokes, the laughter, the smell of good food, everyone speaking at once. Sweet nostalgia clutched my heart.

The corpulent piano player, Mrs. Holden arrived. She pursed her lips as if she'd bitten a lemon and stormed off. Angry banging of piano scales followed.

"We must practise now." Gustav led, shuffling into the

rehearsal room.

I lagged until every person left. Fingering the letter in my skirt pocket, I moved to where Antonio's coat still hung on a hook on the wall. You could tell by the stitching, the coat had been tailored in Russia, not Canada. The pocket had clean, perfect stitches in an arc, not a straight line, to match the cup at the bottom, a perfect place to slip the letter in.

"Katya, come. It is time to start." Gustav's voice had a note of impatience.

The letter rattled in my hand. I tucked it back into my skirt. It was later, after practice that I lost my nerve. I went to the kitchen, lifted the stove lid, and tossed the note in the fire.

The following evening Gustav and Elsie went off to visit friends in the country. Antonio and I rehearsed late again, but not too late, and it was dusk when we arrived back at Gustav's house. Antonio followed me into the foyer. The house was quiet.

"You are trembling." He put his fingers on my neck. My body bucked and drummed.

I stepped aside. "Will you come in for tea?"

"Yes, tea would be good." He removed his coat, then mine and hung them both over his arm. I floated along the hall to the kitchen. He followed. I fetched the kettle and carried it to the water pail.

"Let me do that." He reached for the dipper.

My fingers froze as they disappeared beneath his hand. Fine black hair sprinkled the knuckle of his index finger, and under his nails the white moons shone. The calloused ridges of his fingertips grazed my wrist. What an exquisite hand. I willed my stomach to calm and stepped back.

Antonio filled the kettle while I dug the teapot out of the sideboard. It was an unusual vessel, square not round, and with one finger, I traced the raised edges of the filigreed design.

Antonio came up behind me. "The pot is elegant and rare." His breath inflamed my ear. "Like you."

I turned to him and his hands travelled to my shoulders, his mouth to my neck, his lips brushed the love bite from my fiddle and lingered there. As he pulled me close, a luscious melody rose.

"Are you sure?" he asked before following me up the ladder into the attic.

"I'm sure." I looked down from the top of the ladder.

In my room I lit a candle, removed my dress, my underclothes, and stood in front of him. He came close, ran his finger down my neck, and I felt nothing but that finger. Then he gathered me in his arms and I knew, more certainly than I'd known anything before, he was truly the spirit of Niccolò Paganini, come to claim me for his own.

He stroked me. Sweetly, gently, *a poco a poco*, his fingers played every inch of my skin. Ascending on my nipples, descending to the weeping petal, he scaled again and again—

largo... crescendo... prestissimo... until I was *con fuoco*. He conducted me, and I learnt him by heart, *a Bohemian Melody*. And sweetly, sweetly, he positioned me beneath him, flowed into me until his notes were my notes, a *duet* of fevered pitch. The room disappeared.

Eight quavers... and sixteen semiquavers later, we slept.

Niccolò and I made nighttime symphonies for the next three weeks leading up to the concert. Each night I leaned out the window and watched until Elsie and Gustav's lamp flickered out. Then I stole downstairs and unlocked the door. Sometime in the next hour, the ladder would creak and Niccolò appeared beside my bed. When he was there I had no guilt, no thoughts of home, no thoughts of anything but the room, and him and us. I wallowed in those perfect days, music by day, music by night.

The eve of the concert came too soon. And that night, after he drifted off to sleep, I got up and lit the stub of a candle, found a piece of paper and my pen.

Niccolò,

I don't want our music to die this afternoon. If it could only last forever. But these words are neglected tunes and my thoughts are tomes. The moon casts a weak light on my pen and sneers at me through the window. How bleak it all seems that I must return to the barn, the flat fields, the long days and stony silences and you will go on without me.

You may have been sent by the Devil, or you may have been sent by God. It makes no difference. Only music makes a difference. Nothing truly evil can touch it. But still, my pain chugs up, like steam from the train that takes me away tomorrow.

Tonight, I will play for you. We have tonight, and we will always have the music.

Goodbye,

K.

Niccolò slept like a *pensato* angel on the mattress. Before dawn I woke him, slipped my letter into his coat pocket and urged him to leave. When he'd left, I dressed and crept outside. For hours I trudged along the outskirts of town until the sun became a blinding slit on the horizon. The performance was 720 minutes away. Gustav stood framed in the window of his house and a look of relief spread over his face as I drew near. He had the profile of a French nobleman, with the uplift of his pointed beard. I would always think of him that way.

The ladder groaned as I climbed to my room and put on the blue dress Mama had fashioned for me from one of her Russian evening gowns. Then I sat, hands folded in my lap. The minutes ticked by.

"Katya, it is time to leave." Gustav hollered from the bottom of the ladder.

I stood and picked up a small mirror from the table. "Go

ahead. I'll be along." I strung Mama's black onyx necklace and adjusted the pendant above my cleavage. I did not pin my hair, but left it loose, falling to my shoulders in elegant waves.

"Is it nerves?" he shouted. "Don't' worry. You will be marvellous."

"No, I'm fine. You go ahead. I'll leave in a few minutes. I need to be alone."

"Very well, but you must hurry."

"I will," I told him and the door banged shut. Fifteen minutes passed. I put on my coat, picked up my violin, gathered a few things into a cloth bag, and climbed down the ladder.

The venue we were to play was the Citadel Theatre, in the heart of the city, a fifteen-minute walk from Gustav's house. It was still light when I set out. A southerly wind had breezed through the day before and warmed the city. New green buds pushed out from the tree branches. The smell of spring rain mingled with a waft of roast chicken from the house on the corner and reminded me of Mama. Suddenly, I was alive and filled with vigour.

The theatre came in sight sooner than I expected. It was an elaborate building compared to most in the city, of grey stone with multi-paned windows and an arched entranceway of oak. I climbed the steps and held my breath, fearful the excitement might escape and blow me back to Gustav's house.

Most of the musicians were already on stage and set up. I

made my way up the side steps. A great cacophony filled the theatre as the musicians warmed up. Performers cluttered the stage. Some stood, some sat, but all were intent on their music sheets. Most practised scales or a few lines of some score. Gustav stood to the rear with his piccolo, eyes closed, chest convulsed with exaggerated breaths, his lips shaped to an O on exhalation.

As I set course across the stage, a cello hammered my temples with a few shrill chords. I reached my place in front and Gustav opened his eyes. He waved. The trumpet player nodded, puffed out his cheeks, and blurted out a boom. I placed the instrument case on the chair, took out my bow and tightened it. My string hand cramped. I wiggled my fingers and opened and shut my hand several times, but the fingers remained stiff. I shook my hand. Panic struck when I looked down at the sheet music, the notes blurred splashes on the page.

Only half of the stage lights were turned on, but my eyes stung from the glare. A drop of perspiration rolled off the end of my nose onto the wood of the violin. As I bent to retrieve a cloth, the entrance doors swung open and the audience herded in, shifting and bumping. The musicians on stage ignored them, continuing their discordant practice as if we, on stage, were alone in the room.

Mrs. Holden arrived, and like a bull descending on a pasture, stopped and sniffed the air. She lumbered to the piano, sat, and added to the melee. I kept one eye on the side entrance, wiggled my foot, tapped my fingers on the fiddle, and yawned three times. After what seemed hours, the doors of the theatre closed, the lights dimmed, the entire place went quiet and someone in the audience whispered, "There he is, the concert master, Antonio."

But, they were wrong. It wasn't Antonio. It was my Niccolò who burst onto the stage with a wave of his bow and everyone stopped short. The audience applauded. He held a hand up until the hall was quiet, except for the rattle of my pulse. He took his place beside me, lifted his bow and we readied ourselves for the tuning note. I looked down. The lines on the music sheet had cleared. The violin rose to my chin, and I grinned at him. He'd brought life back into my fingers. He raised his bow, struck the note, and every instrument replied.

Before the vibration of that single note died, the conductor made his entrance. Another wave of applause blasted as he stepped to the podium. After a few moments of rehearsed inactivity, we began.

We opened with Bach. I scanned the sheet, but my attention was on Niccolò. How skilled he was!

The *Concerto in A Minor* started slow and dignified but accelerated to *prestissimo* in the final episode. The walls shook with applause. We bowed.

The first movement of the *Concerto for Two Violins* begins like two lovers who meet in the park. He says, 'I love you'. She says, 'I love you' and he says, 'I love you' and she says, 'I love you,' over and over, each time with more and more passion. Niccolò and I were sequestered on stage, the other musicians, melodious decoration. The centre episode is slow and haunting. By the third movement our two violins sang out as if they were a single instrument, as though Niccolò's bow and my bow were the same tool, as if he'd entered my song and me his, and on the final note, a rain of perspiration flew between us.

"You were brilliant," Gustav said at the reception in the foyer later. He pulled me into a fierce hug and kissed both cheeks. "Your Papa will be so proud. Tomorrow, I write to him."

My legs shook. Niccolò had been swallowed by a cluster of females. "Is there someplace we can sit?" I asked Gustav.

"Not here." He looked around. "But this will not take so long. Soon we return to the house and celebrate, with champagne." Gustav made a fist and punched the air above his head. "Two hundred and seventy dollars. We have money now. Antonio can go to New York. There is nothing to stop him now."

"I need to sit." I pushed my way through the crowd, slipped into the theatre and sank into an empty seat in a back row. Floodlights beamed down at the stage, musical instruments scattered across the wooden platform like bones. I slumped and gave myself over to the void of my mind. The voices faded to a hum.

Members of the orchestra pattered past me up the aisle to

retrieve tubas and trumpets from the stage floor. I opened my eyes. Niccolò was last to come. He retrieved his violin and mine, placed them both in their cases and carried them to where I sat.

"I cannot come with you to Gustav's house." His voice was flat.

"No?"

"I must stay with the Mayor and his wife. She has made the arrangements for my audition in New York." He set the case on my lap, bent and kissed my forehead. "You understand?"

"I suppose." But I really, truly, honestly did not understand.

He disappeared. A program sat open on the seat. I found a paper and pencil in my handbag and revised the comments I'd written:

They say Niccolò Paganini tricked his audience. It was not the strength of his performance that caused his strings to break. It's said that just before the end of a performance he would pause, turn away, put a nick in one of his strings and continue to play until that string broke. He played on with three strings for a few minutes and paused, turned away and score another string. He repeated the same for the third string until he was down to a single string and still he played on. Legend has it, the fourth string was not constructed of lamb gut, but ripped from the cavity of his dead mistress.

I crumpled the paper and tossed it at the chair in front of me.

Gustav and Elsie dropped me at the station the next morning. I bought my ticket and sat on the bench outside to wait. A cruel wind whipped up and in a slanted, piercing stream, it began to snow. It couldn't touch the ice cold stone that was my heart. Niccolò would open my letter, perhaps in a day, or maybe in a week. He did not pay attention to such details, like what nested in his pockets.

By the time the train rumbled up, all signs of spring had disappeared.

A sea of snow stretched across the flat expanse of the prairie like a cold dream. The train chugged along and with every mile, an icy heaviness settled in my arms and legs. By the time we passed the Dari farm north of Sylvite my limbs seemed separate from my body.

Someone had carved his initials in the wood of the bench in front of me. The woodgrain intersected at the bottom of the first letter, so it might have been a B or could have been an R. It was impossible to tell. But I couldn't even muster the energy to raise my hand and trace the ridge of the groove. The train's whistle sounded far off, in another world.

Footsteps approached my seat. I didn't look up but felt the conductor's shadow blacken over me. I shut my eyes and shrank against the wall. My temple cracked on a metal plate. Pain doused a tender spot on the side of my head. I cupped one hand over it and saw spires and cupolas, like a postcard Mama kept in her top dresser drawer. Spires and cupolas that reached to the sky.

"Are you all right, Miss? I believe this is your stop." The voice had no body. Something touched my shoulder.

I gasped for air, forced my eyes open and set them to gaze at the flicking landscape through the window and willed the voice to go away.

"Can I help with your bags, Miss?"

The reverberation of the train's wheels slowed to half time. I shrank farther in my seat.

"Miss, do you need help, Miss?"

"She's the Sadilov girl. Someone should run out and get her father."

"The Sadilov place is just north of town."

"Someone, get a blanket."

My breathing became more regular, but I pushed the voices away and pressed my nose against the cold glass of the window's pane. The train stopped. I felt hands under my arms. Steps moved beneath me, a cold bench, time numbed. I can't say how much later the footsteps sounded.

"Here she is, sir"

"Katya...little nightingale." Papa's voice was a song. He touched my cheek. "She is fine. I will take care of her. Can you get the bags?"

He slipped his arms under my legs, behind my back, and

lifted. The frigid wind juddered my stiff body as he carried me across a hollow wooden platform.

"Vasha, what?" It was Mama's voice.

"It's the old sickness, Olga. She will be fine. Get another blanket."

"Not like before," Mama said. "It can't be."

"No, no, do not worry," Papa said.

They wrapped me up and sat me in the wagon.

Mama's arms circled me. "Katya, you are safe now." She rocked me. Her breath feathered my cheek. The horse snorted and the wagon lurched.

It wasn't until we stopped and a door opened to the soothing smells of Mama's kitchen that I felt safe. Papa carried me upstairs to my old room. "Did something bad happen? Did someone hurt you?"

I pushed his questions from my mind, too weak for the image of that suffocating cloud or the memories that lurked beyond its foul-smelling dirt.

He eased me onto the bed and sat beside me. " Never mind. You are home, little bird. No one can hurt you." He hugged me hard.

"We should not have let her go." Mama's voice came from the doorway, but I didn't look up.

"She is home, and safe." Papa patted my arm. "We will not mention this to George."

"He will hear. People speak."

She was right. People do speak. I resolved right then, not to tell George about what happened in Edmonton. He would never forget or forgive. Mama knew he was a good man and thought I didn't deserve him, and surely the past few weeks had just been a dream, playing with Niccolò Paganini.

"We will tell him she was taken with fever but has recovered," Papa said.

I'm not sure how long Papa sat on my bed, but when he left, Mama undressed me and tucked me in.

My voice came back. "Can I tell you a secret, Mama?" The room was cozy with the smell of the wood stove and roasted chicken. I gathered the quilt up high around my neck.

"What secret?" Mama asked.

"Niccolò Paganini is the greatest violinist in the world."

"He is not alive. Over a hundred years ago, he died." She frowned and shook her finger.

"No, Mama. He's not dead." I knew something of spirits. When I was a girl the old women in St. Petersburg told stories about them. I'd felt their presence too. They were the ghosts of long-dead souls, cursed to drift aimlessly between life and death because they'd never loved during life. When the moon and the stars align just so, they can slip inside a human form and attach themselves for a while. Sometimes they stay forever.

"Do not speak foolish, Katya. You know what is true."

"No, you don't understand. He is music and music has its own life, Mama. Niccolò is a spirit that passes from body to body."

"Your Papa fills your head with too many stories." She leaned over and kissed my forehead. "Go to sleep."

I closed my eyes. Her steps pattered across the floor, the door clicked and I was alone again. Niccolò Paganini's spirit filled my head. I feared that sleep would never come again.

Demon Dream

The flame of a single lamp flickered from the corner table in the parlour. Vasili slumped in his chair and watched shadows twitch along the wall like fish in a black pool. Olga had been right. He should not have arranged for Katya's trip to Edmonton. Angel of god, if something had happened to her. These past seven years, the simple fact that she was alive had made life tolerable in this new country.

Olga trod into the room. "She will sleep. I was afraid."

"Yes, I was also frightened."

"Her face, Vasha, it reminded me of your mother. Remember how she took to her bed, refused to eat, how she laid in her bed for weeks and weeks? I worry."

"You worry too much." It was true, Katya resembled her grandmother, but no, it was different with her.

"It was her eyes. She did not seem to know me." Olga rubbed

the side of her neck.

"Do not let your nerves take control. Come." He stood, put his arm around her shoulder and led her to the window. "See, a dark night. But the sun rises again tomorrow."

"She talks of Niccolò Paganini."

"Yes. She has mastered his songs."

"She speaks as if he is alive."

"He is alive to her. To play his music, he must be. Paganini was the finest violinist who ever lived. Every man who picks up a fiddle yearns to play Paganini as Katya does."

"You have told her too many fairy tales, Vasha. As a wife she should turn her thoughts to George and to her house."

"No, wife. She must never neglect the music. It is a gift. Husbands and houses cannot rival this."

"This gift, it will not protect her or give her a baby to love." Olga slipped out from under his arm. "It is late. George arrives early." She left the room.

Katya's violin case was on top of a stack of books. Vasili opened the case and caressed the wood. Such an instrument, as curvy as a goddess in the Hermitage Hall of Statues. He shut the lid and gazed out once more at the black night before climbing the stairs to bed.

Vasili woke with a start. Sharp images flared through his head from the dream. Olga slept on her side, her arms outside the covers, her breast rising and falling at even intervals. He eased himself up from bed and stole into the hall. The early morning glow shone through a crack in the door of Katya's room. Her figure did not move under the quilt. With a gentle pull, he clicked the door shut.

The linoleum in the kitchen was like a sheet of ice. As he walked barefoot to the stove, he wished he'd taken time to get his slippers from under the bed. He stooped to gather paper and sticks from the wood box. Within minutes, the kindling crackled in the firebox and a puff of spicy smoke escaped the burner lid. The dream stayed with him.

From the shelf by the window he slid out a book of poems and held it up to the morning light. Words blurred across the page. Even Pushkin could not compete with his nightmare. The kettle whistled. He fixed a cup of tea, sat at the table and dropped his head to his arms.

"Vasha, you are up early." His wife's hand rested on his shoulder.

Vasili looked up. "Katya is still asleep?" Olga stood beside him fully dressed and alert.

"She has not moved." She touched his chin and raised his face. "The dream again?"

"Yes." Vasili drummed his fingers on the wood of the table.

"The Bolshevik?"

"Yes, and Mother too, this time."

She patted his head. "I will fix eggs and *maskoska*. Get the meat for me. Get up. Move. Put it out of your mind."

Vasili stood, walked to the storeroom at the end of the hall, pulled the last roll of sausage off a hook and returned to the kitchen. "It was cold this morning." He handed the coil of meat to his wife. "Did you forget to add coal to the stove last night?"

"Only a few lumps are left."

"We will buy another bin."

"We've spent most of the money." She sliced and arranged the sausage in a circle at the edge of the frying pan.

"Harry will extend us credit."

"Why should he? We have not paid the bill from last summer."

"Our crop will be better this year."

"We cannot expect him to wait so long." Olga poured steaming water from the kettle into a teapot on the counter.

"Should I wake Katya?" Vasili stood and gulped down cold tea.

"No, let her sleep. If she is hungry, she can eat later." She cracked two eggs into the frying pan and grease spat up.

"You are not eating?" he asked.

"Bread is fine for me," she said. "I do not want eggs."

"But the chickens, they still lay?"

"They lay poorly without music." She flipped an egg with her spatula.

"They miss Katya too," he said.

Olga slipped the eggs onto a plate, arranged rounds of sausage beside them and cut two slices of bread. "Come, eat." She put the plate on the table. "Do not worry over coal. We will burn cow chips during the day, a little coal at night. It will stretch. This is not so bad."

"You need breakfast too." He picked up the plate and handed it back to her.

"I told you. I want bread, no eggs or sausage." She thumped the food down in front of him.

Vasili sat, raised the fork and wiggled the rubbery rim of the egg. "My dream. The picture will not go away." He set the fork on the napkin and turned the chair to face his wife. "We were in New York. I think it was New York. The Bolshevik had followed us there. Mother was with me. I ran along a dark street, the Bolshevik behind in pursuit. Mother skipped ahead, in a white nightgown, her arms waving above her head and she sang the *Internationale* loudly, as if performing at the Metropol."

His wife sat next to him and placed her palm over his clenched fist. "Eat before the food is cold."

"I remember thinking, if only she would not make so much noise, we could escape. She ignored me when I held my finger to my lips and continued to run and skip and sing. I lunged for her and caught the hem of her gown. It ripped. I stumbled and fell flat to my stomach, a torn piece of white fabric in my fingers. Mother disappeared around a corner, the folds of her nightgown split. Her buttocks shone like bones in the moonlight. I heard the heavy footsteps of the Bolshevik come closer and closer. Then I woke. My hands still shake." He raised one hand in the air to show her.

Olga steadied her husband's hand with both of hers. "Never mind. It was only a dream." She released his fingers, stepped to the counter and wiped up a scatter of crumbs.

"Why does he haunt me again now?" But even as he asked, Vasili knew the answer. When he remembered, whenever he sensed Katya was in danger, when his thoughts strayed back too far, the dream was not too far behind.

"There are chores. Chores rub out the terrors from the night." She lifted her hands out of the water and dried them on her apron. "Now, it's time to milk."

"You work too hard. Come, sit. Let me milk this morning." He pulled on his boots and went out.

Sometime later he returned with a full pail of milk, set it in the pantry, opened his book, and smiled at how beautiful the words were once again. His wife was right. The coal would stretch. Katya was safe, asleep upstairs. The cow still produced milk. They were thousands of miles away from the St. Petersburg and the Bolshevik. Olga knew how to defeat that demon dream.

CHAPTER FOUR

Backwater

I woke to light shimmering through white lace curtains and knew I was safe in bed at Papa's house. A few grave notes rumbled through my mind. These notes afforded me enough energy to lift my hand from under the covers and stretch my fingers. Through spread fingers I watched as a man entered the room. He came close, touched my forehead and spoke. But the notes muffled his words. He was a head with moving lips. Then I felt arms under my neck and my legs. He lifted me. The man's smell was familiar and then I remembered it was George who would come and take me back to his farm. He stood me up and his voice broke through, became clear, like the radio at Walker's store when deaf Harry adjusted the knob.

"Come now. We'll get you dressed."

The nightgown tangled in my arms above my head. A cold draft from the window brushed up my spine. My arms flopped free.

"Give me your arm," he said and pulled it straight.

I looked down at my bare legs and gooseflesh sprang up on my legs. As I stared, it spread from my thighs to my knees, small, perfect bumps that flittered along the skin and sent a shiver through my belly. It made me want to cry.

"You're freezing. I don't know why your Mama keeps the windows open at night. It's a waste of coal letting the heat out every night." He sat me on the bed, stomped to the window, slammed it shut, and almost instantly appeared back in front of me. "How did you get so thin in three weeks? It's no wonder you got sick. Didn't your Papa's friends feed you?"

"They were kind," I said.

"You shouldn't have gone." He stuffed my arm into a sleeve and fumbled with the buttons on my blouse.

"I can do that." I moved his wrist aside and my fingers grappled with the loops of fabric and slippery buttons. The notes in my head faded. George held up my skirt, and I stepped into it.

"Here. Your boots." He squatted and reached for my foot.

"It's okay. I'll manage." Once I'd laced my boots, we went downstairs to say farewell to Mama and Papa. By the time we were settled in the sleigh and halfway home, my mind was as silent as a written note.

Winter had fought off spring. The wind blew frigid across the landscape. Walls of poplar stood beside solitary houses like frozen sentries and dirty snowdrifts nudged the barns and fences. Horses paused in the field in pairs, patient and pressed up against each other with frosted lashes. The entire countryside seemed suspended in time.

George and I resembled Egyptian mummies with scarves wrapped around our faces and layer upon layer of clothing.

He reached up, pulled the scarf off his mouth, turned and said, "It's fine to have you home."

I could barely hear him over the wind but he smiled. Poor George. I had used him badly. He covered his face back up and snapped the reins. I leaned over, pressed my fingers to my temple and pushed away the image of another man, a man in Gustav's attic room, a strand of dark hair flopped over one eye. We arrived at the farm before dark.

When spring comes, in southern Saskatchewan, it lands with a fury. The first week of June 1926 was one of the wettest on record. Rain pelted the farmyard with no relief for eight long days. On the ninth day, sun and light swooped across the plain.

George left for the field earlier than usual that next morning. I woke several hours later, stretched under the covers and fingered the threads of scar on my upper lip. A song buzzed in the pillow. I looked over at my violin against the wall by the washstand, climbed out of bed, and picked it up. I intended to play but a tiny bird on a branch outside the window trilled a simple tune with a rare melody. Distracted, I set the fiddle on the bed, dressed and skedaddled outside.

I meant to feed the pigs and chickens and collect eggs but a warm spring wind, a pasture grown high with spear grass, and the sweet smell of clover lured me. Soon the house was out of sight. I roamed as far as the slough at the north end of the property.

The breeze was fresh as if the very air had been washed clean and hung out to dry. The sky was bruise blue, the pasture emerald. Even the ground hogs appeared to have more vigour than usual. I squatted and watched them dart in and out of their holes. One stood ramrod straight on top of his mound and threw me a kiss with his tiny paw.

I wandered the circumference of the slough. The soil was muddy there and my shoes sank in the muck as if weighted. My feet pulled free of my shoes, first one and then the other. Cool, soft mud squeezed up between my toes. A prickle scuttled up my legs.

A wide pool of sludge sidled the pond, and it drew me in. In the middle my feet disappeared. A curious urge followed. I removed my dress and underclothes, sat in the ooze, and watched it seep up between my legs. My thighs melted to smothered humps. I laid down. The rich dirt squished through folds of skin and wriggled into my armpits. My hair became clotted, my head heavy and I rotated until my face was caked.

Rolling to face the sky, I craned my neck in search of an air hole.

Then I lay there, my entire person swaddled in slosh, saturated and buoyant at the same time. And it was warm, wrapped in this earth, and safe like a dunk into warm plum jam. Deep purple coloured my eyelids. Crystals of sugar swam in the sandy grit, and I sniffed the perfume of overripe fruit. The sun's heat signalled no elapse of time. There was no moment, no memory, only the marrow of me and this extraordinary bath.

"Katya, what in God's name are you doing?" Through crusted lashes, I stared up at him, a hulking silhouette with a wide hat, awash in brilliant light. He stomped into my sanctuary. His fingers found my wrist, and he yanked up hard. With a sweep of his large hand, my clothes were fished up and slapped on my shoulders. I stumbled behind as he dragged me along the path, a vice-like grip on my arm. All the way back to the house he didn't look at me or speak. The vein in his neck pulsed like a pig's heart does after slaughter.

When we arrived in the yard, he stood me near the water pump. The muscle on his arm bulged as he worked the lever. He filled up bucket after bucket of cold water and dumped them over my head. It was cold, chilling, mean, water. Bucket after bucket. My clothes slid to the ground in a soggy heap.

After he'd drowned the earth in a puddle by my feet, still he did not speak. He pushed me into the house, shoved me into the bedroom, and left. I sank to the bed and wrapped my shivering, naked body in the quilt. Sometime later my husband returned with my violin in his hand and placed it beside the bed. He rummaged in the top drawer of the dresser and on his way out he grabbed his hat off the hook and closed the door. I heard a key turn in the lock.

"What are you doing?" I shouted and leapt out of bed, clutching the quilt around me. I flew to the door, grabbed the knob, and rattled it. It would not budge. "George, you've locked me in." I tried again. I shouted. "Why are you doing this? George, come back here right now." I pounded the door. I kicked the door.

"I've got to go out. You'll be okay." I heard the kettle slam on the stove. The door banged shut, and the house was silent.

The bedroom had only one narrow window. I was thin, but not thin enough to escape through that tiny hole. Still, I rushed to it and pushed up on the casement. It was nailed and only budged a few inches. A stream of cool air blasted through.

I tried to consider his point of view. I really did. My mud bath must have seemed foolish, but it didn't warrant imprisonment. He had no right to lock me in this room. George did not understand me at all.

I paced and paced, sure at any moment the door would fly open. He would realize his mistake and release me. Hours later when efforts to convince myself dissolved, I picked up the violin and played Pachelbel's *Canon*. Normally, that piece could calm me, but after I'd gone it through several times I was still shaking with rage. I snatched the clothes out of the dresser and threw them in heaps on the floor. I folded the clothes and put them back in the drawers. I played Vivaldi's *Winter* and the spring breeze became a bitter wind that whistled in under that bolted door. When I tired of the song, I ripped the clothes out of the drawers again, and flung them again, folded them again, and shook with rage again. I played Paganini's *Caprice No 17* over and over the rest of the day. By late afternoon, I looked at the window expecting to see bars. Instead, I saw a crow, sitting on the sill like a prison guard, pecking a claw with his beak as if to dare me, "Just try and get out."

My violin quivered with indignation. I dropped it on a pillow and raced to the door again. I made a fist and punched the door. Blood burst from my knuckles and my hand became a knot of pain. I shrieked, "Let me out, right now". The empty house sucked up my screams. I relieved myself in the chamber pot and threw the contents at the window. The crow side-stepped the splash. I wailed. My throat grew hoarse. My hands shook. My breath came in raspy puffs.

It was dark, and I was exhausted when George's key finally clicked in the lock.

"Katya, come."

I was on the bed staring at the wall, legs up, arms around my knees. I refused to turn around but could imagine him in the doorway, dressed like a peasant, ears stuck out from the side of his head, a boorish lout. My fingers clenched. My knuckle bled through a scab, already crusted over.

The bed squeaked, and I felt his weight.

"I'm sorry, Katya, but I couldn't stay in today and watch you. I had too much work to do."

"I didn't ask you to." I pressed my face into my knees.

"Your Papa told me to pay attention." George rested his hand on my shoulder. "He said sometimes I shouldn't leave you alone."

"You misunderstood what Papa said." My voice sounded like someone else's, not the raging voice inside my brain. But I remembered how Mama used to say the same thing before the sickness set in. "Papa told me not to leave you on your own." But she had never locked me up.

"I was worried, Kat." George squeezed my shoulder. I curled up into a tighter ball. "The mud. That was stupid and crazy."

Tears sprang to my eyes, streamed down my face and I swatted them off.

"What were you doing out there? Tell me," he said.

"You are not capable of understanding." My voice cracked. "Go away.

Leave me alone." I didn't lift my head from my knees. The mattress shifted when he stood.

"Suit yourself." His boots clapped across the floor and the door thumped shut. I got up, flung the door open, ran outside and into the field. I ran and ran until gasping for breath. I collapsed in a patch of clover and cried. When I'd finally sobbed myself sick, after the sun set on the horizon, I hobbled through rippling grass and returned to George's house.

It was impossible to put the day out of my head. I went to the parlour and picked up a book. Words blurred on the page. The click of that lock played over and over in my mind and it made me furious—even more enraged than George's locked room at the back of the house, the room I wasn't allowed into. He refused to tell me why it was locked or what was in there.

George kept his distance. He disappeared into that back room and stayed there for the entire evening. At his normal bedtime I heard the padlock click shut and moments later the mattress creaked. I sat on that chair stone-still and waited for his grunts and snorts of early sleep. Then I slipped into the pantry, pulled out the whiskey jug, tiptoed out of the house and across the yard. More than one person could have secrets.

A single kerosene lamp swung from my fingers casting eerie shadows on the barn walls. I shivered in my flimsy night-dress. The barn doors scraped shut behind me, and I waded through the cloud of manure near Ethyl's stall. The cow shuffled and bumped her heavy frame against the wooden rails.

It reminded me of an elephant Papa and I had seen one summer outside St. Petersburg. A circus company had stopped on the side of the road to water their animals. A throng of gypsies swarmed the watering station as dirt-faced children ran rampant up and down the street. The elephant, caged in a wagon, lifted one foot up and slammed it down with a thud, throwing its bulky rump against the slated confines of the pen. The wood bent and groaned on each impact but didn't split. I stared into the wrinkled eyes of that elephant and for a moment shared a connection with the beast, a bond I'd never experienced with an animal. Those desperate eyes had mirrored my own.

I sat down in the prickly hay, pulled my knees up to my chest and scrutinized the cow. What a dismal and useless existence it had. The barn was a quiet, empty shed. There was no music in the shuffle of a cow's feet.

A wild cat streaked across the loft.

All night, I stayed up sipping whiskey from that jug.

Just before dawn, numb and chilled, I slipped back inside and took up my station in the rocking chair by the window. George got up. I didn't acknowledge his existence. He went out.

Sometime late that afternoon my husband returned and prepared our evening meal.

I managed a little sleep that night and the following morning woke feeling much restored. George and I exchanged a few words over breakfast. It was as if what had passed between us had been sopped up and wrung out. I think we both wanted to set aside that day. At eight o'clock sharp George hitched up the wagon for a trip to town.

As the wagon dipped and pitched along the road, the horse's hooves danced side-to-side to avoid familiar holes. I kept my eyes on the horizon, aware only of my husband's presence by the occasional slap of reins. His silence didn't bother me. How could it when the wind hummed a song so sublime and spear grass swayed across the field like the swish of a stallion's tail?

We rolled into Sylvite and George tied the horse in front of the livery before he strode across the street to Joe's Barbershop. A group of men could be found at Joe's any time of day. Some showed up for a haircut, but most went for the talk. The women of Sylvite socialized in church groups, but the men gathered at Joe's. I was to pick up a few necessities and kitchen goods.

I headed for Walker's Mercantile. An ancient steam tractor as big as Mary Perkins' house, sat rusting behind the building. Even it looked charming that day. I climbed the few rickety steps to the entrance.

The store was empty except for the clerk, Deaf Harry. He was perched on his normal stool, like a drone bee guarding a hive of post boxes on the wall behind him. His nose pointed to the same dog-eared copy of *Popular Mechanics* he'd been reading a month before when I'd come to shop. He peered up over his eyeglasses as I wandered in.

Even though I was less than two feet away, he shouted.

"Morning, Mrs. Brown."

"Good morning, Harry."

"Huh? What did you say?" I waved, smiled and turned my attention to the merchandise. The shop was shelved to the ceiling with every provision you could think of: tools, nails, boots, frying pans, blankets, bags of flour, sugar, beans, and oatmeal. Large wooden cracker barrels cluttered the entrance. A red bolt of fabric caught my eye, and I walked to the back, reached out, and ran my hand along its satiny surface. I picked it up, carried it to the front and dropped it on the counter. Harry's eyebrows shot up.

"You want some of this fabric? It's $2.00 a yard," he said.

"My, that's dear," I said. "But it's lovely."

"How many yards you looking for?"

"I'll take it all."

"But, there's ten yards on this bolt. That'll cost twenty dollars."

"I'm not finished." I hurried back down the aisle. Halfway along, a brown box sat on a shelf, not covered in dust, and the label on the front read *2A Box Brownie Camera* - $3.98. I lifted it, turned it over in my hand, and put my eye to the viewfinder. Framed by the camera, an exhibit of perfume bottles glistened in the next row. How clever of mankind to invent this device that could capture a single moment and record it for all time. I tucked the Brownie under my arm and headed for the fragrances. With its slender-necked bottle held to my nose, I twisted off the cap. *Lily of the Valley* is one of the most divine smells on earth. I closed my eyes and imagined how it would feel to step out of a bath and splash such a scent on my skin. But there was the problem of the threadbare bath towel I'd been forced to use since moving in with George. I scampered along and found a stack of towels, ivory white and thick. There were only six. After gathering them up, I rushed to the front of the store.

The red fabric lay right beside a glass jar of Liquorice Whips. Side by side, they formed a lovely picture, and I resolved that would be my first photograph.

"I'll have those Liquorice Whips," I placed my purchases in front of Harry.

"How many?"

"I'll take them all."

He leaned forward and cocked his ear. "All of them?"

I raised my voice and moved my lips with the sound of each word. "Yes, all of them."

He reached under the counter and pulled out a paper bag.

"No," I said. "I want the jar too."

"The jar too?" he hollered. "I have to charge you a dollar for that jar."

"I want the jar." I looked him straight in the eye. "Wrap up the whole jar."

"Will that be cash?"

"No, put it on our account," I said.

"You'll have to sign for it." He pulled a ledger out and picked up a pen. He wrote line by line by line, formed each letter with ridiculous care and glanced out the window and up the street between each word. Finished at last, he pushed the ledger toward me. I signed his stupid book.

Deaf Harry swivelled on his stool and reached up into our mail slot on the top left. "Oh yes, you've got mail in from New York."

My heart bumped my ribcage as he passed me the letter. "Oh, it must be the new sheet music Papa ordered." I stuffed the envelope in my bag.

Moving at the speed of an earthworm, Harry wrapped the perfume, Liquorice Whips, fabric, and towels in brown paper and put the camera in a bag.

Once outside, I stowed my purchases in the back of the wagon, retrieved my violin and set out toward the outskirts of town along the railway tracks. Within minutes I'd passed the park at the edge of town. A wisp of wind drifted through poplar trees that lined the road leading to the rail yard. A wooden fence and grooved path strung out to the horizon. Asleep between the tracks, a grey cat stretched out, rag-like, nose to the sun, tail extended up and dream-twitching. I side-stepped around him.

Across from the rail yard there was a tree, the kind that children love, with sturdy limbs curved close to the ground. One branch offered a sling-like seat and I sat. My hand shook as I withdrew the envelope from my bag. The letters were spaced close together, but distinct, the return address too simple, 130 13th Avenue, New York, New York. I tore open the envelope.

Dear Katya,

I did not get the opportunity to say goodbye or to thank you for the performance in Edmonton. I am in New York now. My audition was successful and I am to be given a chance to perform with the Philharmonic. Many skilled musicians fill the practice rooms and the days are long with music. The red mark on my neck grows larger every day but life is interesting here.

Gustav secured a room for me in a house run by a Russian woman. She is a good cook, but strict. There are six of us and we all take our shoes off in the hallway and do not expect dinner if we are late as much as five minutes.

I think many times of the music we made together. If one day you travel to New York, I hope you will see me.

Yours truly,

Antonio

I read the words over and over until they blurred on the page. The lilac bushes were heavy with flower, effusing a ponderous aroma I could taste. I gazed out past a freight train stalled in the yard. A crow spiralled in the northern sky. As I watched, the bird became outlined in exquisite yellow light. Bathed in the halo, he glided down and landed less than twenty feet away atop a boxcar. His black eye flashed. He looked at me and nodded.

My maiden name initials were printed on the side of the car, *K.P.S.* and right below, *New York, New York.* Before I had time to think, I was at the car, my violin pushed through the narrow opening of the door, my hands on the door handle, and my body hoisted into the empty boxcar. I took my violin out and played. What a haunting sound that vacant boxcar churned out. An hour later, or perhaps two, the train moved and the engine's grumble tried to mute my song.

Astray

Olga had stood in the doorway tapping the garden fork on the floor until Vasili got up and accompanied her outdoors. His wife believed if she did not sow seeds before the first good rain they would shrivel and the earth would refuse to send up shoots. It was an old, tired Russian superstition. Vasili was not so superstitious and muttered a prayer for rain.

He tipped his head and inspected the sky. If the swallows flew low, it would rain. This was not superstition, but based on scientific fact. A flock of high-flying swallows in a clear blue sky dashed his hopes. After turning over one more clump of earth, he stopped to study the landscape, now green, when only weeks ago the fields had been white with snow.

Canada was not so different from Russia. Winter ran on and on and then without notice, spring came. One day Vasili might be blissfully settled in a comfortable chair with a novel and the next day outside with a spade in his hand. A wagon rumbled up the road in the distance. Vasili wedged his shovel into the ground and turned to his wife. "It looks like George. Katya is not with him."

Olga was on her knees between the horseradish and rhubarb, fingers deep in the soil. She drew her hands out and shaded her eyes.

The wagon arrived. George reined in the horse, jumped down and rushed over to them. "Is Katya here?" He squinted at the house.

"No, she is not with you?" Vasili asked.

"She was with me, but now she's disappeared." George spat the words.

"What do you mean, disappeared?" The handle of the shovel slipped from Vasili's fingers and landed in the dirt with a thud.

"I stopped at Joe's this morning. She went to Walker's for supplies. When I went to get her, she was nowhere to be found."

Olga hefted herself up with one hand on her knee. "Do not worry, our daughter, she likes to wander."

"Well, I drove every street in Sylvite and even out past the train yard. There was no trace of her. Mrs. Chambers said she saw her on the South Road hours ago."

"Did you and Katya argue, George?" Olga asked.

"She was fine this morning on the way to town."

"But did you quarrel?" Vasili was familiar with the expression on his wife's face as she asked this. It was the same look she always gave him when he sat too long reading.

"I don't know what got into her. She tried to buy everything in the store. When I came out of Joe's, she was gone."

Olga glanced at her husband, but spoke to George. "What does that mean, everything in the store? What did she buy?"

"Fabric, perfume, a camera—nothing useful, nothing we could afford." George reached up and massaged his neck.

"We will go to town and search for her." Olga's voice sounded calm, far too calm. Vasili sensed the panic underneath.

"You stay here, *Lyubov moya*. If she is off walking, she will come home. I will go with George."

George sprinted to the wagon. Before Vasili could follow, Olga squeezed his arm hard and spoke in a whisper. "Ride up the road to Lloydminster," she said. "Remember how far your Mama sometimes got?"

"We will find her." He patted his wife on the shoulder. "Perhaps she is at tea with a lady in town."

"What lady in town would invite her to tea?" She shook her head.

Vasili knew she was right. Katya had no lady friends in Sylvite.

So Vasili and George set out, a ten-minute ride by wagon. Vasili told his son-in-law he should not worry—women were not predictable and she would be walking in a place he had not thought to look. After all, Katya liked to explore and wasn't she young and full of energy? George did not appear too angry, but his knuckles were white as he gripped the reins. Every few minutes he flicked his wrist and the leather straps spurred the horse faster.

When they reached Sylvite they drove up and down each street and asked people in their yards, "Have you seen Katya Brown?" But no one had. This did not take long. The whole town consisted of only three streets and four blocks. They headed along the main road, toward Lloydminster. When they'd made ten miles George turned the horse around, declared it impossible she could have gotten so far on foot, but Vasili was not so sure. It was near dusk, when back in Sylvite, they stopped on Main Street. John Dari stepped out through the exit of the Legion.

"She has been gone for five hours," Vasili told him. "I worry. It will be dark soon."

"I'll get a few of the boys." John turned and hurried back into the building.

George tied the horse up in front of the church. Then he sat on the steps and dropped his head to his hands. "Damn it, where could she be?"

Vasili leaned against the hitching post and gazed at the

church steeple. "Do you think she has run away?"

"We argued, but I thought she was over it." George stared at his fist, clenched upright on one knee. "She took her violin."

"That is not strange," Vasili said. "She takes it always."

Four men staggered up behind John spewing a cloud of stale beer. A lanky fellow who resembled Abe Lincoln spoke up. "We should check Jackson Coulee. My nephew twisted his ankle there last year. Treacherous, that path down there."

And so they set out for Jackson Coulee. By good luck, the sky was clear, and the grass torched with silvery light from a full moon. They called out for her by name near barns and sheds along the way. Howling dogs replied. They lined up side-by-side and marched through the gully.

Vasili thought the coulee resembled a wrinkle on the flat sheet of the prairie. Vegetation at the top was sparse but as they walked into the furrows, small bushes and thick grasses brushed against Vasili's legs. Cactus prickled and snapped under his feet and he was grateful for his sturdy leather boots. They tramped over a rock formation that discharged pebbles in an avalanche with each footfall.

After they had been to the far edge of the coulee and back, John raised his hands. "We've covered every inch of land to the river. She's not there."

The other men murmured in agreement. The Lincoln man spoke for them. "Let's hold off until tomorrow. She might even be at your house by now, Vasili, fast asleep.”

“Or in a hayloft somewhere,” Jim Hall said. The men nodded and muttered confirmation. Minutes later, they filed off back to Sylvite. But George would not quit. He was like a man sleepwalking: up one path, down another. Vasili followed behind. They covered every piece of ground that led to and through the coulee again. As they plodded along, Vasili considered the road to Lloydminster. He knew how many miles a woman could hike when determined to run away. When the eastern sky oozed out its first morning light, too tired to take another step, they returned to town, climbed into the wagon and made their way back to the house.

Olga greeted them at the door with an anxious face. “You did not find her?”

“No, *Moya zhena*. We did not find her but we will not give up.” He put his arms around his wife, kissed the top of her head and she leaned into his chest. “She will be asleep in someone’s hayloft, no? And now George and I must lie down before our bones collapse from lack of sleep.”

They slept a few hours and when the morning sun was high, George and Vasili set out again.

CHAPTER FIVE

Custody

I stood with my nose to the part-open door of the railcar and grinned. So, this was what they meant by 'riding the rails.' I was a loner, a vagabond, wild and free, thrilled to be out on the beaten track. A cold blast of wind whipped a strand of hair against my cheek. I shivered. A waft of chimney smoke from a lonely farmhouse stung my eyes.

After a while I sat cross-legged and watched the countryside whizz by. The wood floor was too hard to sit on for long and I stood again, stretched and rubbed the bruised bones of my buttocks. Gooseflesh textured the threadbare fabric of my blouse but the chill didn't dampen my mood. I took out the violin. While playing I paced from one end of the railcar to the other and matched my step with the draw of the bow across the strings. The empty car lent an eerie quality to the music. Later, in the complete black of night, the notes, the wind and the churn of the wheels on the track fused in perfect harmony. By daylight I must have covered the length of that car a thousand times.

A raw torrent of air gnarled my hair as I craned my neck out the crack in the door. The morning light brimmed with hope as a city skyline appeared on the horizon. I gazed at the buildings and experienced a pang of yearning for the spires and cupolas of St. Petersburg. But this place did not compare with my home city. Three chimneys jutted up behind a line of low structures. The landscape slowed. Ahead, I could see the dark outline of a man beside the track. I'd heard of railroad detectives who worked near cities, who hauled bums out of cars and threw them in jail for stealing free rides.

I needed to get off soon. The train no longer chugged rapidly along but the ground below still moved at a terrible speed. Drawing a deep breath, I cradled the violin case, closed my eyes, squeezed through the opening and leapt. A squawk sounded, like a terrified bird, and I knew it had come from my own throat. My body hurtled through the air. I hugged my violin closer, wrapped myself around it. An instant later something exploded against my skull.

The sky turned black. My mind drifted away from me.

Then the vision comes. It's familiar, the dim corridor, stairs going down, down, down. I'm half carried and half dragged to a cave-room at the bottom. A man hovers over me and his shadow engulfs me and his evil eyes bore into me.

I've seen him before, near the orchestra pit, one arm draped over the shoulder of a skinny boy while I played, this man's eyes, the only eyes in the hall, his form, larger than the conductor. He wears a military jacket. His dark hair falls in strings over a cratered face.

Even in this shadowy chamber I can make out his contorted expression. I back into the corner. The wall reeks of decay. His hands loom above me. He forces my shoulders down. Cold mud slaps my bare limbs. His liquor-foul mouth sucks away my breath. The sleeve of his coat swats my cheek like the sting of a wasp. My head snaps back, cracks against something hard, erupts with pain. My collar chokes me. Fabric rips. Icy fingers claw my chest, my ribs, my legs, and I twist away. I hear a snarl. Then his teeth clamp onto my upper lip, a vice on my upper lip, ripping, tearing my lip away from my teeth. Then blackness.

My eyes popped open. A face with a bushy moustache inspected me from above. My head throbbed.

"Miss, are you all right, Miss?" He had a kindly face with clear skin, and he wore the hat and overalls of a railroad man.

I let out a deep sigh of relief. "I thought you were someone else."

"What's a young lady like you doing riding the trains?"

"I don't know."

"Darn foolish. You could've been killed." He offered his hand, helped me up and my teeth chattered. "You're frozen stiff, girl. Your lips are blue. Holy Mother, look at that head. You've got a goose-egg the size of my elbow." He took off his coat, put it over my shoulders and led me along the tracks to the station ahead.

It turned out I'd landed in Winnipeg, not New York, in a nasty crevice on the outskirts of that city. I couldn't even run away with any success. Now I'd have to go back to the farm with George—back to the threadbare towels, barnyard stink, and chores.

The switchman spoke to the conductor. They told me they wouldn't throw me in jail. I never thought they would. They said it just to scold me. Then they returned me to Sylvite on a passenger train.

Once home, I limped to Papa's.

As I neared the house, Mama ran out the door and screamed, "Oh, Katya. Oh, Katya," over and over. She scurried along the path toward me, her short legs moving faster under her housedress than I would have ever thought possible. She hugged me and cried as if I'd been away for a year, rather than a day.

Later, in the sitting room, bruised, disappointed, and still freezing, I had time to collect my thoughts. It was good to be safe in Mama and Papa's house. The whole exploit had been an error in judgment. My foot throbbed, propped up on two pillows on the ottoman. Every muscle of my body ached.

I smiled as Mama set a tray on the tea table. "Thank you."

She turned and cocked her head to the rumble of a wagon. "They're home." She scooted into the kitchen. I poured my own tea.

Several minutes later I heard angry voices. Then George appeared in the doorway. His eyes were narrow slits above dark bags. He walked into the centre of the room without taking off his hat and planted his boots right on top of Mama's favourite rug. "What do you have to say for yourself?" Hands behind his back, he paced. "The shopping was bad enough, but to run away?" His mouth was bone tight. "I had every man in Sylvite out looking for you." He stopped his lecture and wrung his hands.

What did he expect me to say? Any explanation would sound like an excuse. But I'd done nothing wrong. I wished Papa had come in with him. Papa always understood. It was easy to explain things to Papa. George stood in the middle of the room, silent, waiting for me to speak. I stared at my throbbing foot.

At last, he spoke again. "Harry came and got me at Joe's. He knows I can't afford to spend forty dollars. Thank God he took it all back. A camera? Bloody hell, what gave you the idea we needed a camera? And perfume? Did you think of flour or sugar? Were we to do without bread, so you could smell good?" George looked at the ceiling and clawed his hands. He was over-reacting.

"You wouldn't understand," I said.

"Try to make me." He stepped to the window and stared out.

I couldn't tell him about Niccolò. That, he would never accept, but I thought he might understand the significance of the sign. "My initials were on the railcar, George."

"Your initials?"

"Yes, *K.P.S.*, right there on the side of the railcar."

"You don't make sense." He walked over and sat in front of me. A vein in his temple twitched. "What do your initials have to do with anything? Besides, your initials are not *K.P.S.* Your initials are *K.B.*. We're married, or have you forgotten that?"

"It was a prophecy. And then there was the crow."

"What prophecy? What crow? What in God's green earth are you talking about?"

"The crow nodded, George. He was in a ball of light on the railcar and he nodded." It was possible that I'd misread the sign, but I could still see that crow bathed in yellow light and I could recall the wind and the wild pulse of freedom as I rode the rails. It made me smile.

George stared at me until his eyes crossed.

"Do you think it's funny? You disappear overnight! The whole of Sylvite is out looking for you! Your Papa and Mama are sick with worry." He put his hands out as if to grab my shoulders but then stopped and stepped back. He began again, his voice controlled. "There'll be no more trips to town for you for a while. I'll take care of the shopping, here on in." He glared at me for a moment and then stomped away. I thought the hinges might fall off the porch door when he slammed it.

George didn't comprehend a thing. He was crippled in a fashion. More crippled than I was with my twisted ankle. My husband had no sense of humour and not an ounce of music in his soul.

George was a plank of silence on the way home that afternoon. This was the least of my concerns. I ached in every muscle in my body. Each bump in the road flogged a different limb. A pain along my spine competed with my throbbing ankle. The trip seemed twice as long as usual, but we arrived at last. George did not look at me or speak during supper and then he disappeared into his secret room at the end of the hall. I had no idea what he did in there and it irked me more and more each day.

I was whipped of energy, but when the inside lever of that back room clanged shut I sprang up and limped down the hall. The door had heavy metal hinges and a padlock, which hung open now and dangled on the bracket. I put my ear against the wood, held my breath and listened to his shuffles.

"Would you like coffee?" I asked.

"No."

"What are you doing, George?"

"I'll tell you one day, but not today." He didn't sound angry anymore.

I crouched and pressed my ear to the door again. There was a thump, a click, a grunt. "Are you sure you don't want coffee?"

"No."

"Why won't you tell me what you do in there?"

"Why don't you go off and play, Katya? Play one of the songs you wrote."

But I didn't play. I was freezing, weak, and my foot still throbbed. In the sitting room, I curled up in a blanket on the chesterfield. After a few minutes I was hot. I threw the cover off. The ache in the small of my back sent out bolts of pain and every inch of my skin hurt. I shivered. The wool fibres of the blanket poked through my dress like a thousand tiny daggers.

Several hours later I heard the door to George's room shut and the padlock click. When he appeared in the doorway, I was on the sofa, shaking so hard my bones rattled, bathed in perspiration, writhing inside the blanket.

"You're white as a sheet," he said.

"I feel ill."

He walked over, leaned down and pressed cold lips against my temple. "You're burning up, Kat. Let's get you off to bed." He lifted me, blanket and all, carried me to our room, and eased me onto the bed.

I opened my eyes and the first thing I saw was George fast asleep on the chair beside me, his eyelashes like the downy plume of the barn swallows that were busy flying in circles near the ceiling. A crow, perched on my dresser, shook its head.

Mary, the neighbour woman stood in the doorway. She lumbered toward me, growing larger with each step. What was she doing here? Three birds flapped around her shoulders, then clawed onto her hair. Near my bed they flew away, and two vanished into the ceiling. The other one melted onto the quilt. Cold glass pressed against my lips. I swallowed and something wet trickled down my chin.

Then it was pitch black and silent except for the ticking of a clock. The quilt pressed heavy on my chest, pillows packed solid against my ears.

I rolled over and light warmed my eyelids. A waft of roasted meat, the clang of pots, the murmur of voices in another room, the flap of wings again.

My eyes opened. Mary's face was so close I could see the hair in her nostrils, a speck of dirt at the corner of her eye. And her face dissolved and became George's face with his pretty lips, too red and perfectly shaped for a man, and the swallows whirled up again, disappearing, reappearing, swooping down. They landed on the pillow above my head. Their feathers plugged my nose, my mouth. I choked.

"You're awake." Mary set a basin beside the bed.

George's eyes flicked open. I attempted to raise my head but my hair was heavy with bird droppings. He took my fingers.

"Looks like the worst is past," Mary said.

"I've been sick?"

"Yes, very sick," George said and placed a cool hand on my cheek.

"How long?" I asked.

"Almost a week."

"Truly, a week?"

Mary wrung a cloth over the basin. "You were delirious for the most part." She tut tutted. "Hungry yet? You've not had enough to keep a bird alive. I'll fix you up a bowl of soup." She arranged the cloth on my forehead and left the bedroom. George patted my hand.

"Why is she here?" I stared at my husband's face.

"Mary is staying for a while." He had a serious expression. "I've given her the spare room."

"How long?"

"Through harvest. She'll probably stay at least until next spring."

"Why? How ill am I? I'll recover, won't I?"

"You'll get better. You just need a little time." He was speaking to me as if I was four years old. "Mary and I have made a bargain. I'll work her fields and she'll help us here, indoors."

"I can take care of the house." Housework had never interested me, but how hard could it be? If the silly cows in Sylvite could do it, so could I. And Mama managed just fine when we moved here. "You know I can learn."

"You're too sick right now. This is a fine arrangement, Kat. Mary can't winter out on that farm on her own. Besides, the company will do you good."

I wasn't so sure about that. George was up to something. I could tell. Why would he invite a complete stranger to live with us? "I don't need company. You want her to spy on me. That's what it is, isn't it?"

"You're being stupid, Katya. She'll prepare food for the threshing crew in the fall. I can't see you getting together four meals a day for twelve men, even if you do learn to cook by then." He frowned at me. I wanted to sit. I wanted my violin. The case was leaning against the wall. My hands pushed away the covers. I tried to lift my neck but the effort exhausted me. My head collapsed on the pillow.

George leaned over and drew the quilt back up. "I'm sorry, Kat. Let's get you better."

For a moment my eyes played a trick. His hair was long, not short, and it was dark. His solid nose was a more chiselled one. His droopy brown eyes became blue and alert. The hand that held mine transformed into the slender fingers of a musician, not the wide, calloused hands of a farmer and I hung onto those fingers for dear life.

George made me stay in bed for a week, so I slept and slept. When I got up, my legs were so wobbly I could barely walk across the room. But it was good to be moving again and my deathly gloom lifted during those next weeks. Mary was a blight on my days, but she stayed out of my way for the most part, and I out of hers.

From my rocker across the room I watched her at the counter washing clothes in a basin. She shuffled over and hung a pair of George's underwear on the line above the stove. Beads of water sizzled, danced on the stovetop and burped up a waft of soapy musk. I wondered what her life had been like before she moved into our house. There had been no clothesline in the kitchen before she came here. She'd put it up to hang George's socks and undergarments, as she had undoubtedly hung her husband's. I'd never spoken to Mr. Kline, and seldom encountered him. Mary had always come to church alone and she was widowed a month before our wedding.

"You must miss your husband," I said.

Her hands stopped churning the soapy water. She turned and looked at me, eyebrows scrunched tight. This was the first time I'd initiated a conversation with her. "Yes," she said. "I do."

"Did you know about his heart?"

"No, he was healthy. Never even had a cold." She wrung out a pair of socks.

"What sort of man was he?"

"You knew him." After lifting the basin with a grunt she tipped foamy water into the slop pail.

"No, I didn't really know him. Was he kind?"

"He was a good man, a hard worker." Mary lifted the trap door leading to the root cellar, braced it up and disappeared down the steep steps. A few minutes later she emerged with a slab of bacon and a crock of butter cradled in her arm. "I'll fix bacon and eggs." She carried the food to the counter. "A hearty breakfast is what you need. Get some meat on your bones." The trap door closed with a thud.

"You need not concern yourself with my bones."

She slapped the slab onto the cutting board and began to search the cupboard, moving things, lifting the tea towel, cookie sheet and the breadboard. "Have you seen the butcher knife?" she asked.

"No." I moved my chair closer to the window.

"It was here last night."

I could feel her stare at the back of my head, could imagine her standing there, hands on her hips. Sunk in the curve of my seat, I nestled into the heavy shawl. "Maybe George took it," I offered.

"What on earth would George want with the butcher knife?"

I sat up, swivelled the rocker and looked straight into her eyes. "You might search under that messy pile of yours at the end of the cupboard." I pointed.

"This one will have to do." She hacked at the meat with a short knife. "George will be in soon. He's milking the goats." The bacon crackled and spat as she lined it up in the pan. The door swung open. "Here he is now."

I smelled George before I saw him enter the room. Goats are

despicable, fetid creatures. The rank odour spilled into the kitchen with him, overwhelming a pleasant fume of bacon.

Mary rushed to pour his coffee. "We had seventeen eggs this morning." Her voice went up a notch whenever George entered the room. It became girlish, with the sickly sweet tone of a dulcimer.

George bent to remove his boots. "Good, I'll take a dozen over to the Davison farm later. Heard they lost all their hens to a coyote last week."

"Shame," Mary said. "Give them two of my hens too and that nasty rooster. I was gonna put him up as soup soon, anyway. Did you hear about the Anderson girl?"

"Heard talk." George pulled a chair out and sat at the head of the table.

Mary set cutlery in front of him. "Nel Brown stopped in on her way to Lloydminster. She couldn't wait to tell me."

"You've got to be careful these days who you hire on. The guy was a drifter, they say. He ran off. No one bothered to go after him." George stirred a spoonful of sugar into his coffee.

Mary wagged her finger. "Nasty business. Denis is a stupid fool. Hasn't the sense God gave a goose, the girl five months along an all. Good thing that man got out of town or Denis might of killed him. Seems it was her papa caught them at it, in broad daylight too."

Mary had a whole orchestra of voice sounds. It was elated

now, with the fluty trill of a piccolo.

She plunked a pitcher of cream by George's cup. "Nel told me what her husband thought of the whole affair. He said the girl should of known better than to wear those low cut dresses, that Denis should of had his head examined, letting his wife run around like that."

"Well, she's back home at her Papa's." George added cream to his cup. "Denis says he can't stand the sight of her. Says the kid, even if it is his, will most surely be tainted and he won't have the brat in his house."

"Shame, but a girl like her is better off with her Papa. Old man Anderson never put up with any shenanigans." Mary marched to the stove, pushed crisp bacon to the side of the pan and cracked two eggs to sizzle in the fat.

I sat to the table. "No egg for me." I held up my hand. The mere thought of an egg spat bile onto my tongue.

"You need to eat more." She held out a plate with toast and a slice of bacon.

"I will eat when I want to." Pushing my chair back, I glared at her.

In those early weeks I feared that Mary was in our home to stay, a female *Domovoi* sent by her dead husband to haunt us forever. She could have sprung from the loins of that ancient goblin. She was short, not five feet tall, had the long face of a draught horse, protruding cheekbones and an angular chin. It was as if her face had kept growing and her legs and arms had stopped. Her hair was dull-brown but thick and might have been pretty at one time, but she wore it as a matron, twisted at the nape. I tried to pretend she wasn't in the house, but every time I turned around, she stared back at me with her horse face.

After breakfast Mary disappeared into the root cellar again and returned with two pails full of sour milk.

"I'll make cheese today." She set the pails by the door to the pantry.

"Let me help." I stood and put an apron on.

George picked up his coffee and left the room. The padlock snapped open on his door at the far end of the hall.

Mary set a cooking pot on the edge of the counter. "Here." She laid out four squares of cheesecloth and handed them to me. "Hold this over the pot."

"I know what to do." My fingers clutched the corners of the cheesecloth.

"Hold tight. Watch you don't drop it." Mary picked up the pail and began pouring. A suffocating stench rose. Putrid white chunks of curdled milk collected in the centre of the cloth and wiggled like maggots. I think she sensed my discomfort and poured the second pail more slowly than the first. I gagged and wrenched my head away but did not release my hold on the cheesecloth. Mary ignored me and concentrated on pouring. At last, she set the pail on the floor and reached for my bundle. "You fasten it with string." She bunched the four corners, wound some twine around the neck and tied a knot. Soon, a great weeping sack dangled from a nail in the far corner of the pantry. It looked alive, dripping its thin liquid into a tin pan placed below.

"We'll leave it for three days." Mary closed the pantry. "It'll be dry by then and I'll show you how to salt it and put it up in a crock."

I escaped to the bedroom, shut the door, lay on the carpet beside the bed, and looked up to where the butcher knife was safely tucked between the springs. It had a razor-sharp edge. A single touch and a thin line of red seared my middle finger. I sucked off the blood, rolled over, got up and climbed back into bed. I was exhausted and weak. How could George believe having that hag in the house was a help?

Estrangement

Vasili leaned on the shovel and glanced up the road hoping to see a distant cloud of dust. Yesterday a letter had arrived from Katya. They planned to visit soon, but she did not say when.

The lilac bush next to the garden plot was in full bloom and its pungent fragrance peppered the breeze. Vasili turned over a scoop of soil. In a few months time, cucumber leaves would inch onto the path and shade their new fruit like umbrellas. Vasili enjoyed watching the garden grow, but to work in the garden was not his favourite pastime. Gardening was his wife's passion. She had insisted on doubling the plot size a year after they had moved in. 'Mrs. Dari thinks I can sell my preserves,' she'd said. What work it had been. The mere thought of all the stubborn grass he had pulled made him tired. Katya, like him, did not take an interest in gardening, but she enjoyed the lilacs. Vasili wondered if he should cut a bouquet now and take them in to perfume the house.

He bent down, tugged up a weed with a grunt and threw it in the pail. How could something with so little purpose grow such roots? Olga had hauled wheelbarrow after wheelbarrow of manure to make this soil rich. She had not expected to feed these greedy thorns. The weed pail was full. Vasili emptied it into the compost box and returned to the house. The turning of soil could wait for another day.

Olga wasn't in the kitchen but canning jars were lined up on the table and the basin floated with rhubarb. At the sink he picked out a red stalk, chewed off one end and then spat the sour wad into the slop pail. "Ugh." Stalks so red should have at least a touch of natural sweetness. He washed the rest of the rhubarb, set each piece out on a towel, and hummed the *Edward Ballade*, a favourite tune by Brahms.

How Katya had loved that song as a little girl. She would sit, small legs wrapped around the leg of the piano while he played. But Vasili had not touched piano keys in a long time.

A month after they had arrived at this house, as a present to her husband, Olga had covered an old armchair with a jacquard fabric she'd brought with her from St. Petersburg. The chair became his reading place. It sat by the window next to a table and if he rested his eyes only on that corner, the library room in his family home sprang to mind. He chose a book from a stack, opened it, moved to his chair and sat to read the Russian legend, *The Sea King's Daughter*. He had not read the story in years, but remembered it well. The main character, Sakdo was a poor musician in the port city of Novgorod whose occupation was to play his twelve-string *gusli* for banquets hosted by rich merchants.

Olga's voice sounded from the hall. "Vasha, are you inside?" She appeared in the doorway. "There you are. I knew I'd find you here."

He looked up. "Do you recall the legend of *The Sea King's Daughter?*"

"Yes, I remember the story."

"But you have not heard it for years." Vasili read out loud. "*Sakdo was well loved and well fed for his music, but lonely and without money, with no opportunity to take a wife. He would sit by the River Volkhov and play to the river because he loved his city, and he loved the river as one would love a wife.*"

Olga sat down on the chair opposite to his and leaned forward. "Do you know who I spoke to minutes ago?"

"No. Who?"

"Mrs. Dari. She walks to town and stopped to bring us a cake. A coffee cake with raisins and oatmeal."

"It was kind of her."

"Yes, she is a good neighbour." Olga tapped her shoe on the wood floor.

He turned the page in the book. "Listen. Ah, this story makes me think of home. *Late one night, while Sadko played, the King of the Sea came, who was so moved by his playing, he hired Sadko to play at a banquet in the depths of the Baltic Sea, paying him beforehand with a large, solid gold fish.* Do you remember what Katya would say when I read her this part?"

"No, I do not." Olga put two fingers to her forehead and closed her eyes for a moment.

"'Would a gold fish be hard to chew, Papa?' Every time, she said the same thing."

Olga leaned forward with a tense expression. "John Dari has almost finished his seeding."

"Remember this part? *It was not easy but Sadko made his way to the King's Castle at the bottom of the sea. Once he arrived, he played for the King and his subjects. The King was so roused by the music, dancing and waving his arms, the Queen feared he would destroy the earth with tidal waves.* Right here, Katya always put her little hand up to stop me and recited this next part by heart. *To save his beloved city, Sadko cut one of his strings and pretended his gusli had broken.*"

"Mrs. Dari says if the seed is not in by the full moon, the wheat will not grow heads."

It was not like Olga to speak so loudly. Was she losing her hearing? "Yes, John speaks of the full moon. It is his superstition."

"His crop was big last year." Olga got up, walked to the sideboard and picked the seed catalogue out from under a stack of paper.

Vasili turned his attention back to the book. "I should give this to Katya. How she loved this story." He ran his hand over the page and continued to read. *"Still, the King was most impressed and offered Sadko his daughter in marriage. She was beautiful and Sadko married her. It wasn't until after the wedding, at the reception the King told him that if he kissed his new bride or embraced her, he would transform into a citizen of the sea and never again be able to return to his beloved city. With great difficulty, when he lay with the King's daughter in a bed of seaweed the night of the wedding, Sadko restrained himself from touching her."*

"Will we plant our seeds soon?" Vasili's wife rustled the pages of the magazine.

"Our field is small. There is time. Listen, I have nearly finished. There is always a King and a daughter offered in marriage, eh?" He chuckled, squinted and held the book out at the end of his outstretched arm. "I will need longer arms soon. *'For many hours Sadko lie beside his new wife and stared up at the sky of sea above. Sleep finally came. Sadko awoke the next morning on the banks of the river, with the walls of his city at his side. He was a rich man, became successful, married and lived a happy life on earth.'"* He closed the book and cradled it in his lap. "A good story for a child. Perhaps she will read it to her daughter one day."

Olga stood and wandered to the window. "Is that John Dari who walks across the field?"

Vasili closed his book, stood up behind her and put one hand on each of her shoulders. "I am not sure."

"Yes, it is him. See the big hat and the way he walks."

Olga was observant. John had the bowed legs of a horseman. He rode his horse more often than he walked but the awkward gait was most likely caused by his enormous belly. "He looks troubled." Vasili watched as John Dari grew closer and stomped up the wooden stairs leading to the back door, a pile of papers under his arm. Olga opened the door before he had a chance to knock.

John bundled through the door and tossed the handful of paper on the kitchen table, the top sheet stamped FINAL NOTICE in red ink. "Damn government." He looked at his boots, shifted from foot to foot then picked up a sheet of paper and held it up for them to see. "I don't know what they want." He passed it to Vasili. "I'd be obliged if you could read this for me."

Vasili took the paper from his friend, sat and scanned the page.

"Neither the wife or me had much schooling," John said. "My Papa wasn't strict on book learning. Kept me home most days to help in the fields."

"It says you are six months late on your taxes." Vasili pointed at the line.

"I paid the taxes."

"When did you pay them?"

"Not very long ago."

"Did you send payment in the Post?"

"No, John Junior and I went to the government office in Lloydminster."

"John Junior left last spring did he not? Katya left in the fall. He left more than a year ago."

"Yeah, I guess it's been a year. Don't seem that long." John looked up at the ceiling.

It seemed much longer than one year to Vasili. Since Katya left, time floated by as slow as an iceberg in the Baltic Sea. "The paper claims if the taxes are not paid by December 31st, the interest will double."

"This government's gonna drive us all to the poor house." John made a fist and screwed it into his temple.

"It is four hundred and twenty-two dollars. I will write to them and explain."

"Sit down, John," Olga said. "You will have coffee?"

Vasili sat, picked up a pen and composed a letter. Poor John.

His son had left and taken the written words with him. Vasili understood his loss. Katya had left and taken the music with her.

"Oh, I almost forgot. There's a letter for you from Katya." John handed over an envelope.

Vasili tore it open and scoured the page with a frown. "She is not coming. She hopes it will be soon, when George is not so busy."

After John left Vasili shuttled from the kitchen into the parlour, sat in front of the desk, and let his fingers run the table top as if it were a keyboard. It gave him little pleasure though. It was more and more difficult to imagine the sound of the notes.

CHAPTER SIX

Riddles

THAT whole summer following my illness I was weak and tired. Oh, so tired. I spent most days in my chair, reading, gazing out the window or staring at my hands. They were bony hands, white with long slim fingers, long like my legs, which became so thin, I couldn't stand to look at them when I dressed. At least my hair hadn't fallen out from the fever. Had it, I wouldn't be able to glance in the mirror again. My hair was still dark and wavy, the only fat thing left of me.

We didn't go to town in August. Besides George and Mary, John Dari was the only other person I saw. He brought books and correspondence from Papa who wrote of Russia and music. I knew most of the books, but re-reading them saved my sanity. In every letter Papa asked to see me. We would have to go to them. Papa's horse was too old to make the trip and in one letter he expressed worry for Mama, mentioned how weary she'd become since I left.

How I yearned for them both.

I hardly saw George all summer. He was up and out in the field before dawn and back in the house only after dark. But Mary was there all day, every day—the only person I had to talk to.

Mary was like my Mama in some ways, but only in some ways. She could have twelve pots boiling on the stove, the oven full of baking, laundry in the washtub and a half-finished doily waiting on the chair. Her hands took over as if they had a mind of their own. She fit in the kitchen as well as the lid on the butter dish. Mary cooked and sewed, threw scraps to the chickens, slopped the pigs, and did it all with the same grim look on her long stern face.

My mama was as efficient as Mary, but she often hummed as she worked and was always quick to laugh. Even if she wagged her finger at Papa or at me, her face always seemed on the brink of a grin. We never took her scoldings seriously.

Mary was at the kitchen table and busy as usual, rolling the top for a Saskatoon pie. It was unusual to see her sit, but she had twisted her foot earlier, slipped in a fresh cow puddle on route to the barn. She'd limped in leaving a trail of muck, sliced up four cloves of garlic, placed them on her swollen ankle, and secured this with two layers of cheesecloth. An aura of garlic saturated the air. She shifted her leg and winced, but at least she wasn't whining.

I leaned forward in the rocking chair. "Were you born here, Mary?"

"Here?"

"In this province?" I asked. "On a farm?"

"Over by Gravelburg." She pointed to the window.

"How did you end up in Sylvite?"

"I married Fred."

"Have you ever been to Winnipeg?"

"No, heavens. Why would I go there?" The rolling pin stopped. She brushed her hands together and a cloud of flour floated up and settled on her dress.

"I'm only trying to make conversation," I said. "I've been there." I thought to ask her if she'd been to New York, but she would never have travelled so far. "I wanted to go to New York."

"Why?" Picking the piecrust up with four fingers, she scrutinised it and then draped it over the mound of purple berries in the pie pan.

"New York has an enormous concert hall, as big as the Conservatory they say." I closed my eyes and imagined that concert hall with Niccolò in it. He'd be with twenty musicians or more, centre stage, a long strand of hair over one eye, the violin under his chin. The vision became vivid, his fingers working the frets and the bow sliding along the strings. But the hall remained dead silent, Niccolò and the other musicians moving about the stage as if playing but they created no sound. I squinted and tried in vain to hear music. Panic gripped me. I opened my eyes to see Mary bent over the open oven door. She slid two pie plates onto the metal rack with a heinous screech. I covered my ears.

When she'd finished limping around the room, brushing the flour off the table, sweeping up the floor and when she finally sat, I spoke to her again. "Are you ever afraid, Mary?"

"Afraid of what?"

"Silence."

"What do you mean, silence?"

"You know, a void—where there's no music, no laughter, no sounds in the night."

"I've no idea what you're talking about, Child." She reached to rub her ankle. "I like the quiet."

I knew she wasn't lying. She was serious. Music was not important to her. I almost envied her. How much simpler life might be without music, but oh, how tragic.

"Your ankle still hurts?"

"It's fine." Lifting her foot, she pointed her toe and wiggled it. "Much better. Should be right as rain tomorrow." She stood and hobbled to the stove.

I lifted the hem of my dress and glanced at my own feet, at the small bump above the bone on my right ankle. It was as if a pebble from the railway siding I'd tumbled into had slipped under my skin and hitched a ride.

"Mary, what's your favourite song?"

"Don't know that I have one."

"Come, you must have one song you love," I said.

"Well, maybe *Let Me Call You Sweetheart*."

"I know that song. It's a charming tune. I'll play it for you."

I picked up my violin and played. The song, with only two short verses, suited a piano better than the violin but it sounded well enough. Mary sat at the table again, eyes closed and rolled her head to the music while I played it over several times.

"They played that one at my wedding," she said when I stopped. "A real pretty song."

The way she gazed at the wall, I could imagine her as a new bride.

"Tell me."

"What?"

"About your wedding, your marriage. What was it like?"

The corners of her mouth curled into a smile and she stared out the window. "Well, I was young." Her expression turned wistful. "I'd found myself a respectable man and looked forward to a house full of children and a nice garden. 'Six boys,' Fred told me the day of the wedding. 'I want at least six boys,' but then he added, 'You can have as many girls as you want.'"

"But you had no children."

"No, I'd of liked a baby, but God didn't see fit." Mary didn't speak for a moment, the hint of a smile gone. Smells of Saskatoon pie wafted through the room. "It bothered my husband. You see, my Fred was an only child. His Mama died in childbirth."

It was a fact, yes. Women died in childbirth. An anxious twinge pricked the skin above my belly button.

"He never saw his own mom's face." Mary tapped her fingernails on the table. "That crazy old Daddy of his raised him by himself. Used to whip Fred with a riding crop with metal bits on the end. He had terrible scars on his backside and all the way down his legs."

"That's awful." I had an unfortunate vision of old Fred's bottom.

"A drinker," she said. "One night Fred was out tending a breach calf in the west field. His Daddy was home in bed, dead drunk, must've knocked over a kerosene lamp. Fred said he'd never seen nothing like it, this big red glow in the sky at two in the morning. By the time he got back to the house, it was all over. Folks thought Fred had a hand in it."

"They didn't?" The cruelty of people during sorrowful times astounded me.

"They did—those who knew the old man and how he treated his son." She nodded and then smiled again. "But that's how I met Fred. He sold off the livestock and came up to Gravelburg. Took a job with the threshing crew, and worked my Daddy's wheat that fall."

"How old were you?" I asked.

"Fifteen." Mary's lips settled back into a stern line but she continued to gaze at the wall. "It was a long time ago." After a few moments she shook her head. "Better quit rambling, though, and get the bread started." She stood and stumped over to the counter. I watched her measure yeast into a small dish and then add cup after cup of flour and water into the bread-bowl. Within minutes she was up to her elbows in bread dough, pushing, pulling, rolling a soft white ball across the counter as she hummed "Let Me Call You Sweetheart."

It exhausted me to watch her. "I think I'll sleep for a while. Not sure where my energy has gone."

"Run along then." She waved me off. "Don't worry. You'll soon get your strength back."

"I'm tired all the time these days." I shuffled off to the bedroom.

I didn't wake until the next morning. It was Sunday with nothing to look forward to. George had declared, once again, that he was too busy to take us to church. I questioned this declaration of busyness. The sun was up and he was still buried in the covers next to me, fast asleep. I slipped out of bed and tiptoed to the kitchen.

Every pot in the house was on the stovetop bouncing and cracking, filled to the brim with water. Clouds of steam billowed up to the ceiling and beads of perspiration speckled the glass jars on the shelf.

"Good, you're up. Go and get the tub set up," Mary said. "We may not be going to church, but that's no reason to skip our bath."

I got the blanket out, laid it over the rug in the parlour, drew the crinkled old tub down from its hook on the wall and gathered the towels and soap. We began filling it.

"You have the first bath," Mary said. "I can't take it so hot." She bent and dipped her hand in the water. "I think that's even too hot for you. I'll get some cold from the rain barrel." She closed the door on the way out and I undressed. When she returned with two pails of water, I was standing naked on the blanket.

She looked away and dumped the cold water. "You'd better get in. You'll catch your death."

"Can you wash my hair, Mary?"

"Can't you do that yourself?"

"Yes, but it feels wonderful to have someone else do it. I can wash yours too if you like."

"I can take care of my own hair, but get in. I'll wash yours if you want."

I climbed in. The water was still scalding, but I sank in and watched my legs turn red.

"Sit forward." She dipped the pail behind me. Then water spilled over my head, flooded my face and I choked and sputtered. "Tip your head back." She poured another stream over me, then picked up the soap and rubbed it over my hair until a lather built. Then her hands wound through my hair and her fingers massaged my scalp.

"You're good at that." My head relaxed in her hands.

"Used to wash Fred's hair." Her fingers moved in circles at my temples. "He didn't have much hair, but he seemed to enjoy it."

I splashed water over my eyes to take the soap away and peered at her. Squatted beside the tub, her one large breast hung over the edge, eye level, inches from my face, bare under the thin fabric of her housedress, the dark outline of a nipple just visible. I reached up and touched it. The nipple hardened.

"What are you doing?" She swatted my hand.

"You have lovely large breasts. Mine are so small." I cupped each tiny breast in my hands and lifted them up. They were small but sore and somewhat swollen. Mary stared for a moment, shook her head, got up and dumped water over me again, four pails full. I nearly drowned by the time she finished.

"Let me know when you're done." She stomped out of the room. I finished washing, dried myself, threw on my dress, and went to the bedroom. George was still asleep, covers half thrown off, all brawn and biceps, the image of a bronzed Greek God. I crawled under the covers with him and woke him in a way he didn't object to.

Life on the farm droned on. Snow came early, the last week of

September. George barely had the wheat cut and stooked when one afternoon the wind picked up and hurled a fine dusting of snow over our pasture. The threshing crew arrived that week. They worked fast, only stopped to eat, and only for the time it took to devour their food as they rushed to get ahead of the weather.

One day the sun came out. I bundled up and went out to the west field to watch. It was a race between the threshing machine and winter as load after load of sheaves flew into the mouth of the contraption. A storm of chaff churned in the air around the machine. The men who worked the device lifted, cut the binding and tossed the stalks on a belt that delivered wheat into the jaws of the thresher. Other men guided it in, fed and pampered the unit. It chewed up the crop, spit straw to one side and nuggets of grain into bins on the other, bins that would later be hefted, hauled into town and converted to cash at the Saskatchewan Elevator Company.

Four times a day Mary loaded the wagon and set out to the field with steaming pots of stew, bean soup, cabbage rolls and loaves and loaves of bread. She bundled the food in flannel sheets to keep in the heat. After two weeks of this, the machinery rolled back down the road and the crew disappeared over Larkin hill. The whole undertaking was over as quickly as it had started, and I was left with Mary again.

In November winter marbled the fields. Each morning I watched Mary trudge through the yard in gumboots, a pail dangling at her side, a smudge on the white-sheet landscape—Mary, the sturdy, Canadian farm woman. The door would open, a stream of frosty air slipped into the room, the pail clanged on the floor and heavy feet stomped three times. The sameness of her routine was maddening.

"You shouldn't leave the door open so long." I pulled my wool shawl up around my neck.

"You're up. Good." She struggled out of her heavy coat. "I'll put the kettle on." At last, she slammed the door.

Mary poured water into the kettle from a dipper hung on the side of the pail, opened the lid on the stove, and added a few sticks from the wood box in a single fluid movement.

"Cold out this morning." She rubbed her hands together.

This was the same thing she said every morning, except sometimes it was "warm out this morning" or "wet out this morning". It was always warm, wet, or cold—never hot, dripping, crisp or absolutely divine.

Mary had been in the house for five months and during that time, my demons had been quiet, my violin case sat open and music spanned my days again. But I knew the tranquil periods were not to be trusted.

The crow sat perched in his usual spot outside on the fence. The rest of his kind had migrated south months ago. He hopped across the yard on one leg, feigning illness to gain Mary's sympathy and the bits of food she would take to him later. But the crow courted me. He bounced toward the house, an awkward, sideways dance over an icy patch. Mary walked up behind me.

"Oh, look at it," she said. "Must of broken a wing, poor thing." She leaned over my shoulder and tapped the windowpane.

"He has you fooled," I told her. "There's nothing wrong with him."

"Poor creature. Trying to make it through winter," she said.

The black devil stopped and looked at us. In the glint of his eye shone the embodiment of Loki, that trickster god of Norse mythology.

I pointed at him. "Don't you understand what he is?"

"He's a crow, a sorry, dumb bird. I'll take him out a handful of scraps later." Mary turned and marched to the stove. There was a clatter, the rich scent of coffee, the hiss of water as it hit the stovetop.

As soon as she walked away, Loki began his dance... backward, forward and twirling, feathers distended, a frenzied reel... his mating ritual. He kept one eye on me. When his body twisted, his head did not, a whirling dervish, black, black against the white, white snow. Most days I couldn't take my eyes off him, but that day I swivelled the rocking chair and set my gaze on

Mary.

"Do you know why they call it a *murder*?" I asked her.

"Whatever are you talking about, Child." Mary didn't glance up. She cut stiff matrimony cake, lifted the squares out with a fork and arranged them on a plate.

"A *murder*. That's what people call a flock of crows."

"Humph." She walked over and plopped the cake in the middle of the table. "A murder. You make up tales."

"I don't. I read."

"Well, all I know is, it's grim weather for a bird this time of year." She poured coffee into cups, no sugar, a tablespoon of cream. "Here you go." She set a cup of steaming coffee on the windowsill and walked away.

I turned the rocking chair around to face the window. The crow was gone. "Where are you now, Loki? Hiding, aren't you? But you'll be back, won't you?"

The quilt on our bed had a thousand birds in flight, all the same, blue on a rust backdrop—haphazard, like a hundred chickadees that flee when you shake the bush. But if you looked closely, you could see a pattern. I had no idea where it came from but it was this bedcover that drew attention when you walked into the room. At first I thought I'd never sleep with that many birds covering me, but the quilt was exquisite. I slumped on top of it and pulled up the wool foot-blanket.

When I woke from my nap, the house was quiet. I wandered into the kitchen and through the living room. Muffled voices were coming from the end of the hall, from George's secret room. She was in there with him. I moved close to the door and held my breath but couldn't make out any words, only Mary's gravelly voice and laughter.

I tiptoed down the hall, into the sitting room and sat on the straight chair by the window gulping back angry tears. And I had felt sorry for her. Poor Mary, poor Mary. How many times had they met in that back room laughing at me? Her knitting stuck up from a basket by the chair. I bent over, tore the needles out, threw them across the room, pulled on the wool until her latest creation unravelled. Then I started on the balls of yarn. I pulled and pulled with fury, first one ball and then the next until all four balls twisted into a tangle of colour. When I could do no more, I picked up my violin and played.

"Come and eat, Katya," George stopped in the doorway and hollered over the "Devil's Trill." I ignored him and he sent Mary in.

"You can't live on music." She tried to stare me down. Then she noticed her knitting in a tangled heap in the corner. Her hands fisted up and her entire face screwed into an angry knot. "Look at this mess. Do you know how many hours of work you just took apart? Of course you don't. You don't know a blessed thing about work."

I turned to the window, closed my eyes and continued to play. I slipped into the *Bohemian Melodies.*

"You're a spoiled child."

I fled across the room and played to the wall.

"Stay here then. I don't care if you starve to death." She stomped away at last.

But I *could* live on music. I *could* eat the octaves, drink the notes and live like a Queen. They were both brainless imbeciles. I played and played and played.

After several hours, I looked up to see George standing in the doorframe.

"What's the matter with you, Kat?"

"What's the matter with me?" This was too much. I stopped playing. "What do you do in that room?"

"Why are you always on about that?"

"She was in that room with you. I can't go in, but she can?"

"I told you before," he said. "It's a surprise, for you."

"You never told me about any surprise. I don't want a surprise."

He shook his head.

I stumbled to the coffee table and kicked it. A glass candy dish flew off and smashed to the floor, green mints scattered and twirled like tops on the hardwood.

"That's enough." He marched toward me glaring.

I hugged the violin so hard the bridge cut into my ribs.

George's jaw clenched to a bony wedge. Then he turned, and with stiff even steps, left the room. I started to play again, not a song I knew and loved, but a siren tune, a single stanza of three lines over and over again.

Later, much later, I collapsed on the couch, exhausted. The bow rattled to the floor. Notes still rang in my ears though, and this satisfied me, spent as I was. Closing my eyes, I clutched the neck of the violin. My other hand pressed a soft spot on my temple that tingled with remembered pain.

Reunion and Unrest

Vasili moved another stack of books from the table in the parlour to the floor. He glanced at the bookcase and let out a huff of exasperation. It was overflowing and two-layers deep.

His library had expanded since they'd been in Canada. Sergei sent books from New York, and from other places where he was on tour, at least one per month. But to find any single book was an impossible task.

When they'd fled St. Petersburg, there had been little time to gather belongings. He knew things left behind would now be in the hands of the Bolsheviks. But before the boat sailed Vasili had gone back to the house with a wheelbarrow, under cover of darkness, and had packed his books. Leaving them would have been unbearable.

"Where is it? Curse the thing!"

"Where is what?" Olga walked in the room. Then she gasped. "What are you doing?"

"I am looking for the book on Antonio Vivaldi, for Katya. It is here, I know." He picked up another stack, set them on the divan, bent, and sorted through them one by one. "Do you remember what colour it was?"

"I do not remember the book." She inspected the jumble, hands on her hips. "Look at this mess. They'll be here soon."

He surveyed the room. Yes, there were many books, wonderful books. Most of them were leather bound with gold-gilt pages. True, the bookshelf had insufficient space, and he had to stack volumes on the furniture and the floor, but books were never a mess. So what if his collection took up room? There was no reason to serve tea in here when the kitchen had an adequate table. "It is not so tragic. Only a few books."

"Where will our guests sit?" She flipped her hand at the book-covered chairs.

"I'll pile them against the wall as soon as I find it." He patted the stack and glanced up at his wife.

Olga sank down on the only free chair, her right hand on her chest, out of breath. She closed her eyes, her face pale, except for two rosy spots, one on each cheek.

"Do not be upset. If we can put up with a little disorder all the time, George and Katya can tolerate it for an evening."

She groaned.

"Are you ill?" Vasili stepped toward her, laid his hand on her shoulder, and she opened her eyes.

"I feel fine. Just tired. Come, we will straighten the books. I'll help you find *Vivaldi*." They began to sort.

She held up a black book. "Is this it?"

"You amaze me. On top of the pile. I could not see the fir trees for the sticks." He leaned over and kissed the red spot on her cheek. "What would I do without you, *Zhena*?"

Later, when the parlour was organised to Olga's satisfaction, she went upstairs to rest, and he relaxed with the book. He had forgotten how good it was. The page fell open at the place where Vivaldi creeps into the sacristy to compose his musical ideas. He had not wanted to be a priest, poor man, but his family forced him. Sometimes in life, choices are limited. If things had been different, how much more music would Vivaldi have given the world? Would Katya remember the story?

"Papa? Where are you, Papa?"

He looked up from his book. Katya stood in the doorway, her violin case cradled in one arm, her silhouette rimmed by light. He took in a breath. For a moment, she looked like his mama, as she had been in the old days, the days before the distress. On his daughter's face he could read that same passage of sadness and unrest.

"Katya, you are finally here." Vasili hugged her for a long time.

"George ran into Ernie Reeger at the store. I thought they'd never quit talking. Where's Mama? The house is too quiet."

"Your mama is upstairs resting. And George, is he with you?"

"He and Mary are tending to the horse." She scowled and leaned in close. "I don't understand why we had to bring that woman with us today. Did you hear? George has invited Mary to live with us."

"Yes, he wrote to me when you were ill." Vasili would rather have time alone with his daughter. With Mary along conversation would be difficult, but what was done, was done. "It is good, no? Having Mary at the farm? She must be a big help."

"Well, she knows how to cook." Katya cracked a smile and winked. She laid her violin case on the table and looked around the room. "It's nice to be home, Papa."

"Yes, it has been too long."

"I'll go upstairs and see what has happened to your mama." Vasili hurried upstairs and peeked in the bedroom where Olga was fast asleep on top of the covers. He walked in, bent and jiggled her shoulder. "Time to get up."

"What?" Her eyes popped open and her forehead wrinkled in confusion.

"Olga, Katya is here."

"What? Now? Today?"

"Yes, today, for dinner. Remember?"

"But I have no food cooked."

"You worked in the kitchen all morning. Did you not cook? I swear it was *shashlyk* I smelled this morning."

"This morning, are you sure?" Olga closed her eyes and rolled away from him.

"Wake up, *Myshka*. Your daughter is home."

They heard the door slam, the sound of George's voice. "Kat?"

"I'd better go downstairs." He headed for the door.

"I will come, in two minutes."

George and Mary settled in chairs in the middle of the room and chattered to Vasili about the weather and the farm as he leaned against his bookcase. Katya sank into her father's reading chair by the window turning the pages of the book he'd found for her. It was fifteen minutes before Olga's footfall sounded on the stairs. When she appeared in the doorway, Katya jumped up, ran over and pulled her into a hug. "Mama, I'm so happy to be home. How I've missed you." Katya was a full head taller than her mama, but half the width or less, a stick beside a boulder Vasili thought—too thin.

"I did not wake up." Olga wriggled out of the hug. "Dinner will be late."

"That's okay, Mama. We're not famished, are we, George?"

"No, we're fine." George got out his pipe. "But we can't stay overnight. Ernie's coming over first thing tomorrow to help with the butchering."

"Are you okay, Olga?" Mary asked. "Your face is white as a

sheet."

"I am fine but dinner is not. There are things to do."

"Let me help." Mary followed her into the kitchen.

"Why not play, Katya, while we wait?" Vasili lifted the violin from its case and held it out to his daughter. "I have missed your songs. There was no music this summer, even at church. Mrs. Bradley, the organ player, has been away in Lloydminster. Her daughter had twins."

Katya was halfway through the first stanza of *Arioso* when a crash sounded from the other room. She paused mid-stroke.

Vasili flinched and yelped. "What was that?"

They heard a clamour and Mary's voice. "Goodness sakes."

Katya hurried toward the kitchen with Vasili and George close behind her. Olga was flat on the floor near the icebox, pots and pans strewn across the linoleum.

"I don't know what happened," Mary said. "I heard a crash, I turned, and she was down on the floor."

"Olga?" Vasili rushed to his wife, squatted and put his hand under her head. Her eyes popped open. She shook her head.

"Mama, are you okay?" Katya crouched next to her Papa and patted her mama's arm.

"No fuss." Olga struggled to sit. "I am only clumsy."

"Lie still for a minute." Vasili placed a hand on her forehead.

She twisted her head away and struggled to stand. "Dinner is ready soon."

Less than an hour later, they sat to eat. Vasili kept an eye on his wife. Mary was right. Her face was too pale, and she pushed her food around on the plate.

Katya took her papa aside before they left. "You should call the doctor in to look at Mama."

"You know how your mama hates doctors."

It was nearly dusk when the guests rumbled away in George's wagon, but for Vasili, the world turned dim. His daughter's place was with her husband, he understood this, but knowing the fact did not make it easy.

When Vasili joined his wife under the covers that evening, her feet were like frozen potatoes. He made her stay in bed the next day. She did not even complain that they missed church. In the afternoon, Vasili walked over and borrowed a bag of coal from John Dari. The house stayed warm that night.

The next day Olga's face was still pale, but she seemed improved. She was up at dawn making *voreniki*. The kitchen table was overspread with a flattened square of dough. An empty molasses tin sat upside down next to a large bowl of mashed potatoes and onion. There was barely space for Vasili's elbows on the table. The aroma of butter-fried onions filled the room. The smell always outweighed the taste, so he could wait. But the scent reminded him of Russia and Russia reminded him of music and the thought of music made him long for his piano.

Vasili tapped his fingers on the edge of the table, closed his eyes and visualised his piano. It had been a Style-7 Blüthner Grand and the envy of every musician in St. Petersburg. He had chosen it himself, made the journey to Leipzig, the year he'd finished his studies. He could still see where it had sat in the music room, the colour of burnt umber, and as he tapped, could hear the lyrical notes of the *Slavonic Dances.*

Olga's rolling pin slammed into his fingers. "So, Mary will live with George and Katya. This is not good." Olga sounded out of breath again, as if she'd run from the barn to the house. One corner of her dough was thick. She grunted and pressed it flat, then using the tin, punched circles into the slab.

Vasili's fingers stopped mid-beat. "It was you who suggested Mary visit Katya, at church that day."

"But I did not suggest her to move in with them." Olga slapped the side of the tin and a piece of dough fell loose.

"It is a good arrangement. George will work her fields and she will take care of the house."

"Our daughter has been married less than a year. It is not right."

"Katya will have more time for her music."

"She needs to learn how to care for her house and husband." After pressing out the last circle, she put the tin to one side, lifted the bowl and spooned potato mixture into the centre of a patty.

"She is young. She will learn." Vasili tapped his fingers on his leg.

"When she was thirteen, you said the same. To her, the kitchen was a place for a meal. She would have eaten with the violin under her chin if I had allowed it. And now she is a married woman and cannot fry an egg."

"She will watch Mary, and learn."

"Did she watch me? Did she learn? And Mary will not stay forever. What will happen if she relies on her for everything and then the woman leaves? What if Mary finds a husband?"

"Mary's prospects for a husband are not good." Vasili pushed his chair away and stood as Olga circled the table.

"She is plain and getting older, but Aylmer Harris might welcome a housekeeper. Mary has no children to burden him with. She works hard too." Olga dipped her fingers in a glass of water, folded the dough into a pocket and pinched the edges together.

"Aylmer Harris does not have the courage to speak of marriage. He has trouble conversing with his dog. No, it will not happen. It is lucky Mary is there. It is useful for Katya and convenient for George."

"Two women, one man—the first year of marriage. This is normal?" She stopped her chore and stared him in the eye.

"It was not so awful for you, was it?" he asked. "My mother, she did not get in your way?"

"No, she never put a foot in my kitchen, just like our daughter. But she was in your thoughts always. She might as well have been with us in the bed."

"So, you were glad to be rid of her? Happy when she died?"

"No." Olga planted her hands on her hips. "Do you still blame me?"

"Of course not. I've said it many times. It wasn't your fault."

His mother's episodes of melancholy had been severe. One moment she was cheerful and full of fun, the next on the brink of suicide. Four times, she attempted to take her own life. On the fifth try she had succeeded. Vasili had never forgotten the blood in the bathroom—so much blood. He knew it was his fault, not Olga's. He should have stayed home more. His wife had never learnt how to read the signs.

"Well, that is past. We were talking about our daughter and her husband." Olga waved one hand above the bowl.

"Well, it's not our decision, is it? Often, you tell me to keep my nose out. So, we will not interfere." He walked away.

"Where are you going?"

He pointed to the cold-room door.

"Why do you always hide in there?"

Vasili didn't reply. Olga would never understand.

At the end of the hall, he slipped through the door and closed it. He descended the few wooden steps. His way was lit by a shimmer of light from cracks around the door.

It was a small room with earth walls supported by planks where roots grew in crevices. The enclosure was cool, always the same, winter or summer. Jars and crocks crowded ledges that lined three sides. A bin of potatoes from Olga's garden sat beside an empty wooden box that he picked up and flipped to sit on. Vasili took a deep breath of the thick air.

It wasn't the odour of vegetation in the cellar, but the hum that attracted him. Complete quiet, except for the drone of the earth, a deep sound, barely audible like the far-away rumble of a church organ. He shut his eyes and let the vibration enter him. Whenever the longing for music coursed through his body like river rapids, the undertone of this chamber smoothed the torrents to a flat pond. Why did people lift their eyes to heaven when all they needed to achieve peace existed a few feet under their shoes?

CHAPTER SEVEN

Patchwork

IN those days and weeks that followed, I missed Mama and Papa. At times it felt as if my husband had confined me to the edge of the earth but still, I didn't experience desolation. Who needed people milling about? Music was a constant companion. All day long, music occupied my mind. It romped through my dreams at night. I could wake with the *Caprice* and dance to it as I dressed. Notes swirled through the cream in my porridge. And some mornings on the farm had such buoyancy. The bubbles in the dishwater seemed to burst in double-time. One morning I woke with a medley of wind and brass sounds, an exquisite *alta capella*. I dressed and rushed to greet the morning.

The kitchen, however, had become Mary's domain, and she commanded it like a Head Mistress. She was there as usual, in her horrible housecoat, purple socks pulled halfway up her calves, staring at a bowl of apples with an intent look—an unalterable presence planted in her private domain. Sometimes the woman did not bother to dress the entire morning and often she traipsed the house in tattered old slippers the whole day.

"Good, you're up. I was thinking we should bake pies. You can mix the crust. No time like now to learn." She dragged a bag of flour out of the pantry. "I'll go to the cellar and get the lard."

"Isn't that lard in there?" I pointed to a tin on the pantry shelf.

"Yes, but you need cold lard to make pastry. That'll be too warm. Get out the big bowl and the measuring cup. Measure two-and-a-half cups of flour." She wagged her finger at me. "And it has to be exact."

She was soon back from the root cellar with a brick of lard wrapped in cheesecloth.

"See, I put them in a mould and cut them into one pound blocks. Most women use butter, but butter makes a soggy piecrust. Lard is best." She unfurled the brick from its gauze wrapping and it landed on top of the flour I'd measured out. "Find me an egg and that jug of vinegar." She pointed at the cupboard.

"You use an egg for pie crust? I don't think Mama ever did."

"Ah, but that's the secret, one egg and a teaspoon of vinegar. It turns out perfect every time. Watch how I work the knives." Her fingers worked the knives like scissors through the floury lard.

She handed the blades to me. I tried to match what she'd

done but my fingers fumbled with the task. A lump flew up and bounced to the floor.

"You can't take all day. The lard is warming up as we speak."

I pretended one knife was a violin bow, and each lump gave off a note. As I played the bowl, a flurry of flour escaped and settled on the table. The knives chimed like notes in a Chinese opera.

"That's enough." She poked around the mixture with her finger. "The lumps can't be much smaller. That's where most make a mistake. They overwork it and the crust gets hard." She cracked an egg into the measuring cup, added a teaspoon of vinegar, beat it with a fork, and then passed the cup to me. "Now, fill it to the line with water. Right to the line, mind you."

I wanted to be useful, but people overrated daily chores as far as I could see. How important was it to produce a perfect piecrust? A piecrust didn't last, didn't make the world a better place. Why spend hours creating a thing to be devoured in minutes?

"No, no, no. Pour some out. Right to the line, not over it." Mary certainly knew how to fuss over nothing. I tipped a few drops into the sink and held the cup up for inspection.

"That's the way," she said. "Drizzle it over the flour now. Then get your hands in and mix. Not too much, mind."

There was something vile in the texture of the stuff, like driblets of dung coated in dirt.

Mary sprinkled flour on the table. "Dump it here."

The mess spilled out. "It's falling apart." I struggled to gather the bits up and stick them on top.

"Now knead. Push the heels of your hands into the dough. You've got it. Keep doing that." Mary clapped. "Your hands will warm up the dough and it'll stick together and as soon as it does that, you can roll it out. Never knead too long. You want a real flaky crust. Too much kneading will spoil it."

After lunch, I cut a warm apple pie into six pieces. Cooked apple, touched by cinnamon is a heavenly smell. When I placed the plate in front of Mary she turned to George and said, "Won't you look at that perfect piecrust? She made it herself."

George took a bite and grinned. "This is delicious." The afterglow of his smile stayed with me for hours. He hadn't approved of a single thing I'd done for a long time.

Later that afternoon when Mary had gone out to collect eggs, George came up behind me at the kitchen sink. "Close your eyes, Kat." He put an arm around my waist, one hand over my eyes and led me forward.

"Where are you taking me?" I attempted to push him away.

"You'll see."

"We can't, Mary will be back soon." I squirmed, but he held fast.

George squeezed my shoulder. "It's not what you think." He urged me forward again. "Don't peek." I heard the padlock on his backroom door snap open.

"We're not going in your room, are we?"

He didn't answer but pressed his hand over my eyes more tightly, and panted in my ear. I smelled his maleness and it wasn't the clean male scent, but the rough male smell, and I realised that anything could happen once he got me into that room. Minutes earlier I'd been sparking with cheerful tunes sprinkled through my mind. The music had stopped now, and I felt George's heart pumping through his skin against my shoulder blade and his hot breath on my neck. He propelled me forward a few more steps and then stopped short.

"Okay, you can look now." He took his hand away.

I opened my eyes. Pinned up on the wall hung the most magnificent quilt I'd ever seen. Musical notes were stitched across a sky-blue background, the images arranged in a symphony of shapes. A loon craned its neck in the far-left corner. The stitching was so fine, it could have been a painting by Alexei Venetsianov but the colours were more vibrant than any painting —the blues, the bluest blue, a fresh-blood red on the neck of the loon.

"It's gorgeous." I stood staring, stunned. "Where did you get it?"

"I quilted it."

"You didn't," I said. But no sooner were the words out of my mouth than I noticed the quilting frame, bobbins of thread, and bits of blue fabric scattered on the floor.

"I planned to have it finished before the wedding, but it took longer than I thought and then we were seeding, then baling, then it was time to harvest." He rubbed my arm as he spoke. As he regarded his handiwork, his expression was pure pride.

"How did you learn to make quilts?"

"It's a long story." He gazed at a box of quilting pins. "Mrs. Warner, our neighbour—I used to help her as a boy. She gave me a penny a week to do chores, but she didn't care about chores. She made quilts. Won prizes for them too." He picked two pins out of the box and rubbed them in his fingers. "My job was to stand next to her as she sewed and wait to thread needles. Her eyesight was going, you see. And then, before she went blind she taught me how to do the stitching."

"Oh, George, it is the most exquisite thing I've ever seen." I turned and put my arms around his neck. He pressed his body up against mine and caressed my buttock. Then we heard the back door slam.

"Twenty eggs today." Mary hollered as she stomped down the hall.

"She's back." I straightened my skirt.

George walked up to the quilt and ran his hand over it much the same way he'd stroked my bottom.

Mary flapped into the room. "The border design came out fine."

That night, after both George and Mary had retired for the night, I curled up on the chesterfield wrapped in my new quilt. George had never learnt to play an instrument, but the notes he sewed onto the quilt were a single line of sheet music with a melody I could hum.

The next afternoon, George sat at the kitchen table and sipped coffee from a cup with a hairline crack. His summer tan had faded, but the leathery creases around his eyes remained. An ashy stripe had wormed its way into his cowlick. He cocked his head. "Sounds like we've got company." He stood and stepped to the window.

I swear, if a hen laid an egg in the barn, my husband would hear it drop. I peeked over his shoulder to see two men on horseback and a wagon approaching our gate.

George turned to face me, put his hands on my waist and squeezed. "Don't mention the quilts, Kat, okay?" He grabbed his coat and headed outside to greet them.

They talked for a while outside before disappearing into the barn.

"Who is it?" Mary asked as she scraped leftover porridge from a pot.

I squinted. "Looks like Sam Olgilvie, John Dari and Aylmer Harris."

"That bunch," she said. "Likely on about that plan they've

cooked up."

"What plan?"

"Some scheme to do with the Grain Growers Association." She made a sour face and shook her head. "Men have too much spare time in winter."

"Yes, George mentioned it." I was lying. My husband rarely discussed such things, and I never paid attention if he did, but that was something Mary didn't need to know.

A half hour later, the men emerged from the barn. George loaded a piece of furniture into the wagon. I couldn't tell what it was, maybe the old chest of drawers that John Dari offered to fix. He enjoyed restoring old cast-offs in his spare time.

They came in and gathered at the kitchen table. I poured coffee. Mary flipped wedges of pie onto plates.

"I'll serve." I picked up the plates.

"What do you think George?" Aylmer Harris filled his cup to the brim with cream. He rubbed his feet together under the table. There was a hole in the toe of one sock.

"It's a good plan." George nodded. "But the Grits will move heaven and earth to keep us down."

"Not if we support the Progressives." Sam slapped the table and coffee splashed out of his cup.

Except for George, these men could be triplets, the same broody faces and lined eyes. It was difficult to estimate their ages. John Dari and Sam Olgilvie must have been in their early forties but Aylmer looked fifty at least. He might be near the same age as Mary. I couldn't be sure of Mary's age either. She was like an old boot, hard to tell if the leather was old or just well-worn. But she had a pleasant manner when she let her guard down, a nice big bosom that farmers seemed to find attractive, and Aylmer could use someone to darn his socks.

"Mary makes the best custard pie I've ever tasted." I smiled at Aylmer.

"It's only pie." Mary tramped from the stove to the counter.

"Damn fine pie, Mary." Aylmer shovelled a forkful into his mouth. The other men grunted in agreement.

I slipped into the pantry and pulled a jug off the bottom shelf, careful to choose the one I hadn't diluted. "A drop of whiskey, gentlemen?"

Aylmer's face broke into a big toothy grin. George raised an eyebrow, but his eyes had a festive glint.

I found four glasses and poured a healthy measure into each. "George, why don't you tell the fellows about your back room project?"

The festive glint vanished from my husband's eyes.

"Want a shot of whiskey, Mary?" George asked.

"Heavens, no." She leaned over the pie pan armed with a metal scrubber.

"Something lighter then?" George stood and marched into the pantry. "There's chokecherry wine on the shelf. Made it myself last winter. It's as good as Joyce Watson's." He emerged with the bottle, poured two glasses, took Mary by the arm, and led her to the table. "Come and sit."

I retrieved my violin from the corner of the room. "Shall I play some music?" George's friends were not much of an audience and not musically discerning, but an audience nonetheless. I took a swallow of wine and began.

The lively tunes that erupted surprised me—a mix of my favourite folk songs, punctuated with country fiddling. Sam Olgilvie stomped his foot. Aylmer's bare toe twitched through the hole in his sock, a stubby sausage dancing a jig.

"Can you play *Little Stream of Whiskey?*" Aylmer asked when I paused for a moment. "My Grandpa used to plunk that one when I was a boy."

"Don't think I know it."

"I'll hum a few bars." He closed his eyes and hummed.

I played along and in no time we had a song going. It must have differed from his childhood song, but Aylmer continued to hum, and when he remembered, belted out an occasional off-key line. My husband bobbed his head. Mary tapped her foot. Then Aylmer pulled John up from his chair and they danced around the table like a pair of roosters. Mary covered her mouth to smother a grin.

"How about *Kitchen Girl?*" Sam asked when we'd exhausted that song.

I knew the tune. Country fiddle pieces do have a lively cadence. When I'd played it twice, George and Aylmer sat, flushed and out of breath. I changed the tone and played a Chopin *largo* piece, an extraordinary work that always moved me. Near the end, my audience sat half asleep, no longer tapping their feet. A Celtic fiddle jig got them twitching in their seats again.

"Want to dance, Mary?" Aylmer jumped to his feet and bowed, extending a hand to her.

"No, I don't dance." She crossed her arms over her bosom.

"Ah, come on. A little jig?" He weaved slightly, fastened on her arm and pulled. She resisted but Aylmer was a solid man with wide shoulders and a thick neck. She was halfway out of her chair when he let go. He almost toppled, but held his balance. With one hand on his hip and the other curled up over his head he tried to twirl on that one bare toe. In the middle of this contortion he fell with a crash. My bow clattered to the linoleum. Mary's chair teetered and next thing, she and Aylmer were in a tangle on the kitchen floor.

He recovered first and offered his hand.

"Leave me alone." Growling, she pushed him away. "I'm fine. Don't touch me." She struggled to her feet and limped to the stove.

"He was only having fun, Mary." I scowled at her, but she didn't turn or respond. An awkward silence descended.

"Well, I guess it's time we're on our way." Sam pushed back his chair.

Mary fled the room, mumbling under her breath. "Darn foolish men." Her door slammed moments later. Sam and George snickered. The creases on Aylmer's forehead tightened to a V.

I took George aside before our company left. My matchmaking effort went off on the wrong note but that didn't mean friendship was impossible. "Why don't you invite Aylmer for supper? He'd be thankful for a home-cooked meal."

"That's nice of you, Kat." He gave me a peck on the cheek. "I'll do that."

When he followed the men outside, I retrieved my bow, tuned the strings on the violin and played a rendition of *Musette*. With each stanza, I imagined Mary in Aylmer's kitchen, darning his socks, then in his bedroom, snuggled up with him under one of George's quilts. This remarkable composition was the first full song I'd learned as a girl, and it taught me that anything is achievable.

The crow stared in at me through the kitchen window.

"Hello, Loki. George rode to town yesterday and didn't tell me. He's afraid I'll ask for a new hat or something *extravagant*."

He tapped his beak on the windowpane twice and cocked his head.

"You, brazen bird. You think you want in here, but you don't. It's colder in this house than in that icy field."

The black scoundrel flapped his wings as if to dismiss what I said. He twisted his neck and peered inside.

I squatted and stared him right in his inky little eye. "I do not imagine for one moment that you can't fly. You could soar off to town if you wanted. I'm stuck in this house all day, every day."

He nodded, the brazen featherhead, and leapt down to the crusty snow.

I took two steps back.

On one foot, the black scourge hopped in a circle, twisting and bobbing his head, wings in a flurry, a spinning shadowy top. At the end of the performance, he bowed. Then he leapt to the sill again and clicked his beak against the pane once more.

"But Aylmer Harris is coming for dinner next week. I'm counting the days. At least it'll be a different face at the table. And maybe after supper I'll play for them."

Mary walked into the room. "Who are you talking to?"

"No one."

"You were talking to that crow, weren't you?"

"There's no one else I can talk to here."

"You're a queer girl. Come away from the window." She tugged my arm, nudged me into the centre of the kitchen and slapped the windowpane with one hand. The crow flapped off across the yard.

"You didn't have to scare him. He wasn't doing any harm." I took a green apple from a bowl and held it to my nose, the smell of autumn still on its skin.

Then Mary dropped a rolling pin. The crash as it hit the floor coursed through every nerve in my body. She stooped to pick it up without a word of apology. This woman blundered through her days with no sense of beauty or grace, and I would be her permanent cellmate until the cows came home. Even so, I needed to talk.

"Do you ever think about getting married again, Mary?"

"No," she said. "I don't waste my time on such things."

"Why not?"

"I just don't." She stopped at the far end of the table and rolled bread dough into a floury rectangle. Her stout arms moved back and forth like the wheels of a train. She buttered the slab, sprinkled it with a brown sugar cinnamon mix, and then tossed on a handful of raisins.

"What about Aylmer Harris?"

"What of him?"

"He's a bachelor."

"So?"

"You could marry Aylmer Harris." What a perfect solution. Aylmer's socks would get darned and I'd be rid of her, a remedy for us both. I had to make her consider the idea.

At that moment, I resolved to treat her with kindness despite how painful it would be. If she thought we were friends, I might change her way of thinking.

"Don't talk nonsense." She marched to the counter, thrust her arms into a sink of soapy water and the only sound in the room was the splash of water and clang of cutlery. I went to the window. The farmyard was stock-still.

"Shall I play for you, Mary?"

"Suit yourself." She dried her hands on her apron and returned to the slab of dough.

"When I was eight years old," I told her, "I played my first concert at the St. Petersburg Conservatory."

"Where?"

"St. Petersburg, in Russia." I clapped. "Oh Mary, it's such a magnificent place, like a palace, lovely stained-glass windows as high as a four-storey house. And I had a wonderful teacher, *Maestro* Auer. He was tall and thin and always wore a black coat and white gloves, even in summer."

"Charlie Watson used to teach fiddle to the boys in town." Mary punched the dough.

"Yes, I know." Charlie and his three old cronies summed up what passed for the musical society in Sylvite.

"He plays at the Saturday night dances." She dusted her hands.

"Yes, I've seen them." Two out-of-tune accordions and Charlie with his screeching fiddle. "Mary, do you remember the song I played at the concert last year?"

"I wasn't at any concert," she said.

"It was Bach." It was doubtful Mary had even heard of Bach. *Partita No 2 in D Minor*. He was one of the finest composers who ever lived. He lived in Köthen with Prince Leopold. Oh Mary, the stories Master Auer told me!"

"Your Master Auer filled your head with fairytales."

"No, no, he knew every composer, all their histories. The best musicians, from across Europe stayed at the Prince's court, at least until the Prince married the awful *amusa* Princess. She made them leave, the nasty woman." I paused for a moment and shook my head. "I've never understood how anyone can hate music, do you? Did you know that Bach once walked to Lubeck, over two hundred miles, to study the work of Dietrich Buxtehude?"

"Ben Hyder comes from Gravelburg to play with Charlie." Mary dipped her fingers in a glass of water and wet one edge of the dough. She rolled the thing into a long log, then pinched it together at the moistened seam. I strode over, picked up my violin and played the *Partita*.

As I played, the court of Prince Leopold and a richly costumed audience replaced Mary, the table, the kitchen counter, the pantry door. I could hear the piano, the cello, the flute. Such ecstasy, to play with a full orchestra, swept away by music and I was a girl again and standing on stage trembling and well into my performance and with every wave of stage fright, an equally strong surge of sound flew from my violin and I welcomed that fear because it was the source of this remarkable music. One eye on the conductor's baton and one on Papa's friend Sergei Rachmaninov, his long fingers curved over the keys of the piano. He looked up at me and smiled. Behind him and off stage, Papa stood with his arms folded. His curled moustache vibrated as the piece built to a climax. Sergei's fingers pounded. My bow skated across the strings. The lure of the music swept over me, and tears rolled down my face, gathered at my chin, and dropped to wet the front of my dress. The baton dropped as slick as a guillotine. Then a dirge of silence... one minute... two minutes... a burst of applause.

"You sure can play that fiddle." Mary was standing by the table watching me, hands covered in flour again, a pan of cinnamon buns cut and laid out.

I put the violin away and stepped to the window. The crow was back. In his beak he had a curved stick that resembled a bow for a miniature violin. His crossed tracks dented the crust of snow. He strutted to the well, flapped his wings, hurtled onto the rock wall and dropped the bow over the edge. Then he twirled and shot me a look that said, 'So there.'

I backed away from the window. "That crow is up to mischief again."

"He was in the barn yesterday." Mary shuffled up for a better view. "Must go there to keep warm."

"Chances are, he's plotting with the cow to take over the house," I told her. "Or hiding his booty. Did you find the brooch you lost the other day?"

"No, but it'll turn up. I've misplaced it, that's all."

"Believe what you want." I walked to the door.

A week passed. Aylmer Harris was to come for dinner that evening but we hadn't even made it through the midday meal. It would be hours before he arrived. George sat beside me at the kitchen table with the newspaper he'd brought from town. Mary fussed with the stove, creaked open the oven door, banged it shut again, and then pushed the kettle to the back burner. A grating screech sounded. Water sprayed up and hissed as it hit the hot surface. I hid in my book.

"Smells good, Mary." George sipped his coffee. "Doesn't it, Kat?"

"Um, yes." I wanted to be agreeable, but the thought of food set my stomach roiling. Since her arrival, Mary insisted on three meals a day. We'd barely scraped our plates each day, and we were back eating again.

"Cabbage rolls." Mary glanced at me with a sour look. "But she'll pick at them."

"You'll eat, won't you, Kat?" George lowered his chin and eyed me.

I nodded and tried to ignore their chatter.

"You make prize cabbage rolls, Mary." George flipped the page of his newspaper. "First to go at last year's Labour Day Barbecue."

"Dorothy Sellars made a good batch too. Hers were first to go." Mary handed him a jar of dill pickles to open. I struggled to focus on my book. The seal popped off the jar and a tangy waft of dill cut through the cabbage-laden air.

"What're you reading, Kat?" George tapped his spoon.

"It's the Vivaldi book from Papa."

"Any good?"

George liked to read, unlike most of the farmers around Sylvite. The closest most of them ever got to the written word was a page torn off a Sears catalogue in the privy.

"Yes, Papa's friend sent it, from New York."

Mary thumped a bowl of bread on the table, glanced at the book, and her lips curled as if she'd bit into a chunk of spoiled meat.

"Do you have any favourite books, Mary?" he asked.

"I've got no time for reading." She dropped a plate in front of me with one red-slimed cabbage roll on it. "Eat this now. Waste not, want not."

"Put the book away, Kat. It's time for lunch." George tossed the newspaper under his chair.

I placed the book in my lap, picked up a fork, and poked at the cabbage, steaming and slick with tomato sauce. The fork holes closed within seconds as if the thing could heal its own skin. I eased it onto the edge of my plate.

"Aylmer should be here before dark. He's likely not had a good home-cooked meal for a while." George cut into a cabbage roll.

"Oh, I figure he has." Mary sat. "Folks seem to have plenty of time for old bachelors."

"Aylmer's a decent man, Mary." George set down his knife. "When he was here last, he was just having fun. He meant no harm." He glanced at her. "Maybe you can whip up your Yorkshire pudding with the roast."

"Guess I could mix up a batch. Plenty of eggs this week." Then she mumbled something I couldn't make out, her mouth full of food. She sat up straight. "See, I told you." She pointed at me but looked at my husband. "She picks at her food."

"Come on, Katya, eat." George leaned forward and with his knife, pushed the cabbage roll into the middle of my plate. Mary shovelled her last bite, marched to the counter, tossed her dish in the dishpan and left. I got up and scraped my food into the slop pail. George scowled.

The afternoon went on forever. I paced back and forth in the parlour, my head twitching with too many thoughts, of Niccolò, the crow, and how the birds on my quilt came alive in the middle of the night. And Mama was sick. I knew it. Papa wrote and said she was better, but he'd never tell me. What if she was ill? What if something terrible happened? Mary was almost a welcome sight when she stomped into the room.

"Dinner is in the oven. You could set the table." Settling in her armchair, she picked up her knitting basket and within minutes the needles twirled like twigs in a whirlwind. I wondered if Mary's thoughts ever matched the speed of her knitting and I decided no, they couldn't, because the rest of her was so immobile. Head bowed, she stared at the commotion her fingers were making.

"Mary, I'm worried. Do you think Mama's sick?"

"Well, she didn't look good when we stopped by."

"She doesn't trust doctors. Papa says she never has."

"It might be her time of life." Mary looked up and then whispered as if sharing a terrible secret. "The whole body changes. Some women go mad. I recall this woman up in Gravelburg. She always seemed real nice. Shot her husband and son one night, just like that. They said it was 'the change.'" Mary let her hands drop and levelled her gaze on my face. After a few moments she spoke again. "You shouldn't worry, though. Most get over it." She resumed knitting.

Even with my agile imagination, I could not imagine Mama standing over Papa with a smoking rifle.

"Mary, what month were you married?"

"August."

"In Sylvite?"

"No. Gravelburg."

"How old were you?"

"Old enough."

"I mean, did you ever wish you'd waited?"

"No."

"Do you have any sisters?"

"No. Four brothers." The knitting needles clicked.

"Have you considered going to live with one of them?"

"Why? Do you want me to?" She glowered at her hands.

"It seems strange you didn't."

"Well, my brothers all have eight kids, except for Samuel and he has seven. They have no room." She dipped her head low and her fingers moved so fast, it made me dizzy to watch.

George had tossed his newspaper on the table. I craned my neck and tried to focus on the headlines. A vision of Mama, a gun and birds in flight caused the letters to blur. I pressed hard on my temple, digging my fingernails into the skin.

After a while, Mary placed her knitting in the basket beside her chair. "Time to milk." She got up, frowned at me and shuffled off. "Good thing someone pays attention to what needs doing around here."

I stood at the window and watched her disappeared into the barn. The wagon wasn't back yet. George had gone to help Ernie Reeger with a sick cow. I stole into our bedroom, groped in the closet, drew out the empty bottle hidden behind a stack of blankets and scurried into the kitchen. The jug was on the bottom shelf of the pantry.

The drivelling dowagers of the Temperance believed whiskey was not a drink for ladies. They deemed it the root of all evil. But what did they know of evil?

I lifted the heavy jug, poured a half-cup and filled my empty bottle. After I'd replaced the whiskey with two cups of water, I returned the jug. It was a shame to dilute it that way, but George had gone out to help Ernie, one of the busiest bootleggers in the province, known for his 'damn fine whiskey.' George would come home with another jug.

Appreciation of fine liquor did not extend to every citizen of Sylvite. Mrs. Stanley had hung a poster at Walker's Store. It depicted a room full of jowly men seated at a table. They were drinking from a bottle labelled 'Poison' complete with a skull and crossbones drawn in red.

I stood, wrapped both hands around the cup and sipped. Whiskey is a soothing elixir. Within a few minutes my thoughts and visions slowed, and it was possible to ruminate on one thing at a time. I thought of birds. Birds are wondrous if you ignore the sorcery that goes along with them. And if I concentrated, the music began and my birds flapped in sync. I could even make them fly in sequence and dance an imperial waltz.

After the first cup, I poured another and finished it in two large gulps. I rinsed the cup, took a peppermint from the candy dish on the tea table, stowed my small bottle back in the closet and sank into the rocker.

By mid-afternoon the entire house was sopping with the rich aroma of roast beef. Mary fussed behind me in the kitchen. The door banged and my husband's voice trailed into the room. After a few minutes I rose and followed him to the bedroom. He stood bare-chested by the washstand, sharpening his razor.

I perched on the bench in front of my dresser and brushed my hair. "What do you think of Aylmer, George?" My husband had a fine set of muscles and as I watched his reflection in the mirror, a lovely bulge swelled his upper arm. He swiped the razor up and down the length of the leather strop.

"What do you mean?"

"You know. People say he's simple."

"No, Aylmer's not simple," George said. "It's that massive head of his. Makes folks think of a big dumb ox."

"Do you think he likes Mary?"

"Don't set your sights on matchmaking, Kat. Aylmer's been a bachelor forever. Got to be a reason." George bent, splashed water over his face, dried off and reached for his white shirt.

I finished knotting my hair and inserted a few pins. "Have you seen my gold necklace?"

"No."

"It was here, hanging on the mirror." I squatted and peered under the dresser.

"When did you wear it last?"

"I don't remember, but I bet that crow took it. I know it's him. He covets our pretty things."

"You make no sense, Katya. Why would a crow want your necklace?"

A clap of horse hooves sounded outside.

"Come on. It sounds like our guest has arrived." George buttoned up his shirt, tucked it into his trousers and cinched his belt.

We were in the kitchen when Aylmer knocked. Steam billowed up from pots. Mary flopped the oven door open, lifted the cast iron pan with both hands and slid the Yorkshire pudding onto the middle rack. George welcomed our guest with a slap on the arm.

Aylmer took up the entire doorway. He stood and shuffled one foot to the other, hunched over to keep from bumping his head on the doorframe. He held a bottle of Scotch in one hand and a tin of shortbread cookies in the other. It was the Christmas tin from Walker's Store that had been in the window for as long as I could remember. He left his boots on the rug and lumbered into the kitchen.

"Smells great." He faced Mary, bowed his head, and handed her the tin. "Hope your leg is better."

"You bought these?" She held the tin at arm's length. "Why on earth buy shortbread?" She clanged the tin on the counter.

Aylmer handed me the bottle of store-bought Scotch.

"You didn't need to," I said and took the bottle, the neck of it still warm from his hand. "Shall I pour you each a drink?"

"Yes, please." Aylmer grinned.

"Good to have harvest done," George said when they were both settled into chairs.

"Yup, sure is. Got a better price than I expected this season." Aylmer sat and rubbed his feet together. He wore the same damaged sock, big toe exploding from the wool.

"It's a gamble each year." George shook his head. "Sometimes I think we're fools."

I found two glasses, poured, and put the bottle in the pantry. Safely out of sight, I took a long swallow myself. The whiskey burned my throat and warmth settled into my belly.

"How's that dog of yours?" George said as I emerged from the pantry.

"Gone blind now, poor old bugger." Aylmer spoke with a slow earnest tone. "Arthritis too. Walks stiff and bow-legged like Old Man Wilson used to. Hardly moves from his blanket by the stove these days."

"You should put him down." Mary poured steaming potato water into a bowl.

"Couldn't do that." Aylmer took a long sip of his whiskey. He plunked his glass on the table and turned sideways to face George.

"It's cruel not to." Mary mashed the potatoes. Her stubby arm pumped. The masher thumped and clicked in the pot.

"How's your hay holding out?" George knew when to change the topic.

"Should get me through to spring."

And the conversation progressed to cattle, seeding and the benefits of keeping pigs. I sat in the rocker and set my mind on whether any melody in my repertoire resembled the snorting of pigs. As a few songs rolled through my head, I rocked.

Mary opened the oven. The squeaked of its hinges derailed 'The Well-Tempered Clavier.' "Time to set the table." She gave me a stern look. I turned off the pig songs and went to help. "The Yorkshires didn't raise today." She hauled the heavy pan out of the oven. The pudding was solid and brown in the bottom of the pan. She cut it into pie-shaped pieces. "It'll have to do."

Soon, the table was crammed with bowls of billowing potatoes, carrots slick with butter, steaming gravy and a platter of roast beef topped with wedges of Yorkshire pudding.

"Delicious." George forked a wad of the pudding into his mouth. "Not too puffy—just fine."

Aylmer fumbled with his napkin, then gawked at his knife and fork as if unsure what to do with them.

"Is everything okay?" I asked him.

"Yes." He dropped the napkin in a ball on his lap. As he placed the knife on the plate, his fork clattered to the floor.

"I'll get you a new one." Mary leapt to her feet.

"No need." Aylmer bent, picked up the fork, wiped it on his pant-leg and dug into his food.

Mary rolled her eyes and sat. I nibbled on a piece of meat. Smacking noises erupted from Aylmer's open mouth as he chewed. I tapped my fork on the edge of my plate. George shot me a look that meant 'cut that out.'

How unfair to chastise me for a little tapping. I was trying to cover up the rude noises of our guest.

Mary kept her head lowered over her plate. George devoured his food faster than usual and with a piece of bread, sopped up gravy on his plate. The apple pie Mary presented at the end of the meal had a burnt crust.

"Good grub," Aylmer said and pushed a half-eaten piece of pie away. "Stuffed as a tick, I am."

"I'll get you another drink." I left the table to retrieve the whiskey.

"Not for me." George stood, rubbed his belly and picked his pipe off the rack on the sideboard.

"Me either," Aylmer said.

Behind the pantry door, I stole another swallow.

"Let's go into the other room, Aylmer." George thumped the big man's back.

Mary and I cleared the dishes. As I emptied leftover potatoes into a smaller bowl, Mary walked over and stood outside the part-open door of the parlour.

"Shh." She held a finger up to her lips. "I want to hear what they're saying."

"Mary, get away from that door. You're spying." I tiptoed over next to her.

She leaned in closer, opened the door a crack wider, and whispered. "It's what I expected. That man's up to no good."

"Why do you say that?"

"He's trying to get George to join the Masons."

"So?"

"They're an evil, secret lot, the Masons. Worship the devil."

"George wouldn't get involved with them and I doubt Aylmer would." I pushed by her and strode into the parlour.

Aylmer had a determined expression. "But your Papa was a Brother." He threw his hands up. When he saw me he stopped talking. George stood by the mantel puffing his pipe.

"Can I get you a coffee, Aylmer?" I asked.

"No, don't bother. Don't want to leave Sarge alone too long." He was out the door in minutes.

"For a big man, he disappears fast," I said to George after he left.

Mary was making a frenzied search of the kitchen. "Can't find my wedding ring." She lifted dishes on the counter, moved the canisters, peered behind, got on her knees and looked under the cupboard. "I took it off when I cleaned the silver. I put it right here." She pointed to the window ledge above the sink.

George squatted and ran his hand along the linoleum. I knew they wouldn't find it and so didn't bother to help. But the dishes needed attention.

When I'd scrubbed the last pot, they were still looking.

"Follow that crow around tomorrow. You'll find it," I told them.

"How would a crow get in here?" Mary lifted a crock and peered under it.

"Enough about the crow, Katya. Your ring will turn up, Mary." George waited until she left. Then he put one hand on each of my shoulders.

"Crows are dumb animals, Kat. Don't let your imagination run away with you. And I know you have a notion about Mary and Aylmer but old bachelors and old farm women get set in their ways."

Then, as he did every night at precisely nine o'clock, he walked to the stove, added coal from the bucket, took off his socks, hung them on a hook over the warm end, lifted the dipper, drank from it and poured the remaining water into the kettle. "I'm turning in now."

CHAPTER EIGHT

Sentiency

VASILI woke to a quiet house. One hand swam through eiderdown to rest in the still-warm imprint his wife had left beside him. Then he remembered what day it was. A firecracker of pain discharged behind his eyeballs. He took a deep breath and squeezed the bridge of his nose.

A crash of pots and pans exploded from the kitchen as he slogged down the stairs.

"You *kozel*." This was Olga's most scolding tone.

As Vasili entered the room, Olga bent and shoved a stockpot into the too-small space in her bottom cupboard. Then she kicked the door causing another racket.

Her outburst over, she tender-eyed her husband as he shuffled to the table.

"You did not sleep well." She set a mug of coffee in front of him.

"I slept fine."

"I will make you something to eat."

"No, no food."

"You are sad, but we have no choice." She patted his hand. "Push it from your mind."

He picked up the cup. Hot liquid splashed out and scalded his wrist. He pushed the drink away.

"I might put it from my mind, if you quit speaking of it." Vasili got up, pulled his parka from the hook and struggled to get his arms through sleeves twisted inside-out. He gave up, balled the coat and threw it to the floor. The door shuddered it slammed behind him.

In the porch he bent over a bucket of apples and sifted through them until he found a big one with red skin, not too wrinkled, surely sweet. With the apple stowed in his pocket, he set out for the barn.

Old Ned was in his stall, head lowered and eyes half closed, but when Vasili pushed the door open, the horse flared his nostrils, blinked, shook his mane and acknowledged him with a quarter-whinny.

"You are glad to see me." Vasili spoke in a low serious voice.

The horse nodded.

"You are a foolish beast. I am not your good friend."

Old Ned had bones where most horses had muscle. His eyes were rheumy, his mane tattered and there was an unhealthy smell to his breath when he nuzzled Vasili's cheek. His head came to rest on his master's shoulder.

"You know what I have in my pocket, but it does not matter to you, does it? You have never been greedy." Vasili ran his hand along Old Ned's neck against the prickly grain of hair, and the horse shivered. Then he pulled the apple out. Ned turned away, pointed his nose to the ground and waited.

What a difference from the horses that had inhabited Mother's stable when he was a boy. They had been splendid to look at yes, pure black and elegant, but often tore a hole in his trousers to get at an apple. And they could never stand still when people came near but pranced and kicked and swatted their tails, showing off. His mother had claimed she loved them but spent no time in the stables with them.

"You are a gentleman of a horse." Vasili reached out and stroked the silky horse-skin nose. Old Ned snuffled his fingers. Vasili offered the apple with his other hand. The horse did not move or acknowledge the fruit until it was pressed to his lips. Only then did he take it from his master's hand, as a mother cat picks up her kitten by the neck, enough bite to lift it, but not enough to break the skin. Old Ned dropped the fruit and lowered his head. Vasili's throat tightened as he watched the horse munch.

Old Ned's head was a too large for his body and his back curved like a cello bow but it was the hooves, cracked and oozing black that gave him the trouble. He could stand, but if he tried to trot more than a few paces his front legs bent forward, and he fell to his knees.

Olga had waited until John Dari was there for their weekly chess game. "The horse has been a friend, but he cannot work. He cannot even walk, let alone pull the wagon." She'd spoken to John only, turning her back on her husband.

"I can take care of it for you." John didn't include Vasili either. "Pierre Maucroix up in Gravelburg will give you five dollars for him."

"He will not be sold for fox meat." Vasili hadn't been able to control the tremble in his voice. He'd left John with Olga at the kitchen table and walked alone for hours in the west field, forsaking their slotted chess game.

Old Ned finished his apple and limped from the water trough to the feeder but he did not eat the hay. He stood still, lowered his head and closed his eyes, as if he knew.

"He is in the barn." There was no wind to muffle Olga's voice.

The barn door gnawed. Vasili turned. John was at the entrance, a formidable silhouette against the morning light, a gun angled at his side. Vasili walked toward him, past him, and back to the house. Inside, he slipped along the hallway, opened the door to the cellar, ducked in, pressed the door shut and sat. Even the earth's hum could not muffle the blast of that gun.

Life travels along and sadness eases. Vasili knew and respected the practical nature of his wife. A week or two after they retired Old Ned, he stepped outside to investigate a blaring racket in the farmyard. Olga was trudging up the path from the barn dressed in gloves, boots and a pair of britches Vasili did not even realise she owned.

"What are you doing, woman?"

It was a biting cold day. He'd not yet sat for a cup of coffee but there stood Olga, in the yard, pulling a five-foot square piece of galvanised tin up the path.

"The house will burn to the ground." She heaved, and the tin clattered across the bumpy path.

"What?"

"Burn. The house will explode in flames unless we cover the wall behind the stove." A curled corner of the sheet caught on a twig. The piece of metal slipped from her gloves and crashed onto the snow-coated rocks. She turned and eyed him. Her features pleated as if she was ready to weep. Vasili turned, grabbed his parka and went to her. No horror surpassed a woman's tears.

"Now, what is this foolish thought you have?" He put his arms around her, pulled her close and lifted her chin. This was a flawed idea. Tears sprang to her eyes, and she wailed.

Olga babbled and blubbered. "The stovepipe was blazing red this morning. It is too near the wall. I touched the wall. A sausage would cook on it. It frightens me to death. You say you will fix it, but you tell me you will do something and then you do nothing."

She gave one last whimper, straightened up and eyed him. "I could not wait. This metal was in the barn. I do not know how to fix it but I will try. See, I have gloves?" She held her gloved hands up in front of her face.

"Where did you find the britches? You look like Tom Mix from that poster in the store."

She grinned then, her face still wet with tears, and bent shaking with laughter. It took her several moments to get words out. "At the rummage sale." And Vasili laughed too. He grabbed the sheet and pulled it as they walked side-by-side to the house.

Vasili had not completed hanging the tin when Olga returned to the kitchen. She resembled his wife again in her flowered housedress.

"Come, I want to show you something." He led her into the parlour, to a stack of books on the table and opened the book on top, *Dead Souls* by Nikolai Gogol. Vasili had discovered it the day before in a pile of books that had sat undisturbed since their arrival in Canada.

"Do you remember this?" He took a paper out from the middle, unfolded it and held it up for her to see. It was the original placard from a 1910 performance of *The Golden Cockerel*. "Remember the trip to Moscow? The excitement? Remember the ticket-taker let Katya in with no cost?"

"She was young. They did not charge for a child."

"But no one took children to the opera, remember? She had to promise not to cry."

"It was not in her nature to cry." Olga took the leaflet and tossed it on the table. "I do not remember a ticket-taker."

"But you remember the opera? How still Katya sat? How she hummed the tunes for days later? I thought she wanted to become a singer, follow the path of her *babushka*."

Olga frowned. "Yes, that is what worried me, that she might turn into your mama."

Vasili looked at the pamphlet again. The Russian words were old friends. "You did not think we should attend because of the Tsar's ban, remember? But it was an important work. Remember, Rimsky-Korsakov died before they even performed his opera. How sad it was."

Vasili held the paper at arm's length and studied the ink drawing of the Opera House. The artist had done a fine job depicting the columns and the carvings above the arch.

"This opera has played in New York. Just last month. Sergei wrote me. He spoke of the performance in a letter last week. Who would believe—the *Golden Cockerel* at the Metropolitan Opera House?" The brochure shook in his hand.

"Sergei said every Russian in New York attended. Oh, I wish we could have been there." Vasili sat, opened the book, folded the paper and placed it back between the pages.

"Will you finish behind the stove now?" Olga stared at him with raised eyebrows.

"Later. I will read now."

"With you, later never comes. I will finish it myself." She stomped out of the room.

Vasili closed his book, got up and followed her to the kitchen.

Gathering of Crows

The days on the farm followed one after the other. The crow kept his constant vigil at my window. Aylmer Harris did not come back to woo Mary. In fact, we had no visitors other than John Dari. Nor did we go anywhere. My husband was not true to his word. We made no trips to town nor visits to Mama and Papa. It was always 'need to fix that fence' or 'need to mend that hole in the roof.'

It was John who told us the fate of Old Ned. That meant Mama and Papa couldn't visit. But John brought news that Mama was better. Mary was probably right thinking Mama was going through 'the change'. She wasn't the only one going through a change.

Mary didn't want me to help with any chores and that was fine with me. Every morning after breakfast she came in with a basket of eggs. That was my cue to leave, and I wandered off to the parlour to practise. But one day I stayed to watch the egg candling.

Two candles were lit in a dark corner of the kitchen where the wall and cupboard meet. Mary filled a bowl with water and placed it next to the candles. It was a ritual worthy of a Russian Orthodox ceremony. Then she removed the eggs from the basket one at a time and held them up to the candle. After scrutinising each egg, she put it on a spoon and lowered it into the bowl of water.

That this fascinated me, was a testament to how boring my life had become.

"This one has a chick in it." Mary held up the egg. "Bet it's Nelly's. That hen is clever at hiding her eggs. The other day I found one under a pile of straw, tucked way back in the roost."

My belly fluttered, and I pressed both hands into it, willing it to stop. Most days a song took my mind off this movement, but no song presented itself. I counted back to the last smear of blood in my undergarments. It was before Edmonton and before the Concert. Even a violin *concerto* didn't have the power to purge this fact from my thoughts.

"We'll let her sit on it." Mary popped the egg into her apron pocket and continued the inspection.

I lifted the folds of the cardigan I wore every day, tugged at the waistline of my dress and focused my attention outside the window. Loki had returned. Beak pointed to the clouds, he strutted across the yard with an aura of contempt. Instead of the usual dance, he hopped up onto the fence post, ruffled his feathers, balanced on one claw and glanced sideways at me.

"Sometimes that crow makes my flesh creep," I said.

"Nonsense." Mary dropped an egg. It fell to the floor with a splat.

But my flesh did creep. I knew my voice sounded calm, but my fists clenched under the sweater. I pushed my knuckles hard into my belly. If Mary had bothered to turn her head, she might have questioned why my eyes were squeezed so tightly shut.

Later that afternoon, I crept into the bedroom and closed the door. Mary was in the parlour knitting. George had gone to the field. I dropped to my hands and knees and peered under the bed. The knife was where I'd hidden it, wedged between the mattress springs. I touched the bone handle and inspected its razor-sharp edge before I pulled it free.

Balanced on the edge of the mattress, I removed my bloomers, hiked the skirt up to my waist and inspected my nest of dark hair. Legs open as wide as possible, I pointed the tip of that knife right at the middle. I felt the frigid iron against my private folds of flesh and understood how painful it would be to follow through and stab.

For minutes or hours I held this posture without moving, a sledgehammer pounding beneath my ribcage, my hand shaking.

Then the afternoon sun struck the shiny surface of the knife and it gleamed blue, like the strings of a violin. It made me think of Niccolò and how I cried the first time I heard him play *Chaconne*. The knife moved away, and I closed my eyes and stroked the dark triangle of hair. I could hear him, smell him, feel him. I wept for him until my tears ran dry and then collapsed against my pillow. After a while, I pushed away thoughts of Niccolò and swapped them with an old nursery rhyme. I ran it over and over in my head.

A GATHERING OF CROWS

One for sorrow,

two for joy,

three for a girl,

four for a boy

five for silver,

six for gold

seven for a secret never to be told.

The next morning in the kitchen, a blanket wrapped to my ears, I rocked and watched light ooze in through the drapes. A bucket of cream sat on the counter. That meant it was butter-churning day. It was a complicated affair, butter making. My few meagre attempts had not met with success. Mama should have been more persevering. If she had engaged me in more practical activities I'd now be able to follow through with routine chores as Mary did. I'd be a proper wife if she had spent more time on my tutelage. But, to be honest, the mere thought of domestic tasks flooded me with lifelessness.

Memories of Mama in our old home had kept me awake the entire night. In St. Petersburg Mama had spent hours stitching magnificent tapestries and inquiring of my studies. We'd had a serving girl, a simple little thing, charmed with childhood forever, whose only job was to bring us tea. There had been other servants too. I no longer remembered their faces, but it had been a happy time.

Then my memory wandered, and I forced myself to think of other things—how the claw marks of a crow can resemble the opening lines of the *Opus 23 Caprice*, what notes might mimic Loki's morning dance, and how to pull them into a score. Quavers and accents formed a wavering image on the wall.

"Morning." Mary clomped into the room.

I flinched. She padded by me, her brown robe tied tight at the waist like the winter coat of a Cossack. She headed for the wood box, extracted a handful of sticks, and crumpled up a wad of paper to build the morning fire.

The cow lowed from a distance, a plaintive single note. "I'd better get dressed. That cow's bawling to be milked." Mary struck a match on the stovetop.

"I can go later."

"It needs doing now." She dropped the lid into its circular slot. The sound splintered the morning quiet.

"Another half hour won't do any harm."

"I'll go." She marched out of the room.

"Good," I said, out loud after she'd left. "I can work on the song." I closed the parlour door, picked up my bow and conjured up the quavers and accents from my earlier vision. Perfect, the opening lines. I put the violin down, took up my pen and recorded them. The curves of the treble clefs I traced with great care and drew my semibreves in a flawless oval shape. Then I played a new phrase, then scribed the next line. Before long my pages were black with notes.

George popped his head into the parlour. "I'm out to the north field." I looked up and nodded. The door slammed, and the churn squeaked in the kitchen.

Late afternoon I spread my music sheets across the carpet. The entire day composing, but why? It was a deplorable song.

I paced back and forth, opened the curtains and stared out, paced some more, then closed the curtains again. I kicked my scribbled papers around the room and returned to the kitchen. Mary was out but her presence lingered. The churn still sat on the floor beside her chair. Dishes littered the counter. What a messy woman. With every job she undertook, chaos appeared in its wake.

I shoved the rocker out of my way and stood in the window. The crow was by the fence pecking at the scraps Mary dropped for him en route to the hen house.

"Loki, I am so restless today." He didn't glance up when I knocked on the windowpane. "I know you're listening, you ungrateful black monster."

I waved my hand in the air. "Look at the shelves in this kitchen." Half-empty jars sat covered with a layer of dust so thick you couldn't see the glass. Every day Mary jammed stuff on that shelf, little bags of this and that thrown pell-mell. She never noticed when things lost their shine. Neither did George. They both thought it was enough to churn butter, bake bread, and milk cows.

"Loki, she's an untidy woman." The nasty bird turned his back on me. "Loki, listen you devil."

I dashed to the shelf and removed the part-empty jars, putting them on the left side of the counter, full ones on the right. Before long the shelves were bare. A tub of water from the reservoir with soap and a few drops of ammonia took care of the grime. The pungent odour made me nauseous, but only for a moment, and I scrubbed the painted shelf until my hands turned red from the harsh detergent. Next, I emptied the contents of part-empty jars into the slop pail under the sink. I washed the jars with hot soapy water and rubbed with a tea towel until they sparkled. Clean jars went on the bottom shelf, side by side. I wiped the full jars and arranged them on the top shelves according to colour. Mary burst in as I put the last one on the shelf.

"What in heavens name are you doing, child." She took her coat off and threw it on the hook.

"Cleaning the cupboard," I told her. "I'm done. Doesn't it look better?"

She stood shock-still. "Where's the food from those jars?"

"I cleaned them."

"But you saved the food, right?"

"No, I put it in the slop pail."

"You threw out all that food?" Her small eyes became large until they were nearly in proportion to her long, ugly face.

"The jars were practically empty."

"Where are the walnuts? I had at least a cup of walnuts. Do you realise how much they cost? I was saving them for Christmas cake." She planted herself on the doormat. "You are a wasteful, stupid girl." Her voice crackled and her face flushed.

"It's my cupboard and I'll do whatever I please with *my* cupboard." I glared at her. My head pounded. If she'd been closer, I might have slapped her face. She must have sensed this, and with squared shoulders tramped away.

I heard a tap at the window. Loki was on the ledge craning his neck to see into the kitchen.

"Stupid woman." Still shaking, I flew across the room and

rapped the glass above his head.

He pressed against the windowpane and rubbed his head on it, like a cat up against a leg.

"She accuses me of waste. You should see what she puts in that slop pail." I walked over to the counter, bent and grabbed the handle of the pail. As I pulled it toward me a splash of sludgy liquid leapt over the rim and hit the linoleum. "See this mess. She dumps everything in this pail—onion skins, coffee grounds, potato peel, dirty dishwater. I'll show her who's wasteful."

I collected an iron stockpot from the bottom cupboard and tipped the sludge from the slop pail into the pot until it was full. After adding fresh wood to the cookstove I placed the pot over an open flame.

Then I grabbed my violin and played. I played the *Sorcerers Apprentice* over and over until the nasty gruel was bubbling.

It was an hour later when Mary came back.

"What's that stink?" She walked in and headed straight for the stove.

I'd finished playing by this time and sat resting in my chair. "What stink?"

"What on earth is this?" She peered into the stockpot.

"Supper."

Her eyebrows furrowed and her nose wrinkled in disgust. She fixed her eyes on the pot on the stove, then glanced at the empty slop pail on the floor. She stood there, wide-eyed, staring at me.

"You're not right in the head." She composed herself. "Do you think George wants to come home to this stench?" She shoved the iron pot to the cool end of the stove, snatched the oven mitts off the wall hook, lifted it, and poured its contents back into the slop pail. A solid mass had stuck to the bottom, and she shook out the final steaming lump. Then, pail in hand, she stomped out.

I turned my attention back to the window. Loki remained perched on the windowsill with a twinkle in his fierce little eye. He hopped on one leg and waggled his head, making no sound, but I knew he was laughing. I grinned, and this encouraged him. He hopped higher, raised his beak, and then leapt to the ground hopping and shaking across the yard.

Drowning

Sylvite was not much of a town, but at least Vasili could walk to it in under twenty minutes, unlike Katya and George who had a three-hour drive or more over bumpy roads. As he walked along Main Street, he did not see a soul. The air was bitter and he wound his scarf around his neck just as a piercing gust of wind hit. He stopped, clutched the bundle in his hand, shut his eyes and waited for it to pass. Then he hurried past Walker's Store, the Livery, Joe's Barber Shop, a row of houses. By the time he reached the churchyard, his fingers were numb inside his gloves.

Dirty snow pushed up against the church wall and along the

rock barricade that separated the parish from Henry's Junkyard. Folks in town had laughed when the Reverend built that fence. He'd hauled rocks from the coulee in a wheelbarrow and worked morning to night for over two months, fitting the stones together with cement. 'Had to do it,' he'd said good-heartedly. 'Henry's junk was creeping up on the Lord.'

Now, if you ignored the rubble next door, the yard was better, more suited to a parish. Vasili moved along the walkway between banks of snow, turned right at the front steps, and followed a path to the Manse at the back. He hesitated before lifting the metal knocker. The Reverend and his wife might be having their midday meal. But Vasili knew he would freeze to the landing if he stood still waiting for long. He knocked.

Mrs. Manning opened the door and greeted him with a smile. She was a tall woman with a prominent jaw and a helmet of straight brown hair that jutted out from her head. The pastor's wife reminded Vasili of the farm women in the Ukraine who laboured alongside their husbands.

Vasili held out the bundle. "Olga asked me to bring this to you for the social tonight."

"Olga's not coming?" She took the package—four mason jars filled with borsch, each wrapped in paper. "But you must be freezing. Come inside. I've just put supper on the table. There's plenty if you care to join us."

"No, I should go back. My wife is not well."

"Nothing serious I hope?"

"She tells me she will be fine but I plan to stop at the doctor."

"The doctor's in Toronto."

Vasili's pulse pummelled. "For how long?"

"He'll be away until next week, but the doctor in Gravelburg will come if you need him."

"Olga avoids the doctor but I worry. She has felt unwell for over a month. Today she did not leave her bed."

"Go then. You should be with your wife." She shooed him away and shouted as he stepped back up the path. "Thank Olga for the soup but tell her she shouldn't be cooking when she's ill."

The wind grew colder as he hurried back through town. Joe nodded from the window of his Barbershop. The chair was empty, and he beckoned, but Vasili did not stop. The road home stretched longer than usual, and the storm gained strength. Vasili had to lean into it and fight for each step. The sky sent out tiny bullets of ice that pierced his cheeks. He pulled his hat over his ears and squinted. But, he told himself it wasn't so dreadful. More snow meant wet soil for planting in the spring.

The house became visible on the horizon and Vasili pushed onward. An unusual yellow mound came into view on the path ahead. At first it appeared to be a bundle of laundry, torn from the line and tangled in a heap, but as he moved closer, it took on human form. He ran.

"Olga, Olga, what?" He bent over her. *"Chyort!"* Her housecoat was open and flapping with one breast exposed, skin blue against the snow.

"I am drowning." She puffed as if she had run for hours. Vasili pulled the garment closed around her neck, gathered her up and lifted. Olga was not a tiny woman, and he staggered, found his balance, and lunged toward the house.

He had stoked the stove before leaving and a blast of warmth hit as he opened the door. Once inside, Olga's breath juddered. He loosened his hold on her, afraid his grip had cut off her flow of air. She nearly slipped from his arms.

He carried her up the stairs, one careful step after another. The steps had no end. At last he reached the top and moved her to the bedroom. He placed her on the bed, rolled her and grappled with the covers. She squirmed on the sheet like a netted fish.

"I'll find help." As Vasili turned to go, she put her hand up and clutched his arm. "You need a doctor." He rushed downstairs, and once outside, raced toward John Dari's house.

CHAPTER NINE

Slabs of Ice

GEORGE and Mary were building an ice shed. It was the constant topic of conversation every day, how big the slabs should be, how to transport them, how many they needed. Late one morning when they were out I dressed and headed to the barn with my violin. Regardless of what my husband thought, cows were a better audience than no one. Ethyl was not an appreciative listener though. She mooed through 'Tales from the Vienna Woods.' I left the barn and stopped outside to observe George and Mary's glacial undertaking.

It was a sunny day, but frigid. George stood at the edge of the frozen slough with a long ice-pick and swung at the surface repeatedly until a wedge of ice split off. Then he hefted a whale-size hook with a rope attached and hurled it at the slab. Once satisfied the hook had pierced far enough in, he wrapped the block twice around with rope. As I moved closer, Mary noticed me.

"Come to help, have you? Do you plan to push a chunk of ice with that fiddle?" She chortled and walked over to where George had knotted the other end of the rope into a loop, took it from him, dragged it up to the horse, and hooked it to a long piece of metal attached to Gust's harness. As the horse moved to the other side of the yard, George began again with the ice-pick while Mary guided Gust forward, the ice block slipping and bumping across the snow.

I stayed and watched. They transported the slabs one after the other to a place behind the chicken coop with a northern exposure. George's face glistened with perspiration and I wondered that it didn't freeze to a solid mask. My feet were lumps of ice by this time and would have made a fine addition to the icehouse wall.

It was mid afternoon when they stopped for the day, and we returned to the warmth of the house. Mary brewed coffee. I toasted bread on a rack over the stove hole, holding my hands above the open flame to thaw them. We sat to a simple lunch of toast and gooseberry jam.

George dunked a piece of toast into his coffee. "We'll slaughter late. Ice should hold into summer."

Mary nodded. "Barring a heat wave like last year."

A rumble of horse hooves rattled the window. George stood to look and moments later John Dari burst into the kitchen without knocking.

"Katya, it's your mother," John said.

"Mama?"

"She's taken ill. Bad. Your papa sent me."

"Is Papa with you?"

"No," John said. "He's home with your mama. I left Blanche with them. Your papa wants you to come, quick. I'm going for the doctor at Gravelburg."

"Where's Doc Haskins?" George asked.

"At a convention in Toronto." John winced and scowled. "He'd be better off staying home, tending to folks who need him."

"You'll never make it to Gravelburg before dark." Mary fussed at the table, picking up plates.

"I know. I'll stay over at my cousin's tonight. He's three hours on this side."

George put on his take-control tone of voice. "Katya, you'd better go. Mary, go with her. I'll stay here with the animals. When John comes back with the doctor, we'll come."

I faced my husband. "Mary can stay here."

"She should go with you." He glanced from me to her.

"No, I'll go alone. I'll be fine. Mama's sick and there's no time to argue." My voice prickled.

"I can go with you." Mary shot me a look. "But you will need help here tonight, George."

George and John rushed outside to get the sleigh ready. I

picked up my violin, my coat, and wrapped a scarf around my head.

"I don't want you with me, Mary. Stay here and help George." I hurried out to where George was harnessing the horse. He cinched the front strap, and I crawled into the driver's seat and snapped the reins. The sleigh glided off before my husband knew what was happening.

"Katya, wait for Mary."

I didn't look back. "She's decided to stay."

The sleigh's runners slicked over the upper crust of snow and we made good time, Gust and I. The only sound was the footfall of hooves on ice and it was hypnotic. Unruffled fields whizzed by.

How heavenly the house looked when I arrived and slid along the old familiar road. How wonderful it smelled when I opened the front door, a mixed aroma of dill, garlic and fresh coffee, Mama's essence. Blanche Dari stood in front of the sink, hands immersed in soapy water.

"How is she?" It was strange to see another woman in Mama's kitchen.

She shook her hands over the sink, wiped them on her apron and turned. "Not good, I'm afraid. Your Papa thinks it's her heart." She walked over, put her hand out and smoothed back a strand of hair that had come loose from my scarf. "Let me hang your things."

I unbuttoned my coat, and she drew it off my shoulders.

"She'll be all right, won't she?"

"God willing." Mrs. Dari hung my coat and turned to inspect me.

She eyed my stained beige dress. I pulled my cardigan closed and buttoned the middle button across the small mound of my belly.

"You've lost weight," she said.

I had too. It was as if every ounce of fat on my body had shifted to my waist. "It's my cooking," I said and smiled. She did not return the smile, and I knew if the circumstances were different she'd render a firm scolding on skipping meals and keeping up my strength.

"Um." She stepped to the cupboard, reached in, pulled out an onion, picked up a knife, and proceeded to peel and chop. "I'm hoping she'll take a spot of soup." A pot gurgled on the stove, and the moist aroma of chicken soup rose to mingle with mama's redolence in the room.

I watched her work. She had tiny but determined hands, the knife slicing onions, the sharp blade landing too near her fingers. If that were me, a gush of blood would follow.

Father called from upstairs. "Katya, is that you?"

"Yes Papa."

"Come upstairs. Mama is awake."

Papa sat on a chair beside the bed, Mama's small hand held up by his large one, her body sunk into the feather mattress, her cheeks as white as the sheets. Her mouth was agape, wheezing, and she looked straight through me. Was she sleeping with her eyes open? I stood in the doorway, clutched my violin case, and glanced downstairs.

"Come, kiss your mama." Papa beckoned me closer.

I tip-toed to the bed, brushed her forehead with my lips, and then took a step back.

Papa got up, dipped a washcloth in the basin of water by the washstand, and wrung it out. As he folded the cloth to lay it on her brow, his hand trembled.

"Are you all right, Papa?" He sat swollen-eyed, slumped, a played-out skeleton. I had never seen him like this.

"It's the worry." He reached and fussed with the cloth. Mama didn't move. I sat on a stool near the door. The room was dim.

The sun and snow outside seemed a separate world, and Mama's rich clutter that had always pleased me, appeared tawdry now. I focused on the carpet. No song ran through my mind. I closed my eyes and searched for notes, a melody, any tune to drown out the rasp of Mama's breath. Dirges invaded my thoughts.

I stood and walked to the window. "Maybe we should get some fresh air in here." I pulled the curtains over as far as they'd go.

"It is cold," Papa said. "I do not want her to catch a chill."

Mama murmured, "Vasha."

I walked to the bed. Papa lifted her hand to his cheek.

"You must find Katya." Her breath rattled.

"Katya is here, *Myshka*. See, at the foot of the bed. And John has gone to bring the doctor. He'll be here soon to help you. Be strong."

For a moment, Mama's eyes cleared. Then they glazed over, and the struggled breathing resumed. We watched her in silence for what felt like hours.

"Music might help," Papa said at last. "Go downstairs and play for us, Katya. It will remind your mama of happier times. We have missed the music since you left."

So I descended the steps, took out my violin, stood in the foyer at the bottom of the stairs and played. I played for hours, songs I'd never played, great epic romance songs of Russia, hymns Mama used to hum. 'Music has great healing powers,' Master Auer told me, 'an elixir of enormous potency.' My bow reached into Mama's memory and extracted her songs. I sensed that even if I pulled my hand away, the bow would continue to slide across the strings.

Mrs. Dari passed by me, dreamlike, carrying a bowl of soup. She disappeared at the top of the stairs as I sent music up—the only way I knew to help.

Near the end of the *Concerto in E-minor*, the bow stopped. I sensed it before Papa appeared on the stairs.

"Your mama has died." He sat on the step, lowered his face to his hands, and cried.

I dropped the violin, climbed the few steps, and put my arms around him. My Papa never wept. My throat filled, and I choked.

"Oh Vasili. I'm so sorry." Mrs. Dari stepped into the foyer. She offered her arm and helped Papa down the stairs. "I'll make you a cup of tea."

I caught my breath enough to speak. "He needs a something stronger."

Papa rested his thin arm across Mrs. Dari's shoulder, and I followed them into the parlour.

There was nothing more Mrs. Dari could do, and I sent her home. Papa and I sat in the parlour with a bottle of brandy between us. When the liquor was half finished, Papa sang one verse of an old Russian love song over and over. I swallowed in large gulps willing it to burn away the blockage in my throat. When we finished the bottle Papa fell asleep, his long legs splayed out in front and his head bent at an awkward angle. I slipped out of the room.

A strange aura lurked in the kitchen. Mama's smells had vanished, replaced by a musty stench. The stove was tepid but firewood sat stacked on the floor. I stuffed paper and a handful of sticks into the wood-box and then lit a match. Smoke fogged the round opening. A jar of dill pickles stood on the counter, and I twisted the lid off, pried open the rubber seal with my fingernails, and raised the open jar to my nose. A few minutes passed before the stove crackled. Soon, I had coffee boiling. The malodorous phantom skulked away as the rich aroma of coffee filled the room. The kitchen became Mama's once again.

Loss

Vasili woke to a bang, bang, bang.

"Anyone home?" someone shouted. "Vasili, I have the doctor."

His eyes sprang open, but the room was pitch-black. He lost his bearings for a moment. Then a candle glimmered in the kitchen. An empty brandy bottle had tipped over next to a stack of books near the open parlour door. He stood and his head pounded.

Katya sat at the kitchen table, arms wrapped around her knees and drawn up to her chest. There was another bottle of brandy, half finished, in front of her.

"Are you there?" More thumps from the door.

Katya sat motionless, staring at the flickering candle.

"Just a minute." He turned to Katya. "Why did you lock the door?"

"Mama was trying to leave."

"Oh, my little nightingale." Fresh tears sprang to his eyes. He walked to her, bent and kissed the top of her head. Then he walked over and lifted the latch.

John Dari, George and the doctor burst in, a tussle of snow-spattered commotion.

"We came as fast as we could." John dropped his coat and shook it outside the open door. A flurry blew back into the kitchen.

"You are too late." Vasili stepped behind them and closed the door.

John turned to his friend, put his arms out and drew him into a hug. Vasili arms remained stiff at his side.

George extended his hand. Vasili allowed him to squeeze his fingers. Then he glanced at Katya with a sad expression and slowly shook his head. "I'm so sorry, Vasili, Kat."

The doctor pulled off his gloves. "May I see your wife?"

"There is a body upstairs." Vasili pointed. "But it is no longer my wife."

"Come." George took the doctor's arm. "I'll take you upstairs."

When they had left, Katya released her legs and stood. "You shouldn't have opened the door, Papa. She was still here and you let her out. Now she might never come back. I can't smell her anymore. Why did you open the door?"

"She is tired, John." Vasili walked over and took his daughter by the arm. "Ah, little bird. You need to rest. Come."

A Vile Fog

Papa didn't cry at the funeral but sat erect beside me in the front pew with closed eyes. I think his tears had run dry. When Reverend Manning began, "Though we walk through the valley of the shadow of death," I found it difficult to breathe. By the time of the final prayer George's handkerchief was a soggy rag fisted in my hand.

I don't recall at what hour we left the church but when we arrived back at his house for the reception, the earthy stink of rot had returned.

Papa sat me in a chair by the sideboard. Every few moments a knock on the door blasted up the hallway as loud as a cymbal struck next to my ear. Then the door opened and banged shut and opened again—blast after blast of frigid air. Tea cups rattled saucers, and the house resounded with the shuffle of feet. Bodies drifted by.

I gasped for breath. A few words squeaked out of me. "More coffee, please someone, boil more coffee." Only the aroma of coffee could block that horrible smell. But that was the only sentence I uttered because the dirge began, "So sorry for your loss, sorry for your loss, sorry for your loss."

Then it was dark, and the bodies disappeared. A shadow shaped like the wings of a crow unfurled along the floor under the gas lamp. And later, when my husband lay curled away from me on the bed, my limbs convulsed in shudders. The clock in the hall struck three. After that I must have slept.

The next day I remained in bed, crippled with my grief. A piece of hair had lodged in the corner of my mouth. I couldn't lift my hand to remove it. My fingers barely wiggled when I tried.

The bedroom door creaked open.

"Katya, I've brought you a cup of tea." Mary stomped in.

"Go away. I don't want any."

I rubbed one eye and opened it a slit as she set the tray on the bedside table and walked to the window.

"Let's get some light in here." She threw back the curtains and fiery pain exploded behind my eyes.

"Come on, dear. Get up, wash your face and comb your hair. You'll feel better."

"What are you doing here?"

"Your Papa asked me to stay over last night."

"I want you to leave."

I braved the light, one eye at a time and watched Mary dither about. She straightened the towel by the basin, folded my dress over the back of the chair, bent and lined my shoes up next to the wardrobe.

"Go away." I wiggled into the mattress.

"I'll get you a basin of water to wash up."

Mary picked up the pitcher from the washstand and left. As soon as her scuffle receded down the hall, I gathered every ounce of energy I could muster, squirmed out of the quilt, rolled off the bed and slipped to my knees on the icy floor. My nightgown strangled my legs as I crawled. At last my head bumped the door, and I pushed against it with all my might until it shut. I reached up, grasped the key and clicked the lock. Then, clutching the doorknob I pulled myself upright. My legs teetered and threatened to collapse, but I tread to the window, pulled the heavy drapes, first one side and then the other and overlapped them so that not a single sliver of light intruded. I collapsed back on the bed, out of breath.

A few minutes later, the doorknob rattled.

"Katya, let me in." Mary knocked, waited and knocked again. She left, and I sank into the blackness.

In a half hour it started again.

"Please, Katya." It was Papa's voice.

And then George's voice, "Katya, unlock that door now."

I wound the pillow around my head and pressed it against my ears until the voices fused to a mumble. I snuffled, "Please, leave me alone."

The rot smell descended and clogged my nose. The vile fog crushed me into the mattress and I released the pillow from my ears but the cloud had blotted out all sound. I tried, tried, tried, but no music came to mind and it was unbearable to be without music and I thrashed and flailed against the sheets.

Sometime later, I lay sweating and spent. Inside the cloud, a hangman's noose appeared, then disappeared, then showed itself again. It looked strong enough to hold my weight, but I couldn't move against the hulking haze that pinned me.

A wrinkle of noise drifted through the fog. A blurry form hovered over me, light emerged, more shadows, more light and I could see Papa leaned over, the jewel in his tiepin, a dazzling flash. I watched the cloud dissipate, as mist lifts over a lake, swirling upward until the ceiling consumed it.

"Katya, my little bird. You must not lock the door." Papa gathered me in his arms, the waxy tip of his moustache brushed against my cheek and I took a deep breath of cool, clean, refreshing air, touched with a hint of Papa's soap.

CHAPTER TEN

Absence

When Vasili found the spare key to the locked room at last, and the door swung open, Katya was in the bed, her eyes full of terror. He didn't want to, but it made him remember that horrific night long ago in St. Petersburg.

He had been at rehearsal that night. Olga told him what happened. Three men came to the door and dragged his Katya away, for no reason, her only crime, offending a Bolshevik. A mental asylum is what they called the place, but it was worse than any prison.

He should have gone to rescue her at once. But no, he went to the authorities. Only, the authorities no longer held power. Weeks passed before he gave up and did what he should have done at first. He could have saved her the terror of that place if he'd acted sooner. It had been easy to pretend that things remained as always, that the people he begged for help had inﬂuence. It had been easy to ignore the brown-coated Bolsheviks on the streets and believe they would suddenly vanish and Russia would return to normal.

Vasili carried Katya downstairs and stood her up in the foyer. In her face he saw a mix of fear, sadness and confusion. She did not appear to be aware of his presence, did not move or respond as he gathered her to his chest and breathed in the spicy scent of her skin. In the kitchen she sat straight in a chair staring at the table with her hands clamped to her knees. Then like a mechanical toy, she ran her fingers through her hair, liﬅed the coﬀee to her nose, sniﬀed it and then set the cup back down— over and over.

"Here, a nice bit of *borsch* for you." Mary placed a steaming bowl in front of Katya but she did not acknowledge the food or liﬅ her spoon. "Poor little thing. This has been a shock." Mary stood behind her and stroked her hair. Katya dropped her head and leﬅ Mary's hand suspended in mid air.

"She'll be better in a couple of days." George spoke with confidence.

Then Katya began to shiver, hands clenched her knees. She shivered as a kitten shivers in fear when a dog bends for a whiﬀ.

"We have to go back." George hunched over a bowl of Mary's *borsch*.

"Yes, I know." Vasili got up from the table, retrieved a woollen sweater from a hook and draped it over Katya's shoulders.

Mary untied her apron and sat. "I could stay on and help you out for a few days, Mr. Sadilov."

"No, Mary. You go with them. Katya will need you. I will be fine. I need to be alone." But Vasili knew this was not honest. He got up, walked to the stove and added a stick from the wood box.

After George dressed Katya as if she were a child and led her out the door, Vasili fought an urge to call them back but he did not.

He glimpsed himself in the hall mirror and whispered to his image. "You are a fool, Vasili, a fool."

From the window he watched the sleigh until it created a smear on the horizon. He had failed his wife and did not even have the courage to help his daughter through this pain.

It felt like days since Katya left, but it was only hours. Vasili was fine until George and Mary took Katya away. Perhaps it was the worry over his daughter that had made it possible for him to behave as normal.

He paced from the kitchen to the parlour, back to the foyer, halfway up the stairs and along the hall. His hand lit on the cellar door, but he realised the earth's hum would offer no comfort and he swung around. A round of needlepoint that his wife had nearly finished sat on an armchair. What care she had taken to stitch the image of a shopping basket, like those used at the Russian market to carry home vegetables. She had created a

tomato, a carrot and an onion. But the basket was half-empty.
Vasili picked it up and clutched the wooden round to his heart.

Hours later he dropped the needlepoint into the sewing
hamper and examined the room, his books piled everywhere, on
the table, the top of the mantel and the sill of the bay window. He
realised that the hamper was the only possession of Olga's in the
room. The parlour was his.

The first week in the house Olga had unwrapped her
collection of *matryoshka* and placed them on display.

He'd protested. "Put those away. We are in a new country.
They will only make you sick for home."

She'd picked up her favourite one that depicted a gypsy
woman and pulled the first layer off to expose the smaller gypsy
inside. Again and again she tugged until eight matching dolls
stood in a circle on the sill and then she'd said, "Yes, you are
right," and fitted them back together. There were sixteen sets in
her collection, and she'd rolled each into the bright bits of cloth
they had been wrapped in and returned them to their box.

The box was still in the back corner of the closet and Vasili
wondered if she had ever brought them out when he was outside
or reading. Had she pulled them apart and cried for home?

He rushed upstairs, threw open the closet door, fell to his
knees, pulled out the box, and carried it downstairs. In one swipe
he cleared the windowsill of books. They tumbled to the floor. He
took each doll out of its wrapping, separated the nested pieces,

positioned the larger figures on one end of the sill, and lined up the smaller ones. He continued until 128 brightly painted dolls crowded the alcove. Outside the window, Olga's trestle with a few strings of dead rose vine still attached, created a gloomy but wondrous backdrop.

He paced the room until the fire died out and the house creaked with cold. Instead of building another fire he added a sweater, a jacket, a hat, and a heavy winter coat. Vasili knew he did not deserve the comfort of a fire. He had failed both his wife and his daughter. He resumed his pacing, his arms stuck out at the sides, a pseudo-Siberian swaddled in fur.

God's music

Our sleigh slid away from Papa's house. Blowing snow sprayed up from the runners and, over the next hours, only the occasional snort from Gust disrupted the whirr of that wind. As darkness descended, our home appeared on the horizon. The sky was black by the time we pulled into the yard. George and Mary headed straight for the barn to attend to the animals.

It was freezing in the house but at least the air was clean. I lit a lamp, fixed a fire, found a pot of baked beans in the pantry, and before long they were bubbling, the air laden with molasses. But these comforts could not dissolve my restlessness. I paced the kitchen, musical notations tangled in my brain. They were frantic notes from the *Flight of the Bumblebee* strung together in discordant syncopation.

When George and Mary came inside we ate. He hung his socks above the stove and went to bed. I kept an outward calm while Mary and I washed dishes, and then she took her basket of knitting to the parlour.

Later in the bedroom, I crawled under the covers beside my sleeping husband. I tried to stay still, tried to fit the rhythm of George's breathing into a song, but three different tunes played in my head at the same time, and I could do nothing but lie quiet and try to focus, but the songs ran over and over and over each other, and my temples pounded with notes that made no sense. I tossed and turned and dug my fingernails into the skin of my arms.

Hours later, I remembered the two jugs of whiskey on the bottom shelf of the pantry. I slipped out of bed and tiptoed along the hall. Whiskey is calming. After pouring a full cup, I stood by the window. The clamour died with each sip and soon silence prevailed. The barnyard shimmered in the moonlight and I pressed my nose against the pane. Gust was in the corner of the corral, eyes closed, a peaceful giant of a horse. How could he sleep standing up? It was difficult for me to sleep lying prone.

But the stillness subsided and soon my mind scrambled again. If only it could fill with music, but no, it was words and thoughts instead. I sat at the desk and took out my pen. *My violin is weaving spells again. It plays in a dark house, consoling and cajoling. It never sleeps, vexes my fingers…* The nib could barely keep up with my mind. Then a thrum from outside, a swarming sound, brought my efforts to a halt. I rushed to the window.

The noise came from corral.

In a white nightgown, sitting side-saddle on Gust, one long braid draped over her breast, was my Mama. Circled by quivering light, she waved me to come. I swallowed the rest of the whiskey in one gulp, dropped the cup and ran. The snow stung my bare feet as I flew across the yard but she was still there, perched on the horse near the corral. "Mama," I whispered. "Is it you?"

She stared at me and smiled, the tender smile I remembered so well.

"Katya." Her voice filled the night air but her lips did not move. My throat tightened as she gazed at me. "Take your violin to the people." Then she faded, and I called to her, "Mama, don't go." But she soon dissolved into a shimmering mirage against the dark sky.

Then it was all so obvious. I ran back inside and got out my violin. My hand trembled as I lifted the bow. It was music, only music that was important and now it was my duty to bring it to the people.

"Katya." George tapped me on the shoulder. "It's four in the morning."

I jumped when he touched me, stopped playing for a moment, and peered into his eyes. "Oh George. Isn't it wonderful? This song is from God."

"It sounds more the devil's song this time of morning." He swung around and tramped off.

"It's okay," he said by Mary's door. "Go back to bed." Our bedroom door closed with a click. I raised the instrument to my chin and continued to play.

Coping

It was mid-afternoon and the sun shone brightly. Vasili pulled the barroom door at the Gentleman's entrance to the Sylvite Hotel and stepped inside. The stale smell of tobacco and spilled beer went straight to his head. He hesitated in the doorway as the room brightened. Two old men sat hunched over glasses of ale. No one stood behind the bar.

That morning Vasili had woken afraid he might lose his sanity if he did not hear another human voice. John Dari, who normally dropped every few days, was away. Vasili had not seen a soul in over a week.

Smoke fogged the saloon and he heard laughter. Four men holding cards occupied a table in the far corner with a scatter of coins between them. Vasili didn't recognise three of them but he was acquainted with Leroy Crowley, a slight man with a pitted red nose, a veteran of the Great War.

"You've got the god-damnedest luck, Jim." A cyclopean fellow sporting a walrus moustache flung his cards on the floor and cracked his empty beer glass on the table.

"Don't be a sore loser, Reg." Leroy had four fingers missing from his right hand, a war injury, and he waved his one remaining finger in the man's face. "You cleaned my clock last week, or have you forgotten?"

"Well, I'm done in." The big man turned his pockets inside out and stomped toward the exit.

Leroy looked up and noticed Vasili. "Vasili, come on over. Join us."

Vasili shook his head. "No, but thank you. I do not play cards."

Leroy puffed on the stub of a cigar. "Suit yourself."

Vasili took a stool as the proprietor's bald head poked up from the entryway to a cellar. He grunted as he climbed the last steps hefting a wooden box of full bottles pressed against his ample belly.

According to John Dari, Henry Thompson kept a still the size of a house in that basement. Vasili studied the dark hole in the floor.

Henry nodded to Vasili, set the box on the floor, marched over and leaned on the bar. "What'll you have?"

"I will have a brandy."

"No brandy, sorry, but we got whiskey."

"Whiskey is fine." Vasili twisted in his chair and glanced over at the three men intent on their card game.

"Henry, bring another for me and these wayward brothers, will you?" Leroy waved one hand over his head.

It was obvious the two men beside Leroy were brothers, the same round cheeks, thin upper lips, the same heads stacked neck-less on their shoulders like pumpkins on fence posts. Henry dropped a glass near Vasili's elbow and the clap on the counter startled him.

"On the house." Henry offered a serious nod. "Sorry about your wife." He turned and picked up a tray.

Henry's suspenders stretched to the point of bursting but Vasili admired the easy way he moved across the room, a tray balanced on one hand like a waiter at the *Evropyskaya*. His tray did not waiver as he reached his customers. He bent, emptied the spilled-over ashtray, picked up the cards in one practiced swoop, wiped the table with a wet rag, collected coins from the men and placed full pints of beer on mats, all without a splash.

Leroy's slurred voice carried across the room. "Vasili, this here is Jimmy and Roy Ellis. They're just over from Lloyd. Gave their wives the slip this afternoon." He placed his hands as if in prayer, bowed his head and then looked up grinning.

"You're in the wrong room for worshiping, friend." The barman swung around and headed to serve the old fellows in the corner.

"Do you play cards here often?" One brother lifted his drink to

Leroy.

"Only once a day, 1 p.m. til five." Leroy laughed a big hearty laugh that didn't seem possible from such a thin man. "But don't let on to the wife, eh." He punched the shoulder of the brother on his right. "She thinks I'm tending to business matters, eh."

"Don't worry." The man took a deep drag off his cigarette and butted it. "I don't know your wife."

"Well, my wife spends most of her waking hours at church. Ladies to Re-instate Prohibition and the Women's League—that kind of thing. She's so goddamn pious she can turn cleaning the pig sty into a revival meeting."

One brother banged his beer on the table. "God, I know what you mean. My wife knits socks for this missionary traipsing around India. I asked her to darn my socks last week and you won't believe what she did." He paused, leaned forward and gripped his beer with both hands. "She picked them up, walked over to the garbage pail, dropped them in and said, 'darn socks.'" The other men howled.

Vasili turned his back on the poker players, lifted his glass, gazed at the bottles lined up behind the bar and drank the rest of his whiskey in a single gulp. This was not the place for him. He decided right then to attend church on Sunday and sit where he and Olga always sat. He would sing the hymns they always sang. With luck Mrs. Bradley would play well and he would forget for a few moments that Olga was not sitting next to him.

He stood and gave a half-bow to Henry. "Thank you for the drink. I must go now." He walked out of the Hotel, back up Main Street past the store and Joe's Barbershop and continued along the road to his house.

Playing God's Music

For several nights after Mama's visit, it was impossible to sleep, and I slipped out of bed as George snored and stood watch by the window, eyes fixed on the yard. But Mama did not appear again. Just before dawn on Sunday morning I gave up looking for her. Mama had a mind of her own. If she wanted to see me she would, and all my wishing would not produce her. Since I was up with nothing to do, I began cleaning the house. While on my knees in the hallway scrubbing the floorboards, I looked up to see Mary looming over me in her horrible brown robe.

"What in heaven's name are you doing?" she said.

"Washing the floor." I dipped the brush into the pail.

"In the middle of the night?" From her dour expression, you'd think housecleaning was sinful or disgusting.

"It's morning." I scoured a dark spot on the wood.

"Well, I never." She plodded back to her room.

There was no pleasing that woman. Nothing I did was good enough. "Make sure you get way back in the corner... Careful of the good china... See you've missed that spot." Mary wasn't much of a housekeeper but found fault with everything I did. I loved to make the wood floor shine and the little figurines in the dining room glisten. When I'd first moved in the statuettes were caked in greasy dust. Sick, sooty little caricatures. After a good soak and scrub in hot soapy water they assembled on the sideboard like a gay party in Prince Leopold's Court.

Any thought of Prince Leopold's Court always made me think of Bach. I left the last stretch of the floor, got out my violin, closed my eyes and played the violin solo for the *Brandenburg Concerto No. 3*.

When I finished the piece George was standing in the doorway in his overcoat. He shook off like a wet dog and came in. "You still want to go to church?"

"Yes." I put down the violin. "I've laid your suit out and pressed your shirt." I kept my voice low. "Where's Mary?"

"Milking the goats." He removed his gloves.

"I don't want her to come."

"You should try to get along with her." He reached out and rested his glove on my shoulder.

"I didn't ask to have her here." I stepped back.

"That fence in the west field needs fixing." He took off his coat and tossed it on a chair. "It's two hours there and two hours back."

"Sunday is a day of rest," I told him. "And besides, I want to see Papa. He'll be lonely on his own."

"All right, we can go, but please try harder with Mary, okay?"

"I'll try." I crossed my fingers behind my back as he walked to the bedroom to change.

"Pretty," George said when I joined him in the kitchen later.

I'd dressed with care, knotted my hair and even taken the time to rub lipstick on my cheeks. "You haven't worn that dress since our wedding."

"Yes, I forgot I had it." The dress had a high waistline and hid the little mound of my belly very well. George had not once mentioned the change to my shape. He hadn't reached out for me in bed for longer than I could remember, so he'd never touched it. Were men not observant of such things? But Mary would have noticed, and she'd not said a word either. I knew I was thin, but to not notice?

"Maybe we should stay home." He gazed at me, traced the lace collar with one finger and then cupped my breast.

I brushed his hand away. "She'll be back any minute."

George walked to the mirror over the kitchen sink, picked up a comb and tried to tame that one piece of hair that always shot out at the crown of his head. He cut a fine figure in his suit. I could watch him all day but if we didn't leave soon, the service would be over. The door opened and Mary blew in, smelling of goat.

"Going out?" She closed the door behind her.

"To church," I told her, "and a visit with Papa."

"Oh." For a moment she looked confused.

"Do you want us to pick up any supplies in town?" George asked.

"Well, I thought I'd go in myself." She rubbed her hands over the wrinkles of her coat and looked at her muddy boots.

"We'll be late." I took my husband's arm and led him to the door.

"I'll roast a chicken tonight," Mary said.

"Don't worry about supper for us." I pulled George outside and slammed the door.

George helped me into the sleigh and as he did, I turned my head to the corral. Above the railing of the fence the air began to vibrate and the image of Mama appeared again, just as she had in the middle of the night but it was broad daylight now and I grinned. George looked right at her.

"Isn't it incredible, George?"

"What?"

"Mama."

"That mangy cat by the barn door? Hard to believe it's still around."

"Mama," I shouted at her. "I'm going to do it."

"What on earth are you talking about, Katya?" George walked around and climbed into the driver's seat.

I blinked, and she disappeared. "Nothing." I placed my violin sideways across my lap.

"Do you need that at church?"

"Yes," I said and placed my palms flat on the leather case.

The service was underway when we arrived. I waited on the steps, listened as the congregation sang *Thou Hidden Love of God* while George tied Gust to the hitching post behind the church. We slipped into the back row.

"There's Papa." I whispered to George and pointed to a seat halfway up the aisle. "He's not singing. This is one of his favourite hymns. It's not the same without Papa singing."

"Shhh." George patted my arm.

The song ended and Reverend Manning began his sermon. *"For the flesh lusteth against the Spirit, and the Spirit against the flesh..."*

Whenever Reverend Manning used the word *lust* to start a sermon, you knew it would be a long one. I shifted in my seat and tried to figure out how the woman in front of me had pinned her hair into such an elaborate roll, curled strands stacked one on top of another. After what seemed hours, my foot twitching non-stop, I looked over at George. Chin on his chest, his mouth agape, he was fast asleep. Reverend Manning droned on. More minutes passed. I couldn't stand it anymore. I opened my violin case, careful not to disturb my sleeping husband and lifted it out. God's music shouldn't be postponed.

I stood up in the middle of *"If we live in the Spirit, let us also walk in the Spirit,"* and made my way toward the chancel. I climbed the few steps and stopped, not four feet from where Reverend Manning stood rooted, mouth open and speechless. I placed the violin on my shoulder and looked out over the chosen people. The truth of the music burned through me and with the first few notes, Mama's presence filled the church. I closed my eyes, let the composition gather force and gave the congregation their first taste of heaven.

I felt a touch on my arm at the end of *Sola Viola After a Dream*, opened my eyes and there stood my Papa. The church was empty, save for the Reverend who had his back to us as he fussed over something on his pulpit and George who stood at the back of the church scowling with his arms folded.

"Wasn't it extraordinary?" I whispered to Papa.

"It was." Papa took my arm and led me toward George and the door. My husband stood statue stiff, turned as we came close, and we followed him outside.

"She can ride with me." Papa put his arm around me. "I have John Dari's horse and wagon. He is away."

"I'll be along." George did not look at me. Papa drew me in close and we walked to the wagon. I smiled up at him.

Papa's moustache was still black but his hair was white and he had new lines under his eyes. He boosted me into the wagon before he climbed up and we set off. As we rode along the bumpy rode, he reached out and patted my knee.

I squeezed his hand. "The performance, was it good?"

"Wonderful. I have never heard *After a Dream* played so well. It is a shame Rachmaninov could not have heard it." He patted my fingers. "I received a letter from him. You remember Sergei."

"From the Conservatory?" Oh yes, Sergei with his long nose and long fingers. I smiled. "I played with him."

"Yes, he was your champion at the Metropol. He heard you and decided you must be put on stage. He is in New York now." Papa slapped the reins.

"I know. You told me that. Does he love New York?"

"He said winter in New York is foul, dreary cold, not crisp and clear like St. Petersburg. He misses drinks at the *Evropyskaya*."

"Does he still play?"

"Yes, but he has not composed since he left. He feels in exile and claims he knows now what it must have been like for Niccolò Paganini."

The wagon rattled along the road and Papa gripped the reins, his large hands in front and bent over the way his tall friend had once leaned over the piano at the Conservatory.

"I always picture your friend at the Conservatory, in front of the piano, in the room with the high windows. Remember the Conservatory, Papa?"

"Ah, yes, a wonderful place. I can still see it. Many times I stood at those windows and watched ice flows drift on the Neva, banging one against the other. They always moved, even in winter."

"I remember the spires and cupolas of the city from the boat when we left. Why did we leave, Papa?"

"You were in danger." His wistful expression vanished.

"I recall no danger. When we left, I was fourteen. I should remember."

"Better you don't." He focused on the road.

"I remember something, a man with a dirty white coat, a place with corridors and closed doors?" Like a bad dream. My knees shook, and I put my hands in my lap to steady them. This was the image that came in the night, a horrible dream.

"Better not think of it." He snapped the reins.

My breath caught, my heart pounded. Foetid air clogged my nostrils. I gasped for air, wiped my nose on the back of my arm, shook my head, waved my hand in front of my face, closed my eyes and concentrated on a Vivaldi song, a fantastical song.

It didn't take long to reach Papa's farm.

The house seemed lonelier now, plopped on this flat piece of land as if God had leftovers and set it down in a blank space. Papa led the horse to the barn. A great sadness swept over me as I watched him cross the yard. He had always been a tall straight man but now he limped along, arched like a witching stick.

The top of the stove remained warm from the morning fire but the kitchen was chilly. Dishes littered the table. A dried-out loaf of bread sat in a heap of crumbs on the counter. Several dirty pots cluttered the stove. Papa took his parka off and dropped it on a chair. He ambled around the kitchen as if he'd lost something.

"Papa, are you okay?"

"Fine, yes."

"Have you been eating?" I walked over to the icebox and opened it. It was bare except for a half-full glass of dill pickles in the far corner, a full jar of sauerkraut and something that looked like it might have once been an apple in the centre of the rack. "I'm glad you're still attending church." I didn't know what else to say. I wanted to cheer him up.

"It made your Mama happy when I went to church." He took off his hat and hung it on the hook. "She is not in this house anymore, but at church I sense her beside me."

"Yes, she's still with us, isn't she?" I wanted to tell him everything, how Mama appeared what she said, but he was staring off into space and I knew it wasn't the right time.

And rancour had commandeered the kitchen again. The room was rancid. "I'll make coffee." I walked over to the stove, added paper and a few sticks of wood and the fire crackled to life. "Papa, I'm worried. Something awful is lurking in this house."

"You let your imagination run wild, little bird. This is a house, emptier now, but only a house. No evil spirits lurk."

"It's because Mama's gone. She was so good, the spirits kept their distance."

"Don't think about spirits. Your Mama wouldn't want you to. We'll have a brandy with the coffee." He wandered off down the hall.

I heard a horse whinny outside and within moments George opened the door, shoved it closed behind him and marched into the kitchen, eyes squinted to slits.

"What were you doing, Katya?" He put both hands on my shoulders and squeezed his thumbs into the soft flesh above my breasts.

"Making coffee." I tried not to wince, but straightened, pushed up on his hands and he loosened his grip. "George, I'm worried for Papa."

"Don't change the subject. What was that, back at the church?"

"What do you mean?"

"You interrupted Reverend Manning."

"Reverend Manning is a bore."

"Why would you embarrass yourself like that?"

"What are you talking about?"

"You got up and played right in the middle of the sermon, for Christ's sake." The words hissed through his teeth. He towered over me, his hands clenching my shoulders as if he itched to strangle me.

I looked right into his eyes. "You fell asleep in the middle of the sermon. Why would you care what I do? Besides, I was playing for Mama."

Papa padded back into the kitchen and my husband dropped his hands. "George, there you are." Papa handed me the bottle of brandy. "Come, we will take coffee in the parlour."

The aroma of the coffee could not overcome the damp earth smell in the kitchen. Papa was stubborn but weak from his loss and whatever stirred in the house might very well overpower him. Without Mama, he was an easy target for a wicked spirit. He had to get out of the house.

I got out three cups and poured coffee, plenty of sugar for Papa, black for George, a half cup for me, two snifters of brandy on the side. I added brandy to my cup, filled it right to the brim and placed the snifters and cups on a tray. In the parlour I handed Papa his coffee and brandy, passed the same to George, picked up my cup and took a long swallow. "Papa, I've decided," I said. "You'll come to live with us. We can fix you a bedroom in the dining room. We never use that room. You can't stay here anymore, can he, George?"

George side-stepped behind Papa and shot me a look. "No, I guess not."

"Your husband may not want an old man underfoot." Papa glanced at George who had turned his back on us.

"You're not an old man, Vasili." George lifted his glass and inspected his brandy as if a fly were swimming in it. "I guess you could come and stay for a while."

"It's a long way from town." Papa put his hands behind his back.

"Yes." George nodded. "It is a long way."

"When do you go to town, Papa?" I said. "Only for church... and George will drive you in when the weather settles. And you'll be with us for Christmas. You can't spend the holiday by yourself." I tapped my fingers on the side of the cup. "I'll play for you every night, Papa."

"Well, I could sell the cows. Next month at the auction."

"Not next month, Papa. Get John Dari to tend them. He can sell them too. You should come *now*... today."

"Katya, your Papa can't just up and leave. He needs time to think. We can decide next month after the auction." George raised one hand, fingers splayed to whoa, the same gesture he used on the horse to settle him down.

I ignored him. "No. I'll ask John right now. He'll take care of the house and the milking. I know he won't mind. He'll sell the milk in town, when he sells his own. He'll be happy for the extra money, Papa."

"Yes, but John is not home. I told you he is away. He won't be back until tomorrow."

"But you'll come? Today?"

"No, not today, little bird, but next week. I'll come next week. There are arrangements."

"Papa, you don't understand. You must leave this house now."

I walked to him and gripped his hand. Surely he could sense the danger. Papa was perceptive, like me.

"Wednesday. I will come on Wednesday." Papa brushed his fingers down my cheek.

I stood up, picked up my coffee, finished it in one swallow and then flew to the kitchen, trembling with frustration at such bull-headed men. In the pantry I rummaged until I found a jar of meat, an onion and a few potatoes with wrinkled skins. It wasn't much, but Papa would need all his strength to endure three more days.

First, I ladled water into the blue enamel pot Mama had always used for her famous soups, then peeled the potatoes and dropped them in. Soon the water bubbled, and I pushed them around with a fork, inspected the white flesh for any spots, any sign the air had tainted them. Satisfied they were fine, I poked them every few minutes until they were soft and then poured the water off into the slop pail under the sink before adding the onion and meat. Not a stew to make Mama proud, but with sauerkraut, a passable meal.

"Come and eat," I called, set bowls on the table, dished out a sizeable portion for Papa, a smaller one for George and a few spoonfuls for myself. The two men were silent as they entered the kitchen and we sat down to eat. Papa didn't offer to say *Grace*. I knew he'd only ever done it to please Mama.

George didn't comprehend this. My papa was not a religious

man.

After a few moments it was George who clasped his hands and bowed his head. "Thank you Father, for this food and for your blessings."

My stomach roiled from the stink in the kitchen. I speared a piece of meat with my fork and brought it up to my mouth but couldn't get it past my lips. A shot of acid spurted up my throat.

"This is tasty." George spooned stew into his mouth.

"You're learning to cook." Papa took a delicate bite and then he too pushed the stew around in his bowl.

CHAPTER ELEVEN

Shame

GEORGE stepped back when Vasili walked into the kitchen, but his face was livid. His hands were too near Katya's throat. She looked defiant, her long neck ramrod straight, her mouth puckered up, and the scar on her lip protruded like the teat of a cat.

Vasili took a deep breath. Had he miscalculated his son-in-law's anger? "There you are, George." He led the younger man into the parlour.

George stood near the bay window and shuffled from foot to foot. Vasili remained standing too and leaned against the bookcase.

"A peddler came to the house yesterday on snowshoes." Vasili kept his tone subdued. George was a reasonable man. His anger would cool. "The man carried a pack laden with many things, soap to clean your harness, a tonic to ward off influenza, and old leather boots with worn-off heels slung on his shoulders. I felt sorry for the poor soul and invited him into the house." As Vasili spoke George stared at the line of *matryoshka* dolls on the windowsill.

"He looked starved, so I found a tin of biscuits in the pantry. Then he filled his mouth and attempted to talk at the same time. From Poland, I think he told me. I understood little of what he said. Maybe it was his full mouth or perhaps the dialect." Vasili stopped for a moment and bent to pick up a twig on the rug by his feet. "Do travelling salesmen stop at your farm?"

"Huh?" George looked up, hands clasped behind his back.

"They come often in the summer, but I have not seen one in winter before, have you?" Vasili asked.

"Yes, hucksters. No, we don't get many." George picked up the most colourful doll and eyed his father-in-law. "Katya's been acting queer since her Mama died." He fidgeted with the doll.

"That is to be expected," Vasili said.

"No, you don't get it. Remember you said I should pay attention to certain things? Well, her appetite is poor, and she doesn't sleep. I don't have a clue what to do, and today at church, Jesus!" He placed the doll back on the sill and pinched the skin on his forehead until it wrinkled.

"But, she is fine now, no? It is just her nature. And was harm done today? I have not enjoyed church so much since we moved here." Vasili chuckled. "Did you see the expression on Reverend

Manning's face? And Mrs. Stanley," He snorted. "Her mean little eyes exploded from her head." A full-out laugh escaped. "The Reverend, frozen, like a turkey in thunder. I do not think he took a breath for the entire performance."

"Vasili, listen. This isn't funny. I'm worried. Sometimes Katya talks to thin air." George scowled. "She has conversations with a crow."

"You worry over that? Do you not talk to your horse or curse a broken wheel on the wagon?"

"That isn't the same. You don't understand. These are real conversations, like you'd have with a person."

"George, you do not understand. Katya has a gift and her temperament is a part of that gift. When she was five years old, she lifted her cousin's violin and played a tune. It was the first time she'd seen a violin. When she was ten years old, ten years of age, they invited her to play at the Metropol with the Masters. She played with the Masters."

Vasili knew his daughter was a genius even sooner, before she walked her first steps. One day she plunked out a tune with her baby fingers while sitting on his lap at the piano. And he remembered how proud he'd been when they summoned her to the Metropol, how his hand shook as he read the invitation and how excited Olga had been when she told the ten-year-old Katya, "You must practice every day, very, very hard." With the thought of his wife, a tiredness overwhelmed him and he collapsed into the chair. "Yes, Katya is different, but you should not worry, George."

"But I do worry," George said. "And, we'll have to keep a good distance from that church for a while."

Smoke and Mirrors

It was mid-afternoon by the time we left Papa's. The road had a thin slick of snow, and beads of ice pelted our faces. One runner of the sleigh slid into a frozen groove and the seat lurched. I drew the quilt up to my ears. It was difficult to get air in past my frost-filled nostrils.

"Why did you do it, Katya?" George yelled over the wind.

"Do what?"

"Ask your father to move in with us? A women should ask her husband before making an offer like that."

"Yes, and a husband should consult his wife before inviting a complete stranger to take up residence." He had some nerve to criticise.

Our voices tumbled in the flurry.

"That was different," he said. "You were sick and Mary nursed you." He stared at the road.

A blast of air shot bullets of snow, forcing us both to close our eyes. The horse lowered his head and pushed hard into the fury. A blast of wind whipped the edge of my quilt as if trying to unravel me.

The air calmed for a moment and I tugged at George's sleeve and yelled, "I'm worried about Papa. Let's go back. We should make him come now."

"We're not going back. This will wait a few days." George snapped the reins against the horse's rump and Gust picked up his pace to a trot.

When we arrived home, the wind had calmed, and the snow stopped. The crow, perched on the fence of the corral, watched us pull into the yard. George jumped down from the sleigh and did not offer to help me dismount. The corners of the bird's beak curled up in a smile. George removed Gust's harness and led him straight into the barn. I remained in the passenger's seat and scrutinised that black bird.

The outline of the crow began to vibrate and changed shape. Its inky wings flickered and dispersed into thin air. Then the outline of wings came back, curved up and re-arranged themselves as lines, like pen and ink drawings, on the red-brown wall of the barn. The lines formed the shape of a piano, a horn section, and violins that whirled with movement and music. Lines and more lines appeared. They took on colour, and the music wasn't the normal melody deep inside my mind, but sprang from the performing image only a few scant feet away. I could do nothing but stare.

The shapes misted and transformed again. First a long braid

materialised, then the gentle slope of a forehead and the patient face of my mama. Her lips moved, but the music was strong and it filled the air with icy exuberance. I leaned forward, straining to listen but lost Mama's voice in the blizzard of song. I studied her mouth and thought I could make out, "Good girl" and "Papa" but now the tune was thunderous. Lines emerged again and sketched over Mama's image until she was a scattered fragment that flicked in time to a lively tune, an *accelerando*—a *crescendo* that sent pinpricks up my spine. The instruments re-appeared on the barn wall and joined in glorious harmony for the climax.

Then the music hushed and all that remained was immense quiet, bitter cold air, and the crow. I pulled the quilt up tight around my neck. The bird hopped toward the wagon with one leg tucked under his belly. I turned in the seat, let my body slide ,and landed with a thud in the snow. It stared at me and cocked its head.

"So, it's you, is it? You're trying to warn me, aren't you Loki? Warn me about Papa. He's in terrible danger, isn't he?" The crow stopped, nodded and his eyes were no longer merry, but small, shiny, serious black beads. I squatted and held out my hand. He jumped forward to my outstretched fingers. Then his mind touched my thoughts, and I knew what I had to do.

A door slammed, and he hopped backwards, breaking the link. Mary smacked the broom on the porch railing.

"I thought I saw you drive up. Why are you still out here?

You'll catch your death. Let that bird alone. I'll take him a chunk of bread later." The crow turned his back on me and flapped off toward the barn.

"Look what you've done. You scared him away."

"He won't go far. Come in. I've got a nice pot of hot tea."

The next three days dragged on forever. All I could think of was the heavy smell in Mama's kitchen, how weak Papa had become, and what I needed to do. The sky remained sunny and calm. Thank the lucky stars because any hint of snow George would use as an excuse to delay our trip.

When I opened the curtains to greet the day on Wednesday, I grinned. It was a grand clear morning, and the roads were fit for the wagon. Our sleigh wouldn't do. It was not large enough to accommodate Papa's bed, books and whatever else he wanted to bring.

After breakfast George hitched up and he and I set out. Motes of ice circled in the air like sparks from a magic wand, a bewitching day.

Everything would be fine once we got Papa out of that house. He'd know what to do about the baby too. Not that I planned to tell him all the details. In fact, I wasn't sure how to broach the subject, but my Papa always found a solution. I pushed the problem out of my mind. That was easy with the rolling drifts of satin snow and songs that danced in my head. We'd driven over three hours when we saw John Dari's place up over the ridge.

"You needn't ask for John's help," I said. "Papa won't have much. Nothing heavy. I can help with the bed."

"The headboard is solid iron. We'll need a man to help," he said.

When we rolled up to the Dari farm, John was on the veranda, coat unbuttoned, a cigar between his teeth, a shiny belt buckle wedged into his potbelly and his bright boots polished to a glassy glow. George explained our plan.

"I'm surprised he didn't tell me. I'll miss the old man." John stomped the cigar stub and jumped into our wagon.

"You'll just have to visit our place more often," I said.

There was a secondary road between John and Papa's house, and it cut travelling time by half. But only two shallow indents in the snow marked the road. The horse snorted, and the wagon bumped forward. Gust's hooves lifted and thumped down, slowly, cautiously.

"Can't we go any faster?" I asked.

"Not if we want the wheels to stay on," George said.

"Well, I can walk faster. Stop the wagon."

"Don't be foolish, Kat."

"George Brown, stop this wagon and let me off or I'll jump." He would not treat me like a child.

"For Christ's sake." He pulled on the reins and Gust planted both hooves in the snow.

John shrugged his shoulders and smirked. I scrambled down, forged ahead, and the wagon rumbled behind me. Soon, the sound of the wheels grew faint. As I strode up the last stretch to Papa's house I heard only the far-off laughter of the two men.

It was at least fifteen below and there was no smoke coming from Papa's chimney. Panic choked me. I ran the last stretch, bolted up to the front door, threw it open and a wall of mustiness brought me to a dead stop. The air was heavy, rank, and grey with the odour. I thrust forward into the porch and then to the kitchen. It took every bit of effort to put one foot in front of the other and plod across the floor.

"Papa." I tried to yell but my voice disappeared in the rancid fog. I could barely see the dishes stacked on the counter, boots strewn on the mat. "Papa, are you home?" I slogged along the hall to the parlour. Here, the air was not as thick. The fireplace grate sat heaped with dead ashes. Papa's chair was empty.

I looked up. The toxic cloud that engulfed the lower rooms had spread only halfway up the staircase, and beams of light streaked across the upper landing. I pushed my way up the stairs, one leg at a time. My muscles strained against the gloom with every step. It seemed to take forever, but near the top I broke through gasping and filled my lungs with air.

"Papa," I yelled again. This time my voice came out clear, and I climbed the last few steps, turned at the top, threw open the door to Papa's room, and ran inside. It was dark with the curtains drawn. It took a few moments for my eyes to adjust. The bedcovers moved. I ran to the window and flung open the drapes. Sharp winter light flooded the room.

"Papa, are you all right?" I rushed to the bed and knelt. Grey stubble covered Papa's cheeks and his Russian fur hat, burrowed deep in the pillow, hid his eyebrows. He opened his eyes.

"What? Oh, Katya." His arms appeared from under the covers and he lifted one gnarled hand up and patted me on the shoulder. "I must have overslept."

"We're here to collect you, Papa. Come on. Get up. Let's get out of this house."

"Is it Wednesday already?"

"Yes, Papa, it's Wednesday."

He pushed away the quilt and sheets, swung his legs off the bed, and sat up fully dressed. Red underwear burst from his pant cuffs. "It's cold," he said.

"Your fire is out."

"I must have slept well." He stood up, wobbled, and I gripped his shoulder to steady him.

"We have to hurry. Are you packed?"

"Do not worry. I need little."

Mama's dresses were still in the wardrobe, and I tried not to look at them. I shoved them aside and picked out Papa's good suit, his three white shirts, and his dressing gown. I placed these in the middle of a thick blanket on the bed, gathered up his razor, strop, brush, the wedding picture on the bedside table, his good leather shoes from under the chair, dropped everything on the blanket, and tied the corners to make a bundle. The downstairs door banged.

"Upstairs," I hollered, and the men stomped up the steps.

"I wonder how they got through it so fast," I said as George and John plodded into the room.

"Got through what?" Papa wandered over to the window, rubbed his eyes, folded his arms across his chest, and gazed out.

Did Papa not see what was happening in his house? "Never mind," I said.

"Vasili." John strode over, turned Papa to face him, and drew him into a hug. "You are leaving me. Who will I call on now, to help me with those damn government forms?"

"Ah, John, you will manage. George's farm is not too far away."

"Morning, Sir," George said. "You're ready to go?"

"Yes, I am ready." Papa shook his head and peered around the room. "We will gather up the gamut."

"I think we should take the washstand and dresser too," I said.

"Let's get the bed now," George said. "We can always come back another day."

"We should bring them now. Why bother John twice?"

"I don't mind coming back," John said.

"We'll take them. We're here now. I'll cart them myself if I have to." It was vital—we had to strip every item Papa needed from the house.

George and John exchanged a look as they pulled the bed apart. I picked up the bundle and took Papa's arm. "Come, let's get you downstairs."

I stopped at the top of the stairs. The cloud appeared thicker than before and had crept even higher.

"Get a good deep breath, Papa. I'll get you through this if it's the last thing I do."

"I'm not sad to leave," Papa said. "Your Mama isn't in the house any more."

"No, the cloud, Papa. You might find it hard to breathe."

"You are confusing me, Katya. What cloud?"

"It doesn't matter, Papa. Let's get you outside."

Each step down the stairs felt as gruelling as a climb uphill. Struggling to breathe, I clutched Papa's arm, and pulled him through the dense air. There was a pressure to it. A thud, thud pounded both sides of my head as if the evil spirit in the house wanted to crush my skull. I tightened my grip on Papa's arm. "Are you okay, Papa?" His face was grey except for a rosy smudge high on his cheekbone.

"Yes, okay, only a little stiff." He gripped the rail. "Do you remember how your Mama polished this rail? It is dull now, but she made it shine. I used to joke my teeth shone in the reflection."

We clambered down the stairs and through the kitchen. Outside I took a deep breath of delicious, crisp air. Papa held back as I tried to lead him to the wagon.

"My books," Papa said. "I've packed them in the trunk, and your Mama's dolls. They're on the windowsill. We cannot leave them."

"You get the dolls, Papa." I patted him on the shoulder and then rushed to the door, leaned in, and hollered upstairs. "Bring Papa's books. The trunk, in the parlour." Then I headed for the rear of the house.

"Where are you going?" Papa asked.

"I'll only be a minute." I raced around to Papa's old storage shed and opened the rickety door. Cracks in the clapboard wall let in a crisscross of light. The corners were dense with spiderwebs. The roof of this shed had always leaked and old catalogues sat curled and crumpled in one corner. It took several minutes to find the bottle of kerosene behind an assortment of empty cans. Then I searched for matches. There was no time to lose. Just when I thought I might need to go back inside, I found a box under a piece of leather, thankfully dry.

I peered around the corner and watched George and John load the bed frame onto the wagon. Then they disappeared back into the house and brought the washstand, dresser, and trunk and set them in the snow beside the horse. Good, they were out of the house.

Papa was seated in the wagon holding a box on his lap. I ducked out of sight. After screwing the lid off the kerosene, I sprinkled a liberal portion on the kitchen window ledge. The sharp scent of kerosene seared my nostrils. I moved closer and squinted through the pane. Grey fog still filled the house. I saw only an outline of the stove and the table. The cloud was thickest here. For several moments it mesmerised me.

Then, I struck a match and tossed it. Flames licked up the window frame. The acrid smell of kerosene hit my nostrils. Then I scampered to the dining room window, ducking to keep out of sight. The kerosene bottle was half empty. Concerned I wouldn't make it around the house, I only wet the corners. But, the effect was the same—an instant yellow flame and black smoke rising. I eyed the old dry wood on the back porch. This was where Papa kept the winter coal, and it was on this wall I splashed the rest of the kerosene. I swiped a match.

The men rushed around the corner, then came to a standstill.

"Katya, stop!" George moved toward me with one hand out. "Blow out the match." The small flame seared my fingers. I threw it against the porch. An instant flare.

"God damn it, Katya. What in hell have you done? John, get the blankets from the barn. The coal bin is behind that wall."

John turned and ran. His boots crackled on the crusty snow.

George rushed up and pushed me away from the flames. My legs gave way, and I landed on my right hip, hurting and helpless, watching him scoop handfuls of snow over the new flame on the old siding. My fire fizzled.

"Don't do that." I scrambled to my feet. "We have to burn it, don't you see?" I pulled on his arm. He landed a hard slap to the side of my head. I fell back into the snow but it wasn't cold, even though I knew it should be, and the skin on my legs prickled with pain, and the sky dimmed as if dusk had set in, the air around me thick with the stink of decayed earth.

My skull burst with pain and my old nightmare flashed—a dark room, the man, a sting up my spine, wails from the upper rooms, vodka-garlic breath, fused with the stench of evil wet dirt.

I held my nose to block the foulness. My ears pounded, and I heard the far-off sound of John Dari's voice. "Here, wet blankets, I dunked them in the well. I think the flames are out over there. I'll go back and check."

Then George's voice, so faraway, sliding through a tunnel. "I'll keep an eye on it here. I think I got it out."

Then, what a relief—the fog billowed out of the house and circled above me into the sky. Through the cloud Papa's voice called "Katya," and the shadow of a crow appeared, a blanket hung from its beak. It dropped and floated in slow motion through the haze, reaching me in time, engulfing me, forming a barrier between my body and the evil gas. It took all my strength to bring the corner of that blanket up over my lip, over the tender spot on my temple but I knew Papa would keep me safe. He called my name again. Footsteps crunched the snow next to my head and I lay warm and protected.

Then the light faded.

A dream had me in its grip. Niccolò was alone on stage in an orchestra hall, and gilded columns loomed up in the immense chamber. The auditorium had no aisles, only seats fitted together, and they formed an unbroken barrier between us. Me, standing at the back of the theatre—Niccolò on stage with his violin. I was too far away to hear him play. If only I could get closer. I tried to raise my leg over the seat in front of me, but my stomach had grown to an awkward size. My knee wouldn't go high enough. I hoisted my belly with both hands and struggled to shove it off to one side, but it grew larger and tighter as I held it. No matter how I toiled, twisted and pulled I could not lift my leg high enough to scale that seat.

Peril and Protection

Vasili carried his daughter to the wagon, lifted her onto the back bench and held her. At her temple, a vein throbbed, and she looked helpless as a newborn mouse.

The two younger men shovelled snow over the smoking sections and then patted each spot with bare hands. Vasili glimpsed something moving near the barn. When he squinted to get a better look, it disappeared. He assumed John Dari's dog had followed, but thought it odd the hound would keep out of sight.

When George was satisfied the fire was out, they drove off. John rode up front with George.

They rolled to a stop at John's farmhouse. "Bring her inside. Blanche might be able to help," John said.

"No, we'd best get home."

"Good thing we got it out." John swung his paunch sideways and eased down from the wagon.

"I don't know what's going on with her, John. I'd appreciate if you kept this to yourself."

"No need to worry. Anything to help."

George snapped the reins, and they were off to the farm. He said nothing during the ride home but sat sullen and stiff.

Katya did not open her eyes during the bumpy ride. She lay so still in Vasili's arms that he bent and listened for her breath every two minutes.

When they arrived, it was Vasili who lifted his daughter up the stairs and to her room. She remained motionless and appeared to be asleep, dark hair fanned against the white pillow, a patterned quilt tucked up to her chin.

"Vasili, we have to do something." George stood at the foot of the bed, hands clenched.

"What is there to do?"

"She's dangerous."

"She did not mean harm." Katya's eyelashes fluttered and Vasili moved close, leaned down, and kissed his daughter's forehead.

"No *harm?*"

"You don't understand her yet."

George did not see Katya's delicate nature. She had always been fragile, but kind. At the age of eight she had found a baby robin and fed it each hour for weeks. Vasili helped her to build a nest with scraps of cloth and soft twigs. She kept it beside her bed and got up whenever she heard a chirp. The worms she collected from the garden and crushed them up with her own little hands. She saved that bird and did not cry, but laughed and set him free when he was big enough to fly.

Now, buried in the covers, she resembled a bird in a nest.

"What if you'd been inside?" George's voice spat anger.

"But I wasn't."

"And if she does it again? What if she tries to burn up this place while we're sleeping?"

"All you need to know is this. Katya is a gentle girl and would not harm a spider. She is a musician. She brings joy, not sadness." How could he think his daughter a threat?

"Mary thinks I should take her to a doctor." George paced to the window. "She says there's a hospital near Edmonton, a mental institution."

Vasili swallowed a lump of instant anger. "Mary should keep her thoughts to herself. Katya needs no doctor or hospital. She needs rest." He did not turn to look at George as he spoke but pressed his fists together in front of his chest.

"I can't watch her twenty-four hours a day. Someone has to run the farm."

"I am with her now." Vasili bent and brushed his fingers across Katya's forehead. Her eyes opened a slit, and she smiled.

George kicked the bedpost. He glanced at Katya but addressed Vasili. "I will not live in fear of being burned in my bed."

The door swung open, and Mary entered the bedroom. "I've made tea. Oh, she's awake. Come along, George, Mr. Sadilov. Let her sleep." She marched across the room and pulled the curtains shut.

"I'm right here in the room, Mary" Katya said. "Leave the curtains open. I'll get up and have tea." She pushed the blankets off and sat. Then she stood and strode out of the bedroom, her spine straight, as if leaving a stage. George followed her.

Then Mary left and Vasili dropped to the edge of the bed. A mental asylum? The hair on his knuckles rose. George must realise he could never let that happen. A cry erupted from the kitchen and Vasili rushed out. He stopped short at the door.

George had a handful of Katya's hair in his fist and her head pulled back. "What should I do, Katya?" His voice sounded controlled but furious. Katya had no expression on her face, not pain, not fear.

"What are you doing, George?" Vasili asked.

"Stay out of this, Vasili." He yanked. Katya's neck snapped backward. "Don't you realise how wrong it was to set fire to that house? Have you lost your mind?"

"Please let her go. You will hurt her." Vasili walked over and placed his hand on George's arm. If he'd been a younger man, he would have grabbed a fistful of his hair.

George released his hold and stepped back. "Maybe it's grief over your Mama's death, but give me your word. There'll be no more setting fires." He barked this out, like a Bolshevik.

"And, no more roaming in the dead of night or talking to that damn crow. I'll put a bullet in that useless bird."

"Please don't shoot the crow. It isn't his fault." Katya's eyes flashed fear.

Vasili understood, in a way. George wanted to shoot Katya, not the crow. Long ago, he had experienced the same frustration with his mother.

George clenched and unclenched his fingers. Vasili closed his eyes and pinched the bridge of his nose. Again he had placed his child in danger, as he had long ago, but now he might be too weak and too old to protect her.

"I promise I won't set any fires."

"Damn right you won't," he said as Mary appeared.

She looked at Katya, then at George, and raised her eyebrows. "I've made a nice Saskatoon pie." She stepped to the counter. "And I thought we'd kill that turkey. It's Christmas Day tomorrow."

"Forget the turkey. We won't be celebrating." George headed for the door. "I'll be in the barn."

"Shall I perform for you this afternoon, Papa? I'll play *Melodía Rumana*. Do you remember how Mama used to love that piece?" Vasili sat beside his daughter and she reached up and patted his cheek. Her voice rang as if she had wiped her memory clean of George's rage. It was soothing to know that Katya's nature allowed her to block these matters and press on in life as if pleased with the world.

CHAPTER TWELVE

Lockdown

IN our room, I undressed, threw my nightgown over my head, crawled between the covers and turned my back on George, who stood at the foot of the bed stripped down to his underwear. My husband's temper disgusted me. And right in front of Papa too. George was attempting to drive Papa away, but he was using the wrong tactic. Papa would stay forever, if worried for my safety.

I heard a click and sat up. "What are you doing, George?"

"Locking the door. I told you, no more wandering around in the middle of the night."

He dropped the key into his pillowcase, lifted the chimney off the lamp, blew out the flame and climbed into bed, plumping the pillow under his head. Within minutes, the drone of his deep-sleep breathing filled the darkness.

The night was long, long, long. And every hour the clock in the hall chimed and each time the strike seemed louder than the last and it rattled my senses. When five strikes sounded, my teeth chattered. Somersaults inside my belly nearly catapulted me off the bed. George was trying to drive me mad with his locked door.

I hadn't slept a wink when he rose just after six and got dressed. The front door banged as he left the house.

That afternoon, when they had both gone out, Papa and I lounged in the parlour. I asked him, "Do you think Mary and George make a good couple?"

"You should not say that," he said. "George is your husband."

"But, do you think he likes her?"

"Mary is older than George. He regards her as a mother."

"She's not that much older, Papa. It's the dresses she wears. She's not forty yet. She told me."

"Why would George be interested in Mary, when he has a charming young wife?"

"I'm not jealous, Papa. I just think George and Mary would be happy together if I wasn't here."

"But you are here, little bird. And you made a vow to honour and obey your husband. Avoid these thoughts. They are not healthy."

"They want to send me away to a hospital. I heard them talking."

"If you left, Mary could not stay here alone with George. What would people say?"

"She could stay if you stayed, couldn't she? No one questions a woman tending a boarding house." I sat at the table beside Papa. "If I died in that hospital, Papa, do you think George would take up with Mary?"

"What a thing to say, Katya. You must not speak of such things."

"But I will surely die if they send me there. You always used to say it, 'hospitals are where you go to die.'"

"I was being a *glupets*. Besides, your Mama said the hospitals in Canada are not the same as in Russia."

"Papa, I don't want to go to any hospital. I want to play in an orchestra again. I want to go to New York."

"Your husband will forget this hospital idea. You are well again. Everything is fine."

"George will never take me to New York and he will not forget the hospital either. I know him."

Papa closed his eyes, fiddled with the button on his dressing gown and I waited, but he said nothing. So I got out my violin and played *Kreutzer Sonata*.

Another world leaked into the room, Niccolò's universe. I saw the conductor waving his baton, the cello player to my right, the clarinet to my left. As I played, I realised this existence would always be there for me, only a few short strums away, and this was good.

Halfway through the piece Papa began to tap his foot with the energy of a young man. And when I played the *Witches' Dance*, Niccolò rose up beside me. He held his bow high, and it moved across the strings, a wave rolling on the open sea and I played in its wake. My notes blended with his notes until nothing mattered except the ebb and flow. I knew once the *Witches' Dance* began, it was out after control, but I was powerless to resist it.

Sleep was impossible with the door locked and George did not let up. His temper didn't flare again but every night, the click of the key triggered me wide awake, and awake I stayed, with thoughts racing through my mind like trains at a busy station. Thoughts of Niccolò, and babies, vast stretches of snow and small rooms with barred windows. And the next day, I was unable play for the first time in my life. When I picked up the violin, so many songs ran through my head, it was impossible to figure out the right notes. The bow scratched across the strings and screeched loud enough to wound the deaf.

Papa furrowed his eyebrows. "What is wrong, Katya? Play one of the old tunes, from when you were a girl. You will remember the old tunes. Do you feel unwell? Why do you have dark circles under your eyes?"

"I can't sleep." I leaned over and whispered. "George and Mary plan to carry me off in the middle of the night while you're sleeping. They're going to lock me up in a mental asylum."

"You must not speak like this." Papa bolted upright and

stamped away.

A surge of indignation shook me. He didn't believe me. I wanted to call him back and say, 'I'm not making it up. You should see the way they stop talking when I enter the room,' but instead I walked to my violin, rage throbbing through every vein in my body, and poised my foot to kick it.

My foot stopped, suspended in mid air, inches away from the body of the fiddle. I couldn't do it. Instead, I slapped my stomach over and over, tears spitting through the air.

They were all against me—Mary, George and now even Papa.

I was alone, and the house was empty. I went to the pantry, grabbed the whiskey jug, uncorked it and guzzled the last few gulps. Then I slipped outside to look for the crow.

I found him perched on the fence of the corral where Mama first appeared. His head bobbed up and down as I came near, and he flapped his wings several times in greeting.

"At least you're happy I'm here." I stepped up to him, closer than I'd ever been before and he didn't budge.

"Loki, I need help. My hand is not paying attention to the songs. It's as if twenty violins in an orchestra are playing a different tune? It's an awful noise." He sidestepped closer, lowered his head and tapped my boot with his beak.

"I shouldn't have tried to set fire to Papa's house. I'm being punished." I glared at him. "And you told me to do it."

He twisted sideways, ignoring me.

Then, the jangle in my mind unfurled.

"What I did was wrong. What do I care if that foul old spirit cloud wants to stay in Papa's house? It can stay there and it'll keep away from me." Loki had no way of knowing the truth about the cloud. Getting rid of it entirely was probably impossible.

"Papa is here now, and he's safe. He was never in any danger. I made a mistake, that's all. I'll explain it to Papa. He'll understand. He always understands."

The crow looked at me with his wise little eyes.

"And I'll make it up to George. I can be a good wife."

Loki turned, lifted one wing and covered his head.

I laughed. "Well, maybe I can't be a good wife, but I can try, can't I? And I'll tell Papa I'm sorry too. He knows of Niccolò and his pact with the devil. He's the one who told me the story. That was before I met Niccolò in person but he doesn't need to know that part. I could be wrong about everything." I stroked my stomach.

The bird hopped, turned his back on me and strutted away with an awkward, jerky gait, leaving crossed tracks in the snow, a crooked path to the barn door. "Okay, leave. I don't care." And I didn't. He was only a dumb bird. He disappeared into the barn and I went back to the house.

I found a package of pork chops in the icebox, took them out and rooted around under the sink until I found potatoes. Furry tails had sprouted from them, but I'd seen Mama and Mary clean potatoes. I rubbed my hands over them to break the white tubes off and then looked for the paring knife. It wasn't in the drawer or on the counter so I picked up the long knife Mary used to cut chicken and started peeling. Peeling was awkward with a large knife, but not an unpleasant job. I dropped each skinned potato into a bowl of water and soon a school of them floated inside the bowl.

One potato was very bulky and misshapen and it slipped around in my fingers but it was only a potato and I did not intend to let it get the better of me. Then the potato slipped out of my hand. I tried to catch it with both hands without dropping the knife, and when I did that the blade sliced into my wrist before clattering to the floor.

I felt nothing at first. The potato slid across the floor. The knife landed beside my foot and a dark splash appeared next to it on the white linoleum. Then another splatter hit and another. I stood and watched, fascinated by the design, black-red on white and the knife glinted and my arm burned and a dark bead oozed from my wrist like the drip of a pump at the end of its stream. I couldn't take my eyes off it.

"My God!" George appeared in the doorway, Mary right behind him. He rushed in and grabbed my wrist, hard.

My arm burst with pain. "No," I said and pulled away.

"Get a towel." George gripped my wrist harder. "Now!"

Mary ran out.

"My God, Katya." George pushed me into a chair still holding on to my wrist. Blood seeped up between his fingers and the blonde hair above his knuckles, specked with red, stood straight up as if caught in a breeze.

Mary handed him a tattered white towel. He put the towel in his teeth, pulled with his other hand and ripped. Then he wrapped a long strip around and around my wrist and squeezed until I couldn't feel my hand anymore.

Papa walked into the kitchen. "What has happened?"

"You said you'd watch her." George yelled at my Papa.

Perhaps because Papa was looking at me, he didn't see the puddle on the floor. He slipped and lost his balance. A long red streak like a tail appeared behind his heel, but he righted himself and didn't fall. "What has happened, Katya?"

"What does it look like? Why do people slice their wrists?" George glowered at him.

"It was an accident," I said. "I was peeling potatoes."

"This is what I was talking about, Vasili. Look at what she's done." George cinched the towel around my arm so tight I thought he would break my arm.

"I wanted to show you I was sorry. I wanted to make dinner, to prove I can be a good wife." George continued to clutch my wrist. I glanced over at Papa. "I wanted to explain to you Papa, that I was wrong and that I'm sorry."

"She needs a doctor," George said.

"The cut, is it that bad?" Papa stepped closer, his eyes brimming with concern.

"I can fix the cut. I can't fix her head."

"No doctors, no hospital," Papa said. "I will not allow it."

"I've had enough. She needs help." George slammed one foot on the floor.

"Is that so? Have you seen one of those places? I have. You are certain she will not be in danger? Are you willing to take that risk?"

My arm still throbbed, but the pain had eased. Papa was on my side after all. I should never have doubted that.

Mary stood beside the kitchen table, cutting a towel into strips and placing them in rows on the table. She stopped, walked over to the cabinet and pulled down a bottle of iodine which she handed to George.

He pulled out the cork, soaked a swatch of cloth in the reddish yellow liquid and folded it in four. He loosened his grip on the towel, unravelled it and pressed the iodine-soaked square over the cut on my wrist.

What anguish. "Oh God, Papa, it burns, oh it burns like a hot iron." I struggled to pull my arm free of George's grip but he only clasped harder.

Papa touched my other arm, leaned and kissed the top of my head. "It is okay, my little bird. He must clean the cut."

George secured the bandage. "I would never send her

anywhere without seeing the place first."

Mary led me into the bedroom. "You rest now," she said. "I'll come back in a few minutes and make sure you're okay."

"It's fine, Mary. It doesn't hurt so much now." I sat on the bed and waited for her to leave. Then I tiptoed back into the hall. The kitchen door was ajar and I stood out of sight behind it.

I heard Papa's voice. "And what would they let you see? Would they let you see how they tie people to the beds at night, wrists and ankles to the bedposts, how they stuff cloth into their mouths to keep them quiet? Would they let you see them drag the pretty girls into the basement, into a dark room? Would they let you see the faces of the girls who struggle—the bruises and cuts?"

I returned to the bedroom and started to hum Mendelssohn's *Songs Without Words, Opus 19*. It began softly, but grew louder in my head until the music blotted out their words. The pain from my wrist sizzled into the notes.

Cradle

It seemed to Vasili that he spent much of his time padding around George's house like a footsore mongrel. He wandered from window to window and stared out at the vast ocean of snow —as far as he could see, the landscape standing still.

The horse plodded from the feeder to the fence and Mary trudged out of the barn, milk pails hung at her sides. She stopped, put the pails down, turned and held one hand over her eyes.

Vasili followed her gaze and said, "John Dari comes to visit. It will be good to see John again. Perhaps we will play chess."

A chair scraped and he heard Katya's light steps as she crossed the room. "John Dari doesn't play chess. I don't believe it."

"Yes, I taught him. He does not play well." Vasili chuckled as he recalled John's strategy. "But I let him win a game and after that he came to the house twice every week."

"You should teach George."

"I do not think chess would interest him," Vasili said as the door swung open and Mary stepped in, followed by John lugging an awkward canvas-covered bundle. "John, you are a feast for my eyes."

"You're a sight for sore eyes too, old friend." John dropped his load inside the door. He bent and strained to reach his bootlaces, arms too short to span his protruding belly.

"What is that?" Vasili asked.

John pulled the canvas wrap off the package.

"Well, I'll be." Mary reached out to touch it. "A cradle. Where'd that come from?"

"George gave it to me a while ago to fix up," John said.

Vasili inspected his daughter. A cradle? Could it be? She seemed tired of late and always wore the big yellow sweater. As he thought this, she pulled at the sweater and hunched. No, she would have said.

"I'll get George." Katya disappeared down the hall.

"How is she?" John whispered as soon as she'd left. He directed his question to Vasili, but it was Mary who answered.

"Same as usual," she said. "Nuttier than a fruitcake most days."

Vasili shot Mary a black look. He put his hand on his friend's shoulder. "It is a long ride. Come, sit."

Katya returned to the kitchen followed by George.

"Coffee, John?" Katya asked.

"No, not coffee." George walked over and inspected the cradle. "Get out the whiskey, Kat. Thank you, John. You've done a fine job on that."

"Sorry it took me so long to bring it out. I had it finished a couple months ago, and should have sent it when we packed up Vasili's furniture."

"Where did it come from?" Vasili asked.

"I came across it a while back, in the barn stuck up in the rafters," George said. "God knows how long it'd been there. Must've been mine. John has all the tools and offered to patch it up."

"It didn't take long to fix. Furniture isn't so well made anymore." John slid his fingers along the gleaming rail. "Mostly elbow grease."

George slapped the headboard. "Solid as a rock. Mary, do you have any goose-down squirrelled away? We could sew up a mattress. Katya, how about that whiskey?"

Katya paused for a moment. "I forgot to tell you, George. We have no whiskey."

"What do you mean? There should be a full jug and another part of one."

"I poured it out by accident." Katya walked away and plucked a tea towel from its hook.

George lowered his voice. "How could you accidentally pour out two jugs of whiskey?"

Vasili saw that John's arrived was more welcome than he'd realised. George was not pleased, but he would not fly into a rage with John there.

"I've just come from Ernie's place." John thudded across the linoleum toward the door. "I've got a jug in the wagon." He headed outside to get it.

"Katya, what happened to the whiskey?" George asked.

Vasili detected a hiss in his son-in-law's voice, and he could surmise what happened. There was no point in pretending. At times, Katya behaved just as her grandmother had.

Vasili forced a smile. "I wonder how he made the wood shine like that?"

George turned his attention back to the cradle.

When John returned Mary took the jug from him and set

three glasses out.

Vasili watched as Katya picked up a pie and a stack of plates from the counter. Her wrist was still bandaged, and she winced as she transferred the pie to her injured hand.

"Did you hurt yourself?" John asked.

"An accident, peeling potatoes." She put the dishes on the table and settled in the rocking chair by the window. She leaned over, intent on something outside.

Vasili came up behind her, bent and whispered, "Did you drink the whiskey?"

"Shh." She lifted her finger and shook it at a crow hopping across the yard. "You black devil," she said as the bird flapped its wings and bobbed its head.

"I didn't just come to bring the cradle." John cleared his throat. "Thought I'd better warn you. Seems one of the McFarlane kids was out near your place, Vasili, the day we moved you." Vasili squeezed his daughter's shoulder, but she didn't react.

"He saw everything that happened, with the fire and all. Well, you know how things get around." John stared into his glass. "Wasn't long before Mrs. Stanley got wind of it. She's got the *Ladies League* up in arms. Yesterday they went to Constable Reeger. That woman's hell bent on getting the law involved. Heard he told them they should go home and mind their own business, but that old busybody won't rest until she stirs up trouble." John took a lengthy sip of his whiskey. "Figured I'd better head over and tell you myself, in case she gets that outfit riled up enough to show up here. Didn't want you to figure I'd spilled the beans."

"What do you think she'll do?" George leaned forward and covered his eyes.

"She's on a crusade to get the church involved and wants to form a committee of concerned citizens and plans marching over to the police station. She's ranting about how arson is a crime and no one can sleep easy until the law does something."

As John spoke, Vasili studied George's expression—first incredulous, then angry and not without fear. Katya was still in her rocker humming as if she'd not heard a word John said.

Then George steered the conversation to the Wheat Pool and so Vasili took the hint and did not add to the discussion. John departed an hour later.

After he left, they retired to the parlour where George stood staring, a cloud of smoke spiralling overhead as he drew on his pipe. Mary picked up her crocheting and Katya appeared in good spirits, smiling every few minutes at a book she was reading. Vasili's discomfort lifted. Katya had done no harm and John was making monsters out of fleas. The incident would pass.

Vasili warmed his hands over the fireplace. "It is Christmas Day tomorrow."

"Christmas passed two weeks ago." Mary grabbed a pair of

scissors and snipped a thread.

"No, our Christmas. Our calendar in Russia, it is different. Tomorrow is our Christmas."

"Papa, do you remember the 'Holy Suppers' that Mama used to make?"

"Ah, who could forget? I can taste the sauerkraut soup and *pagach*."

"And a small bowl of black beluga for everyone and baked fish. I don't think we've had baked fish once since we came here," she said.

"What was so holy about your suppers?" Mary dropped her crochet hook in her lap and squinted at them in the dim light of the parlour.

"In our tradition," Vasili said, "we have twelve dishes, one for each apostle and so we call it 'Holy Supper.'"

"I remember how scary *Ded Moroz was*." Katya made a face.

"*Ded Moroz* is Grandfather Frost," Vasili explained to Mary. "He is similar to Santa Claus in Canada but he dresses in blue, drives a sleigh pulled by horses and carries a big stick to beat children who misbehave. Katya would cry herself to sleep in fright on every Christmas Eve."

"So, you've been naughty all your life?" Mary chuckled.

George frowned.

"I did so love *Snegurochka.* But yes, he terrified me."

"Grandfather Frost did not have elves. He had *Snegurochka,*

Snow Girl, to assist him." Vasili drew his chair close to his daughter and patted her cheek. "She was lovely but not as beautiful as Katya."

"Never cooked that turkey I fattened up for Christmas," Mary said. "Could chop his head off tomorrow and fix up a Canadian Christmas dinner."

"No, do not bother." Vasili didn't explain. Mary would never understand. Without his wife, he wanted no 'Holy Supper.'

"Maybe next year." Katya patted his arm. She understood.

Mary grunted. "If you're here next year, after Mrs. Stanley gets finished with you."

George dropped his pipe on the mantle. "We'll turn in now. Katya, come to bed."

"I'm not tired yet."

"Come to bed *now*." He walked over, reached for her arm and pulled her out of the chair.

Vasili picked up the poker and swatted at the fire. Then he stared at George's clasp on Katya's arm, blotches of white on her skin from the pressure. George loosened his grip but did not let go.

Mary stretched and pretended to yawn. "It's been a long, old day. Tomorrow we'll get a fresh start."

The former dining room was now Vasili's new bedroom. It was not so bad, but not home, a large space with little furniture but he had a thick, warm quilt. He had hung his dressing gown and shirts in the wardrobe. The trunk at the foot of the bed still held most of his books. He could not bear to unpack them here. A gate-leg table occupied the corner. It was draped with a white doily and on the doily a silver goblet sat beside a bottle of real Russian vodka, sent by Sergei in New York. Vasili poured a full cup.

So, George had John restore the cradle. Maybe now he would remember why he married Katya and abandon his plans to send her away. But he must suspect she drank the whiskey. Why else would he grab her arm like that? He hoped George planned to simply keep a closer eye on her now. Vasili would need to do the same.

The floor had no carpet. Vasili wished he had brought the one from the bedroom at home. He scuffled across the wood floor, sat on the bed, kicked off his shoes and rubbed his toes on the raw lumber. But it was not the cold or the different room that caused Vasili to lie with eyes wide open for many hours.

Chapter Thirteen

Poison

MARY was trying to poison me. I watched her as she stood and scraped a carrot with the chicken knife, the same knife that had attacked me and left my arm in bandages. A bowl of slimy meat sat on the counter beside her.

"Fresh liver," she said. "George butchered that old sow." A sickly waft of pig blood rose from the bowl.

"Let me help." I had to keep a close eye on her, on the slight bulge of her apron pocket. Mary was an uneducated woman, but capable of a simple plan, a sprinkle of white powder on my food, enough to cripple but not kill right away. She had a slow demise planned, a creeping rot to my body and no one would suspect.

"You want to help, do you? Well, why don't you get your princess hands into that liver and wash it up good. I'll go get some bacon fat to fry it in."

"I'll go," I said.

"No, you deal with the liver." She stomped over to the root cellar entrance, yanked the trap door up by its metal ring, propped it open with a long stick and disappeared into the hole.

I eyed the open door. I could slam the door, jamb the broom handle through the ring and lock her away. The thought made me smile. Mary, trapped in the cellar for all time, with her crocks and slabs, forever out of my business. But soon she was back, and I was still by the sink contemplating the bloody puddle of liver.

"Don't just stand there looking at it." With the crock of bacon fat under one arm, she released the prop and dropped the door with a thump. "Get that meat washed. George will be in soon. He loves his liver." She took a dirty spoon out of the sink and popped it into the crock.

"You should clean the spoon before you do that," I said.

"Mind your manners, young lady. Don't worry about what I'm doing."

I took a strainer off the shelf, tipped the bloody mess into it, filled a jug and dribbled water over the raw meat.

"You've got to get your fingers into it." Mary pushed my hand into the slippery mass.

The meat felt warm and slimy. I gagged and plunged my blood-smeared fingers into the jug of water. A chip of vomit rose to the back of my throat.

Mary laughed. "Not much stomach for real chores." She bumped me aside. "Run along." Her sausage fingers sank into the meat. "You just get in the way."

I backed up, but I didn't leave.

"That's it. You watch how it's done," she said after a few minutes. "Heaven knows, you might have to cook one day." Mary snatched up an onion, whacked off the hairy end, skinned and chopped it.

Then I couldn't keep track of her anymore. She was all over the kitchen. Onions sizzled in the fat, and she flung long slithery strips of liver into the pan. She set out plates, lifted lids, poked vegetables, and made coffee. Did she slip her hand in her apron? She darted around so much, I wasn't sure.

Papa stepped into the room.

"Did you have a nap?" I asked him.

"Yes, I woke up hungry and the smell of onions pulled me." He tipped his head back and sniffed with a smile.

"There's George." Mary glanced out the window. She scraped the charred liver onto a platter.

George came in, and threw his coat over the chair by the door. George, Papa and Mary took seats, but I stayed put.

"Come and sit to supper." George scowled at me and then turned his attention to Mary. "It's nippy out today, but no snow. I've got that pork ready to smoke."

"I'll get the smokehouse going tomorrow," Mary said.

"Katya, please sit to the table." George's voice had an impatient undertone.

"Come on, sweet bird." Papa patted the seat next to him.

So, I sat. Everyone lifted a bowl at the same time and heaped food onto their plates, like starving peasants.

"You're not eating?" Papa asked when I passed him the platter of liver, taking none myself.

"No, I'm not hungry. Excuse me." I stood. "I think I'll practice *Fantasy in C.*"

"Sit back down," George said. "You'll eat." He wagged his fork at me. "Has she eaten today?"

"Not that I saw," Mary said. "I made her a nice big bowl of porridge this morning. She never took a bite."

"You know I hate oatmeal." She could keep her poisoned gruel, but I was in no mood for an argument so I sat to the table.

"You hate oatmeal. You can't eat eggs. Beans make your stomach turn." Mary shovelled an enormous chunk of liver into her mouth.

"You should eat something, my bird." Papa picked up the bowl of carrots. He dropped a spoonful onto my plate and reached for the liver.

"I can't eat that." I held my hands over the plate.

"Potatoes then?" He placed the platter back.

"That's enough," I said as he shook a wad of potatoes off the spoon. I studied Papa and George's plates. Their supper was half eaten, and I knew Mary wouldn't dare tamper with the food in the bowls so I picked up my fork. Then I noticed an oily slick of something under my carrots. The hateful hag was putting poison on my dishes. So I held a gob of potato in my mouth, put the napkin up to my lips and spat. I was hungry, and it was punishing, but I got every morsel off my plate that way.

Each morning for the past two weeks, Mary had breakfast set out on the table when I came into the kitchen. I inspected the meal, flipped the eggs over, scraped the toast with my knife. The eggs she prepared were a funny colour. If I squinted, traces of poisonous powder appeared on the toast. I discarded any food she'd touched at the first opportunity.

Starvation was a threat. With the bedroom door locked at night I couldn't even slip out and forage the pantry. And Mary rarely left the kitchen.

George and Mary had licked their plates clean. Papa was still chewing. Mary went to the counter, turned her back to us and poured tea.

"No thank you," I said as she placed a murky cup of tea in front of me.

Later, after I'd cleaned the dishes and swept the kitchen floor and Mary had joined the men in the parlour, hunger got the better of me and I slipped into the pantry with a spoon and released the seal on the cheese crock. Several good portions of soft curds eased my hunger pangs. After smoothing the surface of the cheese, I replaced the weight and lid.

I'd trounce Mary at her own game. The ghastly woman would not poison me, or starve me.

Drunk

At dawn the next day Vasili watched George hitch up the sleigh and ride out. In the afternoon he returned with two fresh jugs of whiskey. With one jug dangling from each hand, he walked to his workroom at the end of the hall. He did not even nod at Vasili. He did not stop to take off his boots. Moments later the door banged shut.

George stayed in his room for hours. At suppertime he staggered along the hallway, stopped and braced himself in the kitchen doorway and blinked at Vasili, Katya and Mary, seated around the table. Then he veered into the bedroom and the bedsprings squawked as he collapsed on the bed.

"Never mind. We'll eat. I'll save him a plate for later." Mary set a bowl of baked beans on the table.

Katya stared into space for a few moments before she got up and joined her husband. Vasili's appetite disappeared with her and when Mary passed him the bowl, he waved it away. He left Mary there alone, went to his room, sat on the bed and listened. But other than Mary's muffled muttering, the house was quiet.

That evening, after Mary retired to the parlour, Vasili slipped back into the kitchen, pulled the rocking chair up to the window and sat for several hours. The sky was ebony. So dark and peaceful, this universe. He concentrated on the emptiness. He wanted the blackness to consume him. Then he remembered Chopin's *Nocturnes, Opus 9 No 2*, and he realised that every moment on earth bore magic, even in the face of worry.

It was late when Mary padded in. "What do you see out there?" She clanged around at the stove. "It's pitch dark."

"Nothing."

"Well, you can't blame George for being upset. That Mrs. Stanley and her lot will make life hell for him?"

"Fear of Mrs. Stanley has big eyes." Vasili rocked the chair, leaned forward and squinted at the pinpoint of a star, barely visible. It flashed and faded, flashed and faded like the opening notes of the *Nocturnes*.

"Well, we need to care." Mary opened the oven door and shoved something in with a clatter. "It's a hard enough life. Sylvite's a small town." Then she marched over and wedged in front of him, hands on her hips.

"Remember what happened to Woody Dow?" She paused as if expecting an answer. Vasili had no idea what she was talking about and his attention drifted back to the night sky.

"Well, I'll tell you. Myrtle Stanley brought a speech-maker in all the way from South Bend, Indiana. That man convinced

Woody's wife and daughters that Woody was no better than a drunkard in a ditch." Mary nudged his shoulder. "You need to listen to this. That speaker raised a ruckus with the women and they forced poor Woody out of his own house. Made him sleep in the barn like an animal. It was bitter weather too, minus 20 or more, but they didn't let him back inside until he swore off tippling."

Mary arched one eyebrow and lowered the other. "If George has any common sense he'll go along with whatever Mrs. Stanley wants. Of course, if Katya had any common sense, he wouldn't be in this pickle."

"Mrs. Stanley should attend to her own affairs and so should you." Vasili stood and headed for his bed.

"I knew talking to you would be a waste of time. You've spoiled that girl rotten and now it's too late."

Disruption

I should have felt free, George sprawled on top of the covers, fully clothed, too drunk to lock the door. But it was as if I'd become a prisoner of my body, my girth heavy and moving. Even with the girdle someone would guess soon, the mound of my belly had grown beyond the capacity of stays and elastic. George snored and a waft of whiskey invaded the room.

I blew out the lamp, stood in the dark and listened. When Mary's bedroom door clicked shut, I searched out a candle and matches and tiptoed along the hall to George's workroom. The padlock hung open on the latch. I stepped in, and lit the candle. The room smelled of lamp oil. A thin layer of sawdust coated bolts of fabric against the wall and a half-full glass of whiskey on the end table glittered amber beside two jugs. I picked the glass up, took a long swallow and sank into George's wingback chair. It was hours later when I hatched the plan to hide away some of the whiskey. I got up, returned to the kitchen and collected two mason jars. I filled them with whiskey, locked George's room behind me, found my coat and slipped outdoors.

There were seventy-eight steps from the house to the barn door. George would pace seventy-four, Papa, seventy-two, he's so much taller than both of us and Mary, with her stubby legs, eighty-five or more. I carried my jars seventy-eight paces to the barn.

A breath of wind doused my candle on the way and I had to walk with care, testing the ground with each step. The blindfold-black night surrounded me and a song grew in my mind, unhurried, measured, like Satie's *Elégie.* Then I abandoned caution and matched my steps to the notes, glissading across the yard.

Gust whinnied and kicked the boards of his stall when I opened the door.

"It's okay boy. It's only me." I put the jars on the floor, dug another match out of my pocket and re-lit the candle. I headed to a heap of crates stacked in a far corner, overflowing with leather straps, old gunny sacks and bits and pieces of rusted metal. I sat, brought my knees to my ears, unscrewed the lid on one jar, and sipped. The other jar I slid behind a crate and then attempted to gather my thoughts.

One of my legs twitched in time with the flicker of the candle's flame. A dull ache swelled in my lower back, but a wondrous song formed notes in my head. It played over and over, a hundred times or more. If I wrote the song out and published it my name would surely go into the history books. My name, beside Paganini, Beethoven and Bach.

I scrambled to my feet. I'd been in one position so long it was difficult to straighten up and walk. In fact, my whole body seized, as if someone had cinched my corselette and pulled the cords as taut as they would go.

The first haze of new light touched the sky as I stumbled out of the barn. I doubled over with a cramp that was so intense, I changed direction and headed along the path to the outhouse. As always, I stood outside the fetid shack and took several deep breaths before going inside it. But the pang dissolved before I sat. I bolted out, gasped for air and set out for the house.

My good pen and a ream of paper were in the parlour. That room was too dim in the morning, so I gathered my writing tools, picked up my violin case and rushed to the kitchen. At the table I dipped the nib to record the opening stanza of my song, but the notes jumbled my thoughts, and my hand shook. The first treble clef became a nasty smudge. If I could play, it might become sharp again. But when I stood and bent for my violin, another furious cramp seized me. It lasted forever and when it eased, I noticed a puddle of water on the linoleum. My feet and underclothes were dripping wet. As soon as I sat, another cramp took my breath away. I dropped to the floor and drew my knees up to my chest.

"What in God's name?" Mary's slippers appeared next to my nose. She tried to lift me. A wave of agony strangled me. Her voice squealed, "Oh, goodness." Then her hand was under my dress. I wanted to scream at her to leave me alone but my throat was as tight as my abdomen and my legs refused to straighten. She eased me onto my side, and tugged at my girdle.

"Stop that," I said, but it was no use. My belly sprang loose from its belting and the garment slipped to the floor.

"George, you'd better come. George," she yelled.

The pain subsided and George appeared in the doorway in his nightshirt, hair standing up on one side. "What?" He had a bewildered expression.

"Help me get her into the bedroom. I think she's having a baby."

"What?" He moved closer.

"A baby."

"She can't be. You're wrong. She reeks of whiskey. She's

drunk."

"I'm surprised you can tell," Mary said. "Considering last night. But touch here." She put her hands on my middle just as another wave of anguish came. I doubled up, but not before George's fingers touched down on my stomach.

"I'll be. She's done a first-rate job of hiding it." Mary got one arm under my shoulder and heaved upward. "Better go for the doctor."

"What's wrong?" I heard Papa's voice as another cramp swelled. George helped Mary lift me and the girdle tangled around my feet. I kicked at it and stepped forward.

"A baby? Did you say, a baby?" Papa asked. "Are you sure?"

"Yes, I think you're slated to be a grandpa." Mary puffed with the effort of holding me steady. "Lord love a duck. I'm not sure where to start. I helped my sister-in-law once, but she was a good strong farm woman. We need the doctor."

"Papa." I screamed as pain wracked my stomach. "Make it stop. It took away my song." They led me to the bedroom, and plopped me on the mattress.

Mary pried my fingers open and moved my hands to the top rail of the bed frame. "Hold on to this." And I did. I held onto the rail for dear life. "Go now George," she said. "No time to waste. Her contractions are close."

"What can I do?" Papa asked.

"Go boil water. The big pot. Lay out fresh towels. And rags, we'll need rags. There's an old sheet in the hall closet. Tattered edges. You shouldn't be in here. Out with you."

Then it was just Mary and the pain, Mary's hands pulling at my clothing, pushing open my legs, the pain and Mary's voice. "Bite on this." She shoved a cloth between my teeth.

I spat it out.

"Suit yourself but that baby's coming. I can see the head." She stomped toward the door.

"Where are you going?" I screamed.

"A basin, rags, something to cut the cord. I'll be back." The door closed. But she didn't come back right away. And the contractions came so fast, I couldn't catch my breath in between them. I clung to the rail. I tried to get up once, but the cramp hurled me back onto the bed.

When she reappeared, I was between pains and took a deep breath. "I can't do this."

"Yes, you can. Just push."

"I can't. Papa, where are you?" I shrieked as another one came on.

"Your Papa can't come in here. You're on your own. Now push."

"No." Another stitch. My stomach was tearing apart—I pushed.

"That's a girl." Mary knelt at the foot of the bed. "Look at the hair."

This suffering would never end unless I stopped it. I gathered up every ounce of energy I had left and heaved with all my might.

"That's it. Good." Mary clapped. "I'll be. You do have a spot of spunk."

I growled between clenched teeth. "I'm splitting apart." And then I felt a whoosh and the spasm vanished.

"There, won't you look at that." Mary cooed.

I closed my eyes. A kittenish whimper sounded.

"It's a boy," Mary yelled. Then she whispered, "He's small."

A weight settled on my belly and I opened my eyes to see a naked, wet creature, puny arms waving in slow motion—tiny perfect hands with fingernails—miniature fingernails and I reached out and touched them, grazing their smooth surface. The little fingers circled my thumb and clasped onto it. The fingernails were biting-sharp. What strength this tiny fellow had. Tears welled up and I couldn't bear to watch anymore but neither could I draw my hand away. Mary leaned over with a knife in her hand.

"What are you doing?"

"Got to cut the cord."

"Get that knife away from my baby." I struggled to sit but Mary pushed me back.

"Lie still," she said.

I squeezed my eyes shut and sank into the pillow.

"There," she said. "I'll clean him up, the little tyke." She pried his fingers off my thumb, lifted him off my stomach and I heard a feeble cry before losing consciousness.

Chapter Fourteen

Swathed

VASILI sat erect at the kitchen table. The kettle bumped and crackled on the stovetop. A few drops of water escaped and hissed, bouncing across the metal surface. Early morning light shimmered on the walls. He studied the heap of rags in front of him. The pile had kept him busy for a while, ripping a sheet into diaper-size portions while his daughter cried out in the next room.

Vasili could not put it from his mind how Katya had screamed, 'Get it out of me. Make it stop,' followed by bawling and the screech of indiscernible words. He had wanted to run to her and run away at the same time, but she was quiet now and he was terror-struck.

The door swung open.

"Is she?" He turned, and the chair legs squealed on the linoleum.

"She's fine. She's asleep." Mary stepped into the room cradling a baby.

"It's a boy, a grandson for you." She brought one hand up, moved the cloth aside and cooed. "A handsome little man he is too, aren't you Pooty?"

Relief flooded through every cell of Vasili's body and he leaned forward to look.

"You hold him. I'll get a basin together." She handed the child to Vasili. "Mind his head." She touched the baby's cheek with a stubby finger and he squirmed.

Without moving a muscle, Vasili sat and held his grandson. "What a mystery. What a miracle." He stared at the tiny red face, the head no larger than a fist and still smeared with blood. "He is small."

"Yes, he's a tiny one. It's no wonder. She was starving the poor thing." Mary pushed the pile of rags to clear space on the table, set a basin down and then headed for the stove.

It was stifling in the kitchen. During his wait Vasili had kept the fire stoked, adding sticks every few minutes.

Mary pulled the oven door open. "He needs a wash but we've got to get the room as warm as possible." She retrieved a blanket from the linen cupboard and laid it across the oven door. "We've got to keep him warm." After lugging a pail over, she hefted it and splashed water into the basin. Then she fetched the kettle and added steaming water, testing the temperature with her wrist. "Mmmm, perfect. We need to move fast before it cools. Bring him here."

Vasili was not sure he could trust his legs. "You want me there?"

"Yes, you can help. We're going to lay him in the bath, right in his towel. You'll hold the corners so he won't bump his head."

Vasili stood and with soldier-straight limbs, carried the child to her.

"Good." She took the baby. "Now, hang onto those edges."

He clutched the corners of the towel.

"Watch he doesn't slip. We don't want to startle the poor tyke. Such a sweet boy. Barely a peep out of him." She propped up the baby's head, lowered him into the water and pressed down as if washing a delicate piece of laundry. The infant wriggled and made faint sucking noises. A waft of female smell rose as Mary unravelled the cloth that swaddled him.

The baby had puny arms and legs, a black clot tied off with a string and a tiny face that screwed up in protest, but he did not cry.

This undertaking was unfamiliar to Vasili. He had not bathed his daughter when she was born. The midwife had cleaned, clothed and tucked Katya into a cradle before they had allowed him into the birth room.

"Could've knocked me over with a feather." Mary rubbed a wet finger into the crease of skin under the baby's arm. A few strands of stringy blood rose to the water's surface. "She must have told you."

"No, I did not know." Vasili clutched the towel as the tiny body floated.

"Well, I suspected she might be pregnant, but at the beginning women can be superstitious about telling so I kept my mouth shut. Still can't believe she was that far along." Cushioning the child's head, she lifted him and splashed his hair with her other hand. The infant let out a weak squawk. "There, there, Pooty, it's okay. You want to be clean and handsome when your daddy gets here with the doctor, don't you?"

Mary patted and swabbed. "I think George was in the dark too. You'd assume he'd have known, but men can be blind sometimes."

"Katya will be fine now," Vasili said.

"You can let go. I've got him. Get that cover from the oven door."

Vasili released his grip on the towel, hurried to the stove and returned with the warm blanket.

"Put it here." Mary pointed to the table with her nose.

Vasili laid the blanket out. "George can forget his plan of a hospital." Vasili stepped back from the table. A newborn changed everything. It was a relief in a way. Young mothers did not go to mental institutions.

"Well, you'll have to take that up with him."

"Will you talk to him, Mary?"

As she lifted the baby out of out of the bath, his small body froze up in her hands and Vasili thought the child had stopped breathing. But Mary wasted no time, and before any cries escaped, had him snug in the heated blanket and cushioned against her breast.

"Sometimes women do funny things when they're with child, but George will make his own mind up about the hospital." She hummed and bobbed across the room rocking the baby.

Antonio

My eyes opened, and I saw a man with a stethoscope leaning over the washstand. When I shifted position, pain flared in my abdomen. A weak cry sputtered, and I watched my baby wriggle and squawk as the doctor pressed the disc of the stethoscope to his chest.

"Don't hurt him," I said.

The man's bushy eyebrows curled up like a smile. "I won't." He focused his attention on the baby, sliding his finger along his temple and cupping his crown, his hand bigger than the infant's head. "He's not the size I'd like to see."

"He'll be all right, won't he?" I twisted around to see George leaned forward in a chair with his hands in his hair.

The doctor's large fingers encircled the child and his whimpering stopped. "I don't like the sound of his breathing.

He's fully formed, has every finger and toe, but you'll need to be mindful." He picked up the baby and passed him to me. How light and warm he was. I ran my fingertips along the blanket and touched the outline of his tiny leg. "What will you call him, Mrs. Brown?"

"I'm not sure."

George rose from the chair and stood beside the doctor. "We'll call him George. George Junior."

"Antonio," I said. "I'll call him Antonio."

"We aren't Italian." George frowned.

"He will be a composer. Like Antonio Vivaldi."

"Very well," the doctor said. "It's settled. His name is George Antonio Brown. Put him to your breast Mrs. Brown. This wee boy needs nourishment. Come, George." He placed a hand on George's shoulder. "Mother and son need to get acquainted." They left.

I opened my nightgown and positioned a nipple against the baby's mouth. His head turned, and he made sucking noises. Dark hair fanned across the pale skin of my bosom. But he lost interest in nursing and tried to open his eyes, his perfect little face screwed in comic concentration. I chuckled, pulled the quilt up and hummed a Brahms' lullaby. Antonio fell asleep.

I don't know how long I watched him. He had so much hair, it could have been a wig, and cupid lips that twitched and pouted as he slept. When I looked up Papa was smiling at us.

"He is a Prince. Perfect, is he not?" Papa whispered. "A gift."

"Yes, you're right, Papa. Look at him. Have you ever seen anyone so beautiful?" I cuddled him and rubbed my cheek against his silky scalp.

Mary burst into the room. "Has he taken any milk yet?"

Antonio jerked awake and let out a squeak.

"See what you've done. He was sleeping."

"Well, he needs to eat." She held a small dish that she set on the washstand. "Goat milk. The doctor told me a new baby can digest goat milk." She strode across the room holding out her arms.

I raised my palm and cuddled him close. "I can feed him."

"Look at yourself. You've hardly eaten in weeks. What have you got to offer?"

"The mother's milk is the best, no?" Papa said. "Let Katya try."

"Well, suit yourselves," she said and tramped out.

"Papa, can you go to the kitchen and bring me a glass of milk?"

Papa looked at the full glass of milk sitting on the beside table. "There is milk there." He pointed.

"Not that milk," I said. "Mary brought it."

"Do you still think Mary puts potions in your food?"

"She does Papa. I know she does. And I can't take any chances, especially now." I rocked Antonio and kissed his warm head.

"Oh, my little bird. I will get you milk because you need to drink, but you must erase these thoughts from your mind. Promise me."

"Yes, Papa."

Papa left, and I set to the business of nursing my baby.

Antonio wasn't interested. I tried and tried. He sucked for a couple of moments and then fell fast asleep. I touched his lips, opened his blanket and tickled his chest, but nothing would wake him. In my arms, he only wanted to sleep.

Papa returned with the milk and a plate of bread and jam.

"I fixed it myself." Papa set the plate on the table and passed me the glass. "This is your Mama's chokecherry jam from a sealed jar. Will you eat?"

"Thank you." I guzzled the milk. Milk had never tasted so sweet. Papa took the glass from me and replaced it with a slice of jam-slathered bread. I bit off a chunk and the tart chokecherries stung the roof of my mouth. "Remember how stained Mama's hands got when she put up this jam?"

Later that afternoon Mary came in, followed by George toting the cradle. He set it beside me, leaned over, kissed the baby's cheek and left. Mary changed the baby, settled him into the cradle and rocked it.

"He hasn't taken the breast yet, has he?" she said.

"No. Maybe if I could get up?"

"The doctor wants you in bed for at least three days."

"I need to relieve myself."

"I'll help you." She reached under the end table for the chamber pot. I swung my legs off the side of the bed and struggled to squat.

"Good." Mary shoved the vessel up under my nightgown. "Slide down now." Once started it seemed the stream of urine would never stop.

"Back under the covers now," Mary said when I'd finished. She placed the pot on the chair near the door. The baby let out a cry.

"I'll feed him now," Mary said. "And I'll have no nonsense from you. This baby has to eat." She picked Antonio up, held him in the crook of her arm, walked over to the dresser, picked an eyedropper out of the cup she'd brought in, and squeezed a drop of goat milk past his closed lips. He coughed and sputtered.

"Now, now. That's all right." Mary bounced him, clicking her tongue.

Then Antonio cried in earnest.

"That's enough. What are you trying to do to my baby?"

"He took a bit." She passed him to me.

Long after bedtime, Antonio and I were still alone in the bedroom. George may have fallen asleep in his workroom. I waited several hours before getting out of bed. My legs shook weakly. Something vile slithered down my inner thigh and made a wet thud on the scatter rug near the cradle. It was too dark to see what it was, but it smelled like the pig shed. I bent, folded the rug in half and tucked it under my arm.

In the parlour I groped on the mantle for the candle. Mary had moved it on purpose to keep me in the dark. My fingers touched a glass vase, the smooth wood of the mantle clock and finally a box of matches. The box made a thundering rattle as it slid it open. The wooden shaft cracked and sizzled when I swiped the striker. Warm light poured from my fingertips. I spied the candle on a corner table and moved toward it, one careful step after another. As the match connected to the candlewick, its flame seared my thumb.

Candle in hand, I tiptoed into the pantry, closed the door and reached for a jar of meat. The lid was tight, and it took my best effort to screw it off. Once open, I picked the salty meat out and stuffed my mouth. In minutes, I'd eaten half the jar. The mat, still wedged under my arm, slipped and landed open on the pantry floor. A disgusting puddle of blood-black liver glistened in the candlelight. My stomach revolted, and I vomited overtop of the glop.

My belly was a raw pit. I refolded the rug, carried it to the porch and buried it beneath a pile of rags in a wooden box. Then I came back to the kitchen, wiped my legs and feet, rinsed my mouth with water and slipped back into the pantry to finish eating the meat. That night my sleep was blissful. The next morning, I felt much stronger.

A week passed and my stamina improved each day. Every night I helped myself to late meals in the pantry. Antonio loved to sleep. I loved to watch him sleep. I had milk, but he remained indifferent to nursing. He took the few drops of goat milk Mary forced into him each day. My breasts became swollen and sore. But this was a minor discomfort and did not shatter my mood.

"The baby loves music," I told Mary one morning. She stood by the washstand folding diapers while I paced, cradling Antonio. "Maybe that's why he sleeps so much."

"They sleep a lot at first," Mary said. "It's nature's way of letting a mother get her strength back. You should quit gadding around and rest."

I hummed a tune. "No, I should play for Antonio." He opened his eyes. "A lively piece, a galliard." I placed him in his cradle. Mary shuffled out with a handful of soiled diapers and I followed her.

I hurried to the parlour. My violin was in its normal place against the wall, and when I unlatched the case, it paralysed me for a moment. Such a flawless instrument. I picked it up, wrapped my arms around it, kissed the neck and played. I began with a movement from *Fantazia Suites*. The sun streamed in through the window.

Papa wandered in and sat. "I haven't heard you play that piece for years," he said when the song finished. "It reminds me of happy times."

"When I was twelve. Remember how I practised it over and over?"

"Yes, and it was perfect every time. Your Mama and I were proud. Every note, a jewel."

"And now I play it for my baby."

"If only your Mama could hear." Papa sighed.

"Mama hears, Papa. I haven't seen her for so long, but I know she's with us, watching over Antonio." Papa was gazing out the window. "Let me bring the baby, Papa. You can hold him while I play."

I propped the violin next to its case and hurried to the bedroom. It was strange. Someone had shut the door. I swung it open. Mary was in the rocking chair cradling my baby, Antonio's cheeks buried in her enormous bare breast. She glanced up with a panicked expression.

"What are you doing?" I flew to her, and she adjusted her blouse. "Give him to me." I held my arms out.

She passed the baby, then stood and marched to the door.

"You're a disgusting woman. Get out. Get out and stay out. This is my house. This is my baby." I followed her into the kitchen.

Then George appeared. "What's going on?" he asked.

"I want her out of this house."

"Calm down," he said. "What's this all about?"

"She was trying to feed the baby."

"Of course she was trying to feed the baby. The baby is small. The doctor said, goat milk…"

"No, she tried to stick her nipple in Antonio's mouth." George stared at me with a blank expression. "Her bare breast. She had my baby's mouth right on her teat."

"She's lying," Mary said. "I did no such thing. I was rocking the baby, and she came in screaming. She's imagining things again."

George turned, frowned and then spoke in a level voice. "I've had it with your imaginings. Go to the bedroom."

He believed Mary over me. I wanted to scream. My hands mitt up and Antonio squirmed. "Okay, I'll go to our room but you keep her away from me. I never want to see her again." I marched out into the bedroom and kicked the door shut.

The baby cried.

"I'm sorry, my love. I won't let that awful woman near you again. Come. We'll find you some milk."

I sat, undid my blouse and raised him to my nipple. He fell asleep. I pinched his cheek and tried to wake him but he slept and slept. After a while I gave up, propped us up against the pillows and drifted to sleep.

Niccolò stood beside the gold-gild column on stage and held out his arms for the baby. We were in the orchestra hall but he was close enough to create a thumping in my throat. I walked up the middle aisle with the baby, coming closer and closer to him. Niccolò smiled, and he looked so handsome in his tuxedo with satin lapels and his fingers were longer and more elegant than I remembered, the silvery half-moons of his fingernails and he tipped his head back and laughed. His laughter filled me with so much joy, I skipped along the aisle. But before I reached the foot of the stage, a big gust of wind tore through the curtains behind him. Snow whirled and whipped in the air above his head and his hair was no longer black, but icy white. His frosted eyebrows, white face, a white rose in his lapel—it was a frozen statue of Niccolò with his arms out, head tipped, a frozen smile. I could barely see him for the lashing snow. I stepped forward into the blizzard and hugged the baby. It was bleak. Frost formed on the baby's blanket and I wanted to run away but my mind would not command my legs to move and the icy wind trapped me. A tear froze on my cheek.

"Katya, give me the baby." I felt a tap on my shoulder and opened my eyes. Papa stood by the bed, George slumped on the chair behind him.

"No, he's cold. I need to keep him warm." I clutched the baby to my chest.

Papa placed his hand over mine and tried to loosen my fingers from the blanket. "Look at the baby, Katya."

I looked. Antonio's skin was white. "He's cold, Papa. There was a storm." I brought him in as close as I could.

"Katya, the baby has died."

"No," I cried. "He's just chilled and needs warm milk, that's all. He needs his mother's milk." I pulled out my breast and touched it to his lips. "He'll eat, Papa. I know he'll eat. We need to give him time. Once he has milk, he'll get warm." A drop of milk oozed out of my nipple and dripped on his tiny blue lips. "See, I have milk for him."

Papa reached out and smoothed a strand of hair that had fallen across my cheek. A howl escaped from George and he crumpled in the chair.

"We will leave you for a while," Papa said.

"That's your answer for everything, isn't it, Vasili?" George's voice cracked. "Leave her. She'll come around. Ignore her. She does no harm. Well, she does harm. She's killed my son."

"The baby was undersized and frail. The doctor said…"

"I know what the doctor said. With proper care, the baby should live. Proper care, Vasili. He said proper care. She couldn't care for an ant."

I buried my face in the blanket and clutched the cloth. "I hate you, Niccolò—you froze my baby and I hate you," but George's sobs drowned out my words.

CHAPTER FIFTEEN

Blue

WHEN George finally pried the dead baby away from Katya, she closed her eyes and remained propped on the bed with her arms cradled as if still holding her child. She did not move and stared at the wall with lifeless eyes.

Vasili sat with his daughter throughout the night. She did not twitch or move a muscle. To stay and care for her was all he wanted to do, but in the morning Mary took his arm and led him to his room where she'd laid out his suit. He had no wish to attend the funeral, and Katya could not be there, not in her present state. Even Mary understood that fact. George did not.

The coffin was shorter than an arm in length, rough boards nailed together. George had built it himself only hours before. When Vasili saw it, his breath caught. He could not bring himself to help George lift the box into the sleigh.

On the drive to town Vasili was thankful of the blowing snow, so loud he did not need to speak. He was grateful too for the cold that numbed his feet and deadened the gnawing in his chest. Mary sat wrapped mummy-like in the rear beside the coffin.

When they arrived in Sylvite George left on foot to collect Reverent Manning. Mary went to the General Store and Vasili plodded through the snow toward the church.

The chapel was empty but warm and quiet. Vasili sat near the front and waited. Thankfully, he did not have long to wait. Getting back to Katya soon was the most important thing.

George and the Reverend Manning arrived with the coffin and carried it to the Alter. The Pastor's wife showed up and placed a thin spray of dried flowers on the lid. George came to stand beside Vasili just as Mrs. Bradley appeared at the organ.

Several minutes later Mrs. Stanley and her entourage turned up, a roost of pecking hens who settled in an adjacent pew. Not one of them had ever shown a kindness to Katya or an ounce of charity to Olga when she was alive, but they did not miss funerals, even on short notice. Everyone stood as Reverend Manning took his place at the pulpit.

Vasili fixed eyes on Mrs. Stanley's hat until she must have felt his eyes and turned. She glanced over his head as if he wasn't there. And it did not matter to him, it never had. Nothing mattered, except keeping Katya safe. He had lost Olga, but he did not plan to lose Katya, not to a hospital or a husband who had no real affection for her.

Reverend Manning directed them to sit and then began to speak in his monotone voice. "Truly I tell you, unless you change and become like children, you will never enter the kingdom of heaven." The Pastor droned on about innocence. "Whoever becomes humble like this child is the greatest in the kingdom of heaven." Vasili noticed how insincere his voice was, like a tired schoolteacher reciting the same words year after year until the words are simply words, without meaning or thought and he knew that words did not exist to describe a coffin so small.

The organ pushed out a few sonorous notes, and everyone stood. Vasili opened the hymn book but did not sing. A streak of light flashed through the stained glass window behind the pulpit and illuminated the blue robe of the Virgin Mary for a moment, and then it faded. A simulation of life itself he thought—a beam so bright and vibrant for an instant before it disappears. Vasili pitied George standing erect beside him, oblivious to the outburst of colour. But no amount of pity would interfere with his daughter's freedom.

After the service George stopped next to the open coffin. The others had gathered in the foyer. "They'll put him in a crypt until the ground thaws." He lifted the tiny corpse, brought it to his chest and gazed up for a few moments before returning it. Then he followed Vasili to join the congregation in the foyer.

Mary met them there and hooked her arm into George's. "We should get back. It'll be dark soon. We don't want to leave her alone too long."

Barren

Mary's head loomed over the bed and I tried to dream her away. "Oh, look at you." Her face refused to disappear. She rested one hand on my cheek. "Ah, you poor thing. That was a shock, losing that baby. But you're young. Plenty of time for more babies."

I fixed my eyes on the ceiling.

"We need to get you well again. That's what we'll work on." She put her hand under my head and lifted. "Here now, some nice warm tea."

I felt the edge of the cup, pursed my lips shut and tea trickled down my chin. She lowered my head back onto the pillow.

"Okay for now. But we'll have to get something into you soon. I think that's half your problem and that's what I told George this morning. Lack of nourishment can hamper the mind." I willed her voice to stop but it didn't. "He's pretty upset himself. Wants to pack you up and take you to the doctors, but maybe he'll change his mind. You need to snap out of it, girl. You need to take better care of yourself, start eating properly." The cup clattered in its saucer. "And fresh air. This room needs an airing out."

Mary's head vanished. Her footsteps clapped on the wooden floor and the window scraped open. "My brother's wife lost her first baby. A little girl it was. Seems cruel but sometimes it's for the best."

Did I know or care about her brother or her brother's wife?
The notes of an elegy began to muddle my mind. Pa dum, pa
dum, pa dum.

"She grieved for a long time. Molly did so want a baby."
Mary's form floated above me again. She lifted my head once
more, plumped the pillows and arranged the covers around my
neck. "Kept busy to take her mind off it. 'Busy hands, happy heart'
is what my grandma used to say. When you're up, we'll get you
busy. I'll show you how to make a decent pie crust. Maybe I'll
show you my daddy's way of smoking meat."

I heard a chair grind across the floor and a creak as her
weight settled into it. "She's got eight kids now, Molly does."

Her hand rested on the quilt over my shoulder. "There's a
place southeast of Saskatoon. They call it Little Manitou. George
should take you in the spring. 'Miracle waters,' they say. People
go for rheumatism mostly, but soaking in that water's been
known to cure the mad."

The first line of *Gray's Elegy* repeated over and over, *the curfew
tolls the knell of parting day*, louder and louder, over and over. It
vibrated against the roof of my mouth. I closed my eyes and
looked for its shape. Black forms floated behind my eyelids, like
the wings of a crow.

"Katya, can you hear me?" George whispered. There was a song, like the snatch of a dream and I held my breath and focused my attention on it lest it slip away. But his breath fluttered at my neck. "Listen, please, I don't understand it either, but it happened and we've got to get on with life." His breath smelled of coffee. "Reverend Manning said some things at the service. He said, 'death is not the most tragic event, the death of an innocent child is a quick journey back to the Creator.' He warned us not to let the loss of a loved one kill our faith."

It was easy for George to go forward, drinking and eating, fixing fences.

He dug under the covers, found my hand, and set it over a smooth surface. "I've brought your violin. Why don't you get up and play?"

I heard him unlatch the case. He opened my fingers and placed them around the neck of the violin. My fingers rested on it, like a lizard on a rock.

"Please look at me or say something, damn it." He shook my arm and then cupped my chin. "What kind of a woman are you, Katya?" He pulled my head to face him but he was little more than a blurry image attached to the song. "You should have been with me. A mother should go to her child's funeral."

His voice faded off, drowned by the melody that grew in my head.

Storm

Vasili sat in the near-dark of early morning close to the open door of the oven. He had been up and dressed for hours, well-dressed, a scarf wound around his neck and a heavy sweater under his dressing gown. He thought it might be his age, this constant shivering. He did not see his son-in-law enter the kitchen, and the voice startled him.

"We need to get away before seven. I want to have plenty of time. The train leaves at three."

As if synchronized with George's voice, the grandfather clock in the hall struck. The echo of each chime was persistent and Vasili wanted the sound to go on forever, to smother George's words or turn back time. But the chimes ended at six. "You must think this over more."

"We have to take her to the mental asylum. She needs a doctor, one who can help with this madness." George placed a hand on each of Vasili's shoulders.

Vasili shrugged. "You think this will help, do you?"

George released his hold on Vasili, turned and walked to the stove. He positioned the kettle over the firebox and it whined. "Go in there and look at her. She doesn't move. It's been four days, Vasili. She won't eat. She hasn't said a word. Has she even talked to you?"

"She only needs a little time. Please trust me in this. I know."

"You are not a doctor." He scowled at his father-in-law.

"You two are up early." Mary arrived in the kitchen and headed straight for the wood box. "Cold out this morning." She bent, chose a piece of wood, moved the kettle back, lifted the lid, rattled the stick in through the opening, and then walked to the window. "There's no wind. I feel a storm coming."

"Can you get her ready, Mary? We're taking her today," George said.

"You should wait and see what the weather does."

"No, I've decided. It has to be today."

"You know, she's had a shock, losing the baby and all. She might come around."

"If you won't get her ready, I will." He stomped across the kitchen.

"I will go," Vasili said. He was suddenly warm, too warm, and he sprang to his feet and trudged out of the kitchen and along the hall to his daughter.

Katya eyes were closed. He walked to the bed and fingered the cover pulled up around her neck. Her eyelashes twitched, but she seemed oblivious to his presence. He sat on the edge of the bed and kept his voice low. "Oh, my little bird. I will dress you and get you ready to go but you will not be on a train to the doctor's. I do not know how I will manage it, but I will stop this. We will go to New York." Her eyes opened a slit and Vasili lowered his voice even more. "I have a little money. John paid me for the cows. Enough for us to get there. And Sergei is there. We will find him. I have his address in New York."

She looked at him then. She did not smile, but there was a flicker of recognition and Vasili went to the closet, collected her wool dress, shoes and stockings. He stood for a few moments fiddling with the flat buttons of her dress. The buttons reminded him of his mama and her frocks. Fastenings, in those days, were covered and often embroidered with bright specks of colour. His mama had always worn bright colours, rich fabrics and rich colours, nothing like this grey wool frock. He had often dressed her, cajoling, urging her on those days when she would have left the house wearing no clothes at all.

He tried to push these memories out of his mind, but he couldn't stop them, because when his mama was dressed and in front of the glass, she had always seemed better.

Katya was so thin, sitting on the bed shivering in her plain white nightgown. It was a struggle to fit her long slender arms into the straight sleeves of the dress but he accomplished the task and then fastened each tiny button. He led her to the mirror, but she did not glance at her reflection. After he'd dressed her as warmly as possible Vasili draped a wool blanket over her shoulders, led her outside and settled her into the sleigh.

The sky was thick and solid white in the distance as they set out. George drove the sleigh and beside Vasili in the back, Katya sat wrapped, her hands secure in her mother's muff, her cheeks barely visible between the earflaps of Vasili's fur cap.

There was one train per day to the West and one train per day to the East. It was a good thing George had insisted on leaving early. They would have to wait for the train. It gave Vasili at least two hours to slip away, buy tickets to New York and then create a distraction for George. Then he and Katya could hide until the morning, and catch the eastbound train. They might hide in the church. No one would there. But what if the ticket man told? George would be waiting for them then. Vasili put his head in his hands.

They had not gone far when the horse stopped, turned his head to his passengers, snorted and flared his nostrils.

"Come on boy." George flapped the reins. The sleigh lurched forward, and the wind whipped up.

Rather than buy tickets, they could steal onto the train. That might work best. In winter, the train crew stayed in the caboose. The conductor did not check for tickets for an hour or more. Vasili would look for the conductor, wait until he was alone and offer him money. A traveling salesman, who always stopped at Joe's, bragged once he had never paid more than a dollar in train fare. Conductors were always happy for extra pocket money. Five dollars would settle it.

The horse stopped again, whinnied, shook his head, and the sleigh jerked to a stop. "What's going on with you, Gust?" George said and then, "Oh, is that what's got you spooked?"

Vasili followed George's gaze to see an antelope in the snow.

It was off to the side of the road with one foot caught in a metal claw. It lay twisted at an awkward angle, his good back leg crossed over the trapped leg and its neck bow-shaped and bent back.

"Looks like he's been down for a while," George said.

The animals's eyes were glazed white and smears of fresh blood stained the snow. Its body twitched.

George wrapped the reins around the horn on the dashboard. "Can't let him suffer." He jumped out of the driver's seat and drew a shotgun out of the rear compartment. It shocked Vasili that George had brought a gun.

George approached the animal, rested the barrel of the gun against the side of its head, pulled the trigger and there was a muffled blast. Blood sprayed out across the snow as if a pot of paint had dropped from the sky.

"We'll leave him for the coyotes," George said. "He's struggled too long. It taints the meat." He jumped back in the sleigh and rested the shotgun on the seat beside him.

Vasili put his arm around Katya, the violin cradled between them. He pulled her head into his chest and the sleigh moved forward again.

They had only traveled a short distance when icy powder blew up from all sides. Before an hour passed the pelting snow threatened to suffocate them. The horse stopped again and George slapped the reins to urge him on.

"We should turn around." Vasili hollered over the squall of wind. The horse must have understood because he turned and set off toward home.

George heeded the horse's instinct and did not try to stop him. A mammoth white cauldron of icy air wiped out any details of the surrounding landscape. The horse was a blurry smudge and Vasili hoped the beast could find its way home. He hung onto his daughter and attempted to concentrate on the passage of time. He figured they had only traveled an hour before the storm began. How long since the horse turned around? Twenty-five breaths per minute was the average. He willed himself to stay calm and counted. When he reached three thousand, he quit. Would this be the end for them, buried under a ten-foot drift of snow, his arms locked and frozen in a ring around his daughter?

Then the house magically appeared a few feet from the sleigh.

"Good boy." George wasted no time. He unharnessed the horse and led him through the swirling snow toward the barn.

Vasili helped Katya into the house and she shook off her layers of clothing. "Oh, Papa, what an incredible storm." She seemed lively and fully recovered. Vasili closed the door, shutting the storm out of the kitchen.

Gales on the Saskatchewan prairie were a new experience for Vasili. In St. Petersburg there had been storms but the many tall buildings formed a protective barrier between his mother's house and the ocean. Bad weather was an excuse to stay indoors near the fire with a book. From the comfort of his boyhood home, Vasili had watched snow skip gayly around the spires of the church as if performing a dance for God.

Here, out the window, he could see no buildings, no barn, no corral, no fence, only a great angry pulse of white. It was relentless and continued to rage through to the next morning.

Before breakfast George came into the kitchen and slipped on his heavy coat. Next to the door, in the front porch, a long thick rope was coiled on the floor. Vasili noticed it when he'd first arrived and had wondered what its purpose was.

"Take the rope," Mary said.

Vasili wondered why George would even go out in such a storm. The animals were safe in the barn.

George looked out the window over Vasili's shoulder. "It should be okay."

"I'll bet that's what Bernie Foster said." Mary bent over the table and swiped the top with a rag sending a sprinkle of bread crumbs across the linoleum.

"Who's Bernie Foster?" Vasili asked.

"I've never told you that story?" Mary stopped wiping. "A few years back Bernie ventured out in this nasty storm that lasted four or five days. He meant to milk the cows but never made it back to the house." She waved the rag in front of her. "His boys set off looking for him with a rope. It was forty below with wind so bad folks walked slanted." Mary paused and tossed the rag into the sink. "They didn't find Bernie until the storm let up. He froze to death, not twenty feet from the house."

"His heart likely gave out," George said.

"No, damn fool man lost his bearings in that storm. It's easy enough to do. Left a wife and six kids too."

George walked to the door and pulled his boots on. Vasili craned his neck as the door opened. George's dark shadow bent into the wind, milk pails in one hand and he and the rope passed from sight less than three feet from the door.

How Vasili missed St. Petersburg in winter. Citizens strolled between bright buildings, skaters glided on a pond in the centre of the city and every family had a sleigh to pull their children through the park. There was never this empty constant squall, snow attempting to bury the house, snow halfway up the windows.

The howling wind and snow did not stop that day or the next.

"Won't budge," George said as Vasili walked into the kitchen on the third morning. George ran against the door—laid one shoulder into it. "It's like running up against a brick wall."

"Worse than that nasty storm in 1920," Mary said. "It snowed us in for four days, but it never got so bad we couldn't open the door."

"I'll try the window. Don't know what my old man was thinking, putting a door on the north side." He turned and glanced at Katya who'd just entered the room. "So, you're awake."

Since the interrupted trip to Edmonton, Katya had been out of bed each day smiling and humming. She spent most of her time assisting Mary with household chores. Even so, George had barely spoken to her. He walked over and opened a west-facing window. Snow had drifted half way up the glass pane and some of it tumbled in onto the linoleum. A blast of wind sent a shiver through the kitchen.

Mary rushed to the closet and pulled out the broom. "I'll sweep that up."

"No, give me that." George took the broom, thrust it through the open window and shoved the snow aside with the straw end. More snow blew in.

Katya stepped to where Vasili sat in the rocking chair by the window and rested her hand on his shoulder. "Mama used to say it's as if Father Winter tries to claim the land back from the farmers. Remember she said, 'We are not at one with nature here but at war with the elements.'"

"It sure seems that way at times." Mary was down on her knees with a rag, snow scooped into a pile in front of her.

George gave the broom back to Mary. "I'll clear a path to the barn." He disappeared out the window, headfirst into the snow.

By the time Mary had breakfast cooked the snow shovel thumped against the door.

"It's still blowing bad." George pushed the door open and snow whipped in.

"Come, have your breakfast." Mary dropped a bowl of scrambled eggs on the table.

"Later. I'd best do the milking before that door's buried again. I'll dig out a few bales of feed too."

"I'll help you." Mary dressed and followed him outside.

Vasili gestured Katya to sit. He leaned over, took her hand and inspected it. "Such beautiful fingers." He clasped his large hand over her smaller one. This was no life for a musician.

"What we need is a good Chinook," Mary said later when she and George returned. "Like a story I heard about once. A guy was driving his sleigh from Sylvite to Lloydminster and he felt the hind bob start to drag. The front of the sleigh was still on two feet of snow but, the back was dragging in the mud."

George laughed. "Yeah, but didn't he lay his whip to the horses and outrun the wind? They say he made it to town ahead of the snow melting behind him." Mary guffawed and Vasili couldn't help but smile. He thought it might be the first time he'd heard her laugh out loud.

Still shaking with mirth, some milk slopped out on the counter as Mary hoisted the pails at the sink. "Like that old tale about Lethbridge. Storm came up so hard, it blew a cow right up against the barn. Story goes, it stuck him up there six feet off the ground for two whole days."

"They say it's so windy down in that country they have to cement up the walls to keep the holes from blowing away," George said.

Vasili scratched his cheek. "What does that mean? To keep holes from blowing away."

"Just a figure of speech, Vasili. It's a joke."

No one suggested a trip to the city. In fact George barely spoke to his father-in-law. Vasili was careful not to say too much, with hope he had changed his mind. Once the weather settled Vasili would devise a new get-away plan.

Katya and Vasili spent the afternoons of the storm in the parlour. Dark smudges still underlined Katya's eyes, but she seemed improved.

One afternoon she picked up the violin and played *Violinschule* while Vasili listened from the armchair near the window, the notes so clear and enchanting. Like a master on stage, his Katya. She allowed the music to die at the end of the song as Mozart intended—a splendid, slow drawn-out ending as if the music had gone to sleep like a good child wrapped into bed with a kiss.

"Bravo," Vasili said when the last note slipped away. "Never have I heard that song performed with such mastery. The best in the St. Petersburg orchestra, they could not play it like you. And you with a bad arm. Does it still hurt?"

"It hurts sometimes. When I wake in the morning, it throbs."

"So, you are sleeping again?"

"Yes. It's good to sleep again. I make my own tea before bed." She lowered her voice. "If Mary makes it I pour it out."

"Ah, Katya, I thought you had forgotten this notion." He placed a hand on her shoulder. "Why would it matter who makes the tea? It all comes from the same jar, does it not?"

"Yes, but I saw her add something to my cup last night." Katya pursed her lips together and fixed her eyes on Vasili's face. "She turned her back, but I could see her dig into the pocket of her apron for her evil potion. Mary wants to keep me wide awake and drive me mad."

"Why would she do that?" This conversation filled him with fresh worry. The episodes always began like this. Vasili's Mama had once accused Olga with almost the same words. He patted his daughter's arm. "What would Mary know about evil potions? She is only a simple farm woman."

"Oh, she knows, all right. Women from the prairie know about herbs and roots, Papa. She told me herself. 'Sweetgrass is for fever and it grows along the creek bed in town. Baneberry will cure headaches.' Mary got her potions from an old Indian woman. She has all sorts of little bags."

"But why would Mary wish to harm you?"

"She wants the house to herself. Don't you see, Papa, how she tries to turn George against me. This morning I walked into the kitchen and they were talking, heads together and they quit as soon as I entered the room." Katya put the violin down and paced.

Vasili sat in the chair and spoke to her in an even voice, surprised at how even, because his blood was pulsing madly. "You must not let your imagination take you away, little bird. Mary does not mean you harm. In fact George told me this morning that Mary thinks you are not eating enough."

"Oh, yes. I'm sure Mary would like to see me eat more. I'm sure she would."

The storm continued to rage and Mary kept lamps lit and the fire stoked. A great barricade of snow pushed up higher and higher against the outside walls of the house. George made another tunnel from the window to the barn.

"We're like troops stuck in the trenches," George said on the fourth day as he paced between the kitchen and the parlour. To Vasili, George seemed more a lion trapped in a cage, but he said nothing.

Vasili had given up hope of seeing anything out the windows. The snow pressed against them and the glass had become like mirrors reflecting the flames of lamps, kept on even during the day.

"Come," Vasili said to George. "I will show you how to play chess."

"I've never played," he said.

"It will engage your mind and help to pass the hours."

He followed Vasili into the parlour. They set the board up on the table and sat opposite one another.

"See the white squares at the bottom?" Vasili pointed to the board. "They call these pieces rooks." He held up two figures, one white and one dark. "You will choose." Hiding one rook in each hand he moved them behind his back. "Choose a hand."

George pointed at his left.

"Good, you will be the white. This is an advantage for you and can make the first move." Vasili gathered up the white and handed them to George. "And this is how the pieces go." He arranged the figures on the squares. "See, the pieces get taller as you move toward the middle. This one is the King." He held up the tallest figure. "As in any country, there can only be one King. You must try to capture my King before I capture yours." George leaned over the table and studied the board.

Vasili did not need to defeat George at chess to prove his mind was strategically superior. He had devised a master plan for his daughter's escape and alternative tactics in the event of unexpected circumstances.

In the kitchen, Katya hummed an old Russian ballad, and dishes clinked as she and Mary prepared the afternoon meal.

After the storm

On the eighth day, the storm lifted, and the wind stopped. Late that afternoon Papa and I stood at the window bathed in orange light. Whipped-cream peaks of tinted snow spiked the horizon and eight-foot waves pushed up against the west wall of the barn. In the distance, the horse whinnied.

George stepped in from outside powdered in white. "Gust's impatient to get out."

"I bet the cows are too," Mary said. "But they won't be moving too fast around the field."

"But look at that snow. When it melts, we'll have damn fine crops this year." George removed his coat and shook the snow off.

"The light is magnificent," I said. "Like the sun through God's eyelids."

"Step outside and you'll see how god-like it is." Mary hugged herself. "It's bitter cold out there."

I went out, but later when they'd all gone to sleep. The full moon hung in the sky above snowdrifts of blue sheen. I slipped along the path George had dug, banked high with snow on both sides. It was freezing in the barn. Even the animals were still. Loki was nowhere in sight, but I found my jar of whiskey under the rusted-out pail where I'd hidden it. I stole back into the house.

I didn't need a candle. Moonlight saturated the kitchen, and the warmth of the stove pulled the moment into an enchanted dream. My violin leaned against the wall in its usual spot. When had I stopped sleeping with it? The words of Master Auer came to me as if he stood in the room, 'It must become a part of you. The musician and her instrument must work as a single body.'

Energy coiled in my belly. I sipped whiskey from the jar but it failed to calm me. My violin sat neglected, tossed against the wall. It needed a stand, something to prop it up, to give it a place of importance.

I got to my feet and rushed toward the back room. George had bolted the door so I tiptoed into the bedroom, opened the top drawer of my husband's dresser and retrieved the key. George snored and burrowed deeper into the pillow. Once asleep, there was no waking him.

George's had covered the cradle with an old blanket which I tossed to the ground. Then I carried the cradle into the kitchen. I glanced around for a backdrop to display my violin. Only the velvet window hangings in the parlour seemed to suit. I dragged a chair over, got up and pulled them down. Then I draped them over the cradle.

The rich brown wood of the fiddle looked splendid against the burgundy fabric. I dropped to my hands and knees and rocked the cradle. A line of music and a line of verse came to mind which made me remember a Russian proverb and one of

Mama's recipes and these thoughts collided in my head but then they fused together and I needed to make sense of them and so I jumped up, ran into the parlour, grabbed a stack of paper, my pen and ink, and tore three pages up into small squares. I scribed several lines of music, one on each piece of paper and tucked these in the folds around my violin. The other thoughts, I wrote them down too, scanning the room for the thing in the kitchen most associated with the thought. I flew to the porch cupboard and found a pot of glue and with a stick from the wood box, smeared glue on the back of each note and pasted them on the wall nearest its object.

Engrossed, I didn't even notice when the blue tinge of the moon became the first weak light of day.

Mary walked into the room. "What in heaven's name are you doing?"

"Oh, Mary. You'll appreciate this one." I ran across the kitchen, got up on a chair and pointed to a piece of paper above the stove. "It's the *Kulich* bread recipe, a sweetbread. I think I remembered the ingredients but I'm not positive how much of each thing, but you can figure that out. I remember Mama making it, and she couldn't make it properly in Canada because cardamom was impossible to find, but she wrote away somewhere and got some and she was so happy that day, and this..." I jumped down and raced the length of the room. "This is the song that goes with the bread but I had to paste it closer to the violin and don't you love how the violin looks now, Mary? The bread needs the stove, but the song needs the fiddle, and we all need songs and food, don't we, Mary?"

"Slow down, child. What are you blathering on about?"

"What the hell?" George wandered into the kitchen and spun around in a circle. He gazed at my thoughts pasted on the walls, stopped and stared at my violin display, his eyes as wide open as I'd ever seen them.

"Here's one for you, George." I skipped to the shelf where he kept his pipe and tobacco. "I'm not sure which one it is, but it's an old Russian proverb, *a drop hollows out a stone*. It reminded me of you, George, and how hard you work and how patient you were when the crop didn't come in as big as you'd hoped. Here it is. This is it." I'd posted many thoughts next to George's shelf, and I pointed to the one in the middle. "It had to be next to the pipe, you see. When you smokey you ruminate, and you present the very embodiment of patience. And another one too, here, *let us run with patience the race that is set before us.*' I'm not certain but that might be from the Bible. It popped into my mind but it goes with the pipe too, patience and God and fire and smoke. But I didn't know at first where to put Papa's. Most of his have to do with music, so I put them on the opposite side of the violin, but some of them have to do with poetry because when I see poetry or music, I think of Papa." I fell to my knees and read from a scrap of paper pinned low near the floor,

"In the day of grief, be mild

Merry days will come, believe.

Heart is living in tomorrow,

Present is dejected here;

In a flash, passes sorrow,

That which passes will be dear.

"I may have forgotten the first two lines but isn't that wonderful, *In a moment, passes sorrow*. That's Alexandr Pushkin. Papa used to have a volume of his poems but I haven't seen it in the longest time but isn't it good that I could remember the whole verse, just about the whole verse... I had to translated it but Papa needs to let his grief go, don't you think, and what better way to do it than with poetry."

"Vasili." George yelled. "Come to the kitchen."

"Yes, Papa, come. I want you to see what I've done and how it fits together. You'll understand." I waved my hand in the air. "I can't believe I didn't see it before now. It comes together like stars that form one glittering body. It's so simple."

"What is simple, little bird?" Papa shuffled into the room in his dressing gown.

"This." I threw my arms up wide.

"She's gone stark raving mad," George said.

"You're the one who's crazy, George," I said, "if you can't see this. Take a minute to read these thoughts and don't you call me names when you haven't considered what this means."

"You're raving, Katya. Look at these notes. The handwriting isn't even legible and what in hell are you talking about?"

"Raving, am I? Listen to yourself. You are nothing but a stupid farmer, George, and most of the time I wonder whatever possessed me to marry you."

His face reddened and a vein throbbed at his neck. He stepped over to the rocking chair, bent, picked up the empty mason jar and sniffed it. "Whiskey. Where did you get this?"

"It doesn't matter where I got it and if I want to drink whiskey, I'll drink whiskey."

George lifted his arm and threw the jar at the door. It smashed into a thousand pieces. "Not under the roof of my house, you won't." He stomped over to me and glared down. "And I doubt they'll be serving you whiskey in the mental asylum either."

I shook from my temples to my toes. Papa stepped forward and nudged in front of George. He put his arms around me. I pushed him away and ran to the cupboard. "You want to hear things break?" I picked up a plate and threw it at the door. I threw a glass, then Mary's large bowl. The bowl was so heavy, it landed short of the door and smashed at George's feet. He was across the kitchen floor in an instant and he pinned me before I could pick up another plate. I kicked at him, but he held on tight.

"Are you convinced now, Vasili? We'll leave as soon as the

snow packs."

George walked me to the bedroom, thrust me in and locked the door.

When that key turned in the lock my thoughts banged against each other. I was sure my skull would split open, and there was no music but a siren pounding in my ears. I was relieved when the foul smelling cloud appeared and forced me flat on the bed.

CHAPTER SIXTEEN

Exposure

THE cloud above the bed lifted. I wasn't sure if it had trapped me there for hours or for days. George's voice rang out. "You've seen her like this before, haven't you?"

Papa was in the room too. I could tell both of them were trying to keep their voices low, but every word was clear. "Only one time. For three days," Papa said.

"You should have warned me."

"Warned you?"

"That she's mad."

"She is not mad."

"Look at her. This happened before and you never told me?"

"In the past she had trouble with melancholia, yes, and I said you should watch her. I told you of her nature."

"But you never told me how insane she is."

"You wished to marry her, George. Love struck you."

"Yes, but she was fine then."

"Olga and I wanted her to lead a normal life."

The conversation stopped and quietness engulfed the room.

Papa drew in a breath with a wheeze. "I should not have brought her here. We should have gone to New York, but I feared for Katya's safety there."

"New York or Timbuktu, what would it matter? She'd still be crazy."

"The city has many musicians—her own kind. They appreciate the temperament that comes with art. No one accepts my Katya in this world."

"Look at her, Vasili, her eyes open and fixed as if she's dead. She hasn't moved in five days."

The room fell quiet again. I didn't care. Let them talk or not talk. Nothing in their words, nothing—not a single thing.

"You need to understand, George, the life we lived in Russia."

I stared upward. The ceiling plaster was cracked, thin filament cracks, like threads of a musical line—straight, curved, crossing this way and that, without purpose or direction, but with an intricate scale. In the ceiling you can create a universe.

"There was a man, in St. Petersburg." Papa's voice softened to a whisper. "He sided with the Bolsheviks. They treated our class of people as the enemy." He paused and cleared his throat. "We heard stories of atrocities, on both sides—terrible things."

Papa stopped talking as if he'd said enough. But after a

moment he started again. "Katya rejected his advances. She was only fourteen and had no interest in men, only music. But that rejection was all it took, because we were a bourgeois family. They came and seized her one night when I was away, and sent her off to a mental asylum. I believe she has pushed these events from her mind."

The covers weighted my body, but a shiver ran through my core.

Papa said, "I wanted to go immediately and break down the hospital doors but Olga told me, 'No, use your friends, the friends at the Conservatory. They have influence.' So I did as she said. I appealed to everyone I knew. I filled out forms. In the lobby of a government official I waited for six days. I did all I could think of, spoke to anyone who would listen. But everything was in turmoil —the military, the regime. I banged on the door of the hospital and pleaded with them to let me see her, talk to her. All to no avail."

I loved my Papa's voice, so deep and sonorous, a trombone of a voice. There was a man…there was a man…there was a man…St. Petersburg—spires and cupolas…to no avail.

He went on. "A month passed and another month. I could stand still no longer. I waited until late, knowing the hospital workers would be drunk on vodka, celebrating the New Year. Good luck came my way." Papa cleared his throat. "The outside guard lay fast asleep, wrapped in fur against the side of the building. He did not stir when I put my hand inside his pocket and took the keys. I planned to kill him if required."

Vodka burned the eyes. Eyes became fiery orbs in their sockets. The ceiling disappeared when that happened. How could you manage without that universe in the ceiling? Because when the music stopped, only the ceiling remained. I twisted my neck to hear Papa better, but at the same time I wanted to yell at him, 'No, don't say more. Let the music return,' but my lips would not move nor speak.

"Inside, the dim-lit hallways stank of urine, so strong it made my eyes water." Papa's words sputtered.

Yes, Papa, urine. It warmed you at first when you released it. Holding it in as long as possible created a diversion, but it was certain to fail. Once you let it go, it only felt warm for a moment. Then the chill crept in, deeper than before. The morning nurse would slap you and scold you, 'Disgusting creature. Look what you've done. Did your mother never teach you not to piss in the bed?'

Papa pressed on with his story. "When my eyes adjusted, I had entered a cavernous room, beds lined against the walls with only two feet between them. Men lay on the mattresses, hands and legs tied to the bedposts. Some of them slept, but the wide-awake men had cloth pushed into their mouths. I crept through that chamber until I came to a door at the opposite end. It led into another room, the exact duplicate, except it was women fettered to the beds."

Oh, Papa, if you only knew. When you struggled, the ropes cut through your skin but it wasn't an unbearable pain. Just like the pain from your bladder, you focused on it and that worked for a while, as long as you weren't intent on getting free. That would drive you mad because the woman who tied the ropes, she was an expert at knots. She hummed when she twisted the rope and laughed out loud at the ones who cried. I had to forget all of these details, for your sake and for mine.

I rolled onto my side and saw Papa hunched on the chair by the window. George sat in the armchair in the corner, staring at my Papa, his face pale.

Papa continued, as if he'd told this story a hundred times. He may have done so, in his head. "The women's faces, I bent to study each. One woman had a streak of white hair, like a skunk, but she did not appear old. Her eyes pleaded, but her face showed no expression except for sad eyes which sparked with hope when she saw me. But I turned away."

George squeezed his fist with the other hand. "Why are you telling me this?"

"Because you'll never understand unless you know what happened." Papa straightened and launched back into his tale. "Light poured from an open door at the end of the ward. In the windowed room, I saw silhouettes of nurses sitting around a table, the sound of laughter, glasses clicking. A woman stood, stepped to the door, and peered out. I froze. She closed the door, turned, and sat again, the laughter and clinks muted. Still, I dropped to my hands and knees, staying out of sight. I crawled from bed to bed, looked in one woman's sleeping face, another woman's anguished eyes and I could hardly bear it. When I had dragged myself as far as the lit room, panic hit. What if Katya was dead?

"I did not recognise her at first. It was her fingers, her long slender fingers I recognised, hanging limp in knotted ropes above her head.

"A thud of footsteps sounded, and I crouched beside her bed. Two men in uniform appeared in the entranceway. I lay flat and rolled under the mattress. 'So, who will be the lucky girl tonight?' one said and laughed. 'Not that one.' He pointed at my Katya's bed. 'She is too skinny now.' I recognised his voice.

"They walked to the other side of the room. I saw his face. My ears had not deceived me. The Bolshevik stood in that ward, the same one Katya rejected. I wanted to get up, run over and strangle him, but I did not move. He bent and cut the ropes that held another young girl. Set free, she struggled, and he caught her plump arm and twisted it behind her back. He produced a knife and held it to her neck. A tightly tied rag gagged her mouth. 'Come now,' he said. 'We will go downstairs for a bit of fun. If you are a good girl, I will take off the cloth.'

"After they left, I remained frozen under the bed and listened.

Muffled laughter sprang from the nurse's room. I rolled out from under the bed, got to my knees, and fumbled at the knots that held my Katya's hands.

"She did not wake. Her skin was white. On her upper lip there was a gash, swollen and crusted with blood, and a blue-black bruise from her eye right down to her chin. They had cut her hair with a knife. Her hair, her beautiful wavy hair, thatched an inch from her head. The ropes came free at last and I lifted her. She weighed no more than a kitten. I held her and ran and did not stop until I reached our house."

"So you went to the authorities? You reported them?" George's voice had an edge of impatience.

"No," Papa said. "This Bolshevik—his father was a friend of Lenin. They would have searched for me. Who knows what they would have done."

"Didn't you have laws, to protect the women and children?"

"Yes, plenty of laws, but a war inside the country too. Many Bolsheviks were good men, but some were monsters. Laws could be ignored or bent to serve the purpose of anyone with power."

"So what did you do?"

"It was too dangerous to stay at home. I collected Olga and a few of our things. We carried Katya to a friend from the Conservatory who hid us. He did this at great danger to himself. The Bolsheviks had control of the city.

"Later, in that room she woke, her eyes fixed to the ceiling as they are now. Her mama dressed her wounded lip, tried to feed her soup, rocked her and cried over her for three days.

"On the third day, my little Katya sat up and asked for her violin, as if nothing had happened. Can you imagine? She asked for her violin."

"This morning, I tried to give her the violin," George said. "It did no good."

Notes of my music soared overhead, a flock of lettered black birds. They split into fragments one by one and vanished into the ceiling cracks.

Papa continued. "That night I walked to the docks and traded a gold watch, Mama's wedding ring and Olga's silver tableware for passage on a ship to Canada. We were lucky that the ship departed two days later."

"Why Canada?" George rose from his chair and walked to the window. "You knew no one here. Didn't your friend Sergei settle in New York?"

"Yes, he did. At first I thought we should go to New York, but the Bolshevik's might have found us there. Many Russians escaped to New York, and my Katya, she was known."

"Why would they care enough to hunt down one young girl escaped from a hospital? Didn't they have bigger issues?"

"That Bolshevik, his father had influence, power." Papa rubbed his fist against his temple. "I did not know how much until later. Not that it mattered."

"Why would he care? He'd lost interest in her, hadn't he?"

"He had, but I did not lose interest in him."

"What do you mean?"

"I mean nothing. It makes no difference now."

Their conversation ceased and the room became a tomb. Papa gazed out the window and George stared at his feet.

"It's a terrible story, Vasili, but it doesn't change anything," George said after a few minutes. "Katya's sick and belongs in a hospital."

"I will take her away."

"And where would you go? New York? You're getting old and it's late to start a new life. Could you even provide for her there? And, don't forget, she's my wife." George leaned forward in the chair and gave Papa a menacing look. "You can't keep running. They can help her at the hospital. We have to take her. We'll drive to the train as soon as the weather clears."

Papa's shoulders slumped, and he sank into his chair. After a long silence I turned my attention to the ceiling, back to its universe of cracks.

Lament

Vasili stood in his room next to the bed. An unnatural silence had settled into the house. He whispered. "So, Olga, did you listen to what I told George? Then you understand my shame."

And in the quiet he detected a murmur, "What shame,

Vasha?"

No, it could not be, but it was, the tender voice of his wife.

"Ah, but I never told what happened, *Zhena* and did not tell George the whole story."

"It does not matter, my husband."

"But it does! Not a day goes by where I do not relive what I did." He walked to the window and pressed his cheek against the icy windowpane. "I allowed the Bolshevik to disease my mind and became as evil as he was."

"You have no evil in you, Vasha." The voice hummed from the walls.

"Yes, I do." He drew away from the window, slumped in the chair next to the bed, lowered his head and spoke.

"You wondered where I had disappeared to, remember—the week we fled?" Vasili shivered and pulled a wool blanket off the bed and spread it over his knees. "For two long days before we sailed, I scoured the streets for him, a hunting knife concealed inside my parka. After dark, I waited the entire night outside the asylum, crouched behind a stone fence—a wolf awaiting his prey. No one came in or out the first night."

"Forget this, my *muzh*. It happened long ago." Now the voice sounded inside his ear and he knew she could hear his thoughts.

Vasili raised his head. "But I need to say it out loud."

"It was after the second night, near dawn. I was ready to give up and almost walked away, but then the side door of the hospital opened and I recognised him, the Bolshevik. He staggered into the alley.”

The vision remained with Vasili, the man’s tight jacket, unbuttoned, with the arms too short. He was wearing an officer’s good leather boots. The Bolshevik was more vivid to him now than he had been that night, so often had he visited this memory.

“I followed him, staying out of his sight. At the end of the alley he stopped to light a cigarette. He wobbled and sang a Russian folk song as he danced side-to-side like a demented puppet—the puppet who slaughters the others on stage and dances around their corpses. Hatred exploded through me.”

Vasili shifted and the chair creaked, or it may have been Olga groaning.

“His match died out. He struck another match and continued to dance. It went out again. He did this three more times before his cigarette ignited, and I watched his face, lit by the yellow glow of the match, convinced my plan was just.” Vasili paused for a moment. “Oh God, Olga.”

“Then I ran at him. He twisted sideways. The knife plunged into his shoulder. He struggled. I stabbed again, this time into his chest. He dropped to the ground. I stood and watched his body jerk. A gurgle sounded. Blood appeared at the corner of his mouth. All movement stopped. It was over that quickly. I ran.”

“Did you kill him?” My Olga, what a gentle voice.

“I could not be certain. That was the night our ship sailed. Do you see? The blame was mine. None of it should have happened to Katya. I should have rescued her in the beginning."

"You didn't know."

"So many mistakes, my *myshka*. I was wrong to wait." A terrible sound escaped Vasili's throat and wouldn't stop. He rocked back and forth for several minutes. "Now we run again. I must take Katya away from here."

But Olga's voice had died away, and he was alone in the room.

A speck in the snow

We didn't speak of the Bolshevik or Papa's story in the days that followed. Papa didn't know I'd heard him recount the events and I wasn't inclined to tell him. I'd caused him enough grief. George was barely speaking to him. Papa needed to leave the past behind.

I was up again and feeling much recovered. During the daylight hours I kept busy helping Mary and playing for Papa, but at night visions of the Bolshevik overwhelmed my brain and even music could not quash his image. The cloud didn't return, but I could not sleep, and for three long nights lay beside my husband like a plank. This lack of sleep took its toll on me and my energy plummeted.

On the fourth night, sleep came at last. I wasn't sure how many hours I'd slept when I woke in bed alone. My legs and arms were rags and my jaw ached as if I'd gnawed for hours on a mouthful of gristly steak. It was still nighttime. Blue light seeped through the windowpane. The bedposts gleamed in the moonlight and the design on the quilt seemed alive, musical notes stitched into the fabric, the quilt that George had made. But the notes were soundless and the room silent, even the routine chamber music, dead and mute in my head.

A faint ping resonated from the window. I strained to see past the black sheen of the windowpane. Was it Loki? No, beaks shine. They don't glitter. But then I caught his outline. It was him. He tapped once more, lifted his wings and left.

I swung my legs off the side of the bed and push up to a sitting position. My hands hurt. To stand was even more difficult. I wobbled on legs that shook and then inched my feet forward like a toddling child.

The window was seven paces from the bed.

Loki was out there, the devil, roosted on the well. A three-foot-wide wall of stone surrounded that well. When I'd first come to the farm it delighted me, the only thing on the property that reminded me of Russia, with its painted wooden pillars and pointed roof. The frame was now entombed by snow. The crow hopped forward throwing up a spark of light and I itched to get closer and see what mischief he had planned. I moved toward the exit.

Mary's bedroom door was closed, but the parlour door sat open. George lay sleeping on the chesterfield, fully dressed, one leg on the floor, wearing the thick green socks that Mary had knit. His head was twisted at a poor angle, and it occurred to me that his neck would be stiff when he rose.

My feet were marble-white against the wooden floorboards. Feet have so many bones, the skin stretched tightly over them, and my right foot had the teat-shaped early signs of a bunion.

George shifted, threw an arm up over his head and I side-stepped past him.

Mary's rubber boots were near the back door, and a pair of George's socks were draped on the clothesline above the stove. Before pulling them off the line, I rested my hands for a moment on the warm stovetop.

For a short woman, Mary had big feet and even with thick socks, my feet swam in her boots. I hiked up my nightgown and scrutinised my rope-thin legs. George's greatcoat, the one he always wore to church, hung on a hook by the door. I yanked it off and slipped into it.

A faint snore sounded from Papa's room that used to be the dining area. Papa snuffles, rather than snores—an even, low sound, like the muted tone from a bassoon. His bedroom at home had been cosy compared to this. He deserved more comfort. I needed to devise a way to make him snug.

Outside, icicles crystallised in my nostrils and I imagined the echo of Mary's voice, 'Warmer out, but not much. Must be ten below.' I breathed in through my mouth. The outdoor sky was lighter and brighter than seen through the bedroom window. The moon was a round, luminous globe against the blue-black heavens which flickered with a jewellery box of stars, the Milky Way a glistering robe tossed into the sphere.

Loki remained perched on the well wall, and I discovered why he sparkled as I grew nearer. The cawing trickster had my necklace draped around his neck and it was not his beak that twinkled. It was Mary's, so-called misplaced wedding ring, attached to his bill like an ornament stuck through the nose of a bull. Mary would be so happy to have her ring back. And she said I'd imagined Loki's thieving ways.

My foot slipped on an icy patch. The rubber boots squealed, and I reeled forward. Loki hopped off toward the north field. His speed amazed me, each leap the reach of a human stride. How could he cover such distance with that jewellery weighing him down?

Off the path, the snow was heavy. It came up over my footwear, but I stayed on his tail. The frozen powder burned my bare upper legs, and I wrestled to pull each boot up and plant one foot in front of the other. Exerting so much energy shook off the chill. I drew in a deep exhilarating breath of freezing air. My limbs no longer ached.

Loki skittered across the drifts and I couldn't catch up with him.

"Stop, you black devil."

He kept me at a distance. If I gained a foot, he gained two. "You think I'll give up, don't you? But I won't. I'll have my necklace back and Mary's ring, you thieving, nasty bird."

I clomped after him. My cheeks grew numb. I put one hand up, touched my lips, and couldn't feel my fingers. George usually had gloves in his coat pocket but my wooden fingers weren't able to find the hole. I took my eyes off the bird, located the slit but found no gloves. I crammed my hands into the pockets, but that made it more difficult to gain ground. Loki was getting away.

"Damn bird."

I thrust my hands back out into the frigid air, wrenched my feet up hard through the snow and gained on him. He was still three feet away, and I surged forward.

Loki let out a demon, deafening caw that cracked the night like the fall of a giant tree. I glanced behind me to the house and barn, small now, alabaster fields of snow stretched smooth as the belly of a sea bream except for the crooked track left by my boots.

My breath came out in raspy puffs, and my throat went raw from the glacial air. The bird stopped for a minute, and I gathered my last bit of strength to pounce. I pushed off, extending both hands and leapt, but my fingers plunged into emptiness. I toppled head first, and it felt as if I'd tipped forward onto a feather bed. Snow jammed up my nose and clogged my throat. I rolled over, sputtered, and choked.

I lay on my back, motionless, so small in the universe, a speck in the snow beneath the vast and jewelled sky. The orange glow of a new day tinted the horizon. My eyelashes were heavy and a great warmth and tiredness set into me.

A twitch of movement flashed inches away from my head. Out of the corner of one eye I spied Loki, within my grasp now, but I no longer had the inclination, the energy, or the spark. My arms lay alien next to my body. My eyelids surrendered and shut.

Gone

Mary was sawing at a loaf of bread. "You're up early," she said as Vasili walked into the kitchen. "How did you sleep?"

"My sleep is like the wolf," he said. "Always one eye open." He shuffled to the door and pulled on his boots. "And Katya?"

"Haven't seen her yet this morning."

Mary had become something of a mother to his Katya. He suspected it gave the woman a sense of purpose. With no children of her own, she must have been lonely on that farm after her husband died.

Mary hummed as she cracked eggs into a bowl.

And Katya seemed friendlier to Mary in recent days. Just yesterday, he'd seen his daughter enter the kitchen, set up the butter churn, and sit to churn without being asked. She'd done it on her own. Vasili would tell this story to George and persuade him to give her more time. Katya wasn't strong enough—not for a long trip to the hospital, not even to escape. Vasili pulled his parka off the hook.

"You're going out?"

"Yes, I need to speak with George."

"Check the barn. He asked me to pack up a lunch to take with you."

"The snow is still deep," Vasili said. "We should delay this trip."

"Good luck in bringing George round." She lined the bread up across the counter, and walked to the pantry.

"I will convince him." He stepped outside. The air was sharp, and he squinted in the early morning sun.

George was crouched beside the sleigh. He glanced up as Vasili approached, lowered his head again, and continued tightening a clamp on the runner support.

"It is warmer today, but still cold." Vasili stopped next to George and clasped his hands behind his back.

"Yep, and clear. Should be the last bad weather for a while."

"The snow is deep."

"Only where it drifts. Roads should be okay. We'll avoid the gullies." He pulled on a strap next to the shaft.

"Is something wrong?"

"No, just making sure it's snug."

"We should wait," Vasili told him. "The horse will find it difficult."

"He's ploughed through worse." George stood, grabbed the

horse's halter off a fencepost, turned and headed for the barn. Vasili followed him.

"We should think this over," Vasili said. "Give it more time. Katya is weak. She has not recovered from the birth." George tramped ahead, breaking the snow with his boots. Then he swung open the gate of the corral, walked to the horse and ran his hand along its mane. Gust nuzzled his owner's chest. George reached into his pocket and brought out a wrinkled carrot. "Here boy."

"George, what you plan is wrong. I am afraid for her."

"I want a wife, Vasili. At the asylum, there's at least a chance they can cure her." Gust chomped on the apple while George rubbed his nose.

"It is not that simple."

"It is that simple. If you have a sick cow, you call Doc Bartlett."

"And, if Doc Bartlett cannot make it or cannot help, what do you do, put the cow down? You cannot do that with a wife."

"And what am I supposed to do? You've seen what she does. I can't trust her." He scowled with his jaw clenched, and Vasili realised he would not convince George to change his mind.

"You can come or not come, Vasili. That's up to you." He threw the halter over Gust's ears and led him over to the sleigh. "We leave in an hour."

The weathered exterior of George's house was the brown of

an old shoe against the white landscape. Vasili crunched through snow on his way back. Rusted machinery parts jutted out of the ground and blended with the west wall. The chopping block, beside the hen house, sat besmeared with blood and feathers from the beheading of last night's chicken, the axe tossed off to one side. And it was quiet, unnaturally quiet, without a hum of wind.

"She's gone," Mary said as he entered the kitchen.

"Gone where?" Vasili felt a stone drop into his gut.

"Just a minute ago, I went in to wake her. The bed was slept in, but empty." Mary took his arm and pulled him to the window. "I thought she was in the outhouse." She pointed. "But it snowed yesterday. See—no fresh tracks. Then I noticed the tracks out past the well. George's good coat is missing and the socks I hung to dry last night are gone." Mary tugged on Vasili's sleeve. "You'd better call George. I think she's run off yonder."

"It must be thirty below zero." Vasili wrestled with panic. Then he rushed to the back door, opened it and hollered, "George, you need to come inside. Katya's run away."

Minutes later, George appeared in the doorway. He stomped his feet and clumps of snow skittered across the floor. "What's going on?"

Mary repeated her account of the last few minutes, pointing out the window at the tracks.

"What in the hell is wrong with her?" George thumped the

heel of his hand on the wall so hard the room shook.

"What is wrong with you?" Vasili stepped closer to his son-in-law. "I told you it was a bad idea to take her away. She must have heard you talk about it. Now, look what you've caused."

"She can't have gotten far." George marched to the door. "The drifts in that field are high. I'll get the snowshoes and go find her." He grabbed his shotgun from the corner.

"What do you need that for?" Vasili's hands curled into fists. Was he searching for her or hunting her?

"The wolves woke me, howling, early this morning."

"I'm coming too," Vasili said.

"Me too." Mary scooted to a wooden box by the stove and dug through a pile of footwear. She pulled out a pair of knee-high Indian moccasins. "You might need extra help if she's gone and hurt herself."

George grunted and stomped to the door. "Suit yourselves. I'm leaving now."

Mary forced Vasili to stop long enough to put on his fur-lined cap and George's leather mittens. "No sense you risking your life too," she said. "If we find her and she's hurt, you'll need your strength."

By the time Vasili and Mary bundled up and stepped outside, George was a furlong into the field.

The imprint left by George's snowshoes had packed the snow for them. Mary slogged ahead, a rotund bundle of sweaters and scarves and overcoats. Vasili followed in her footfall, finding it difficult to keep up with the younger woman even though each step must have been an effort for her, the snow up past her knees in the higher drifts.

"Do you think the wolves present a threat?" Vasili asked. He pushed a vision of Katya's mangled and bloodied body out of his head.

"Biggest risk is freezing to death," Mary said. "It's warmer today, but not toasty. Good thing she had the sense to dress up, because being sensible is not your daughter's strong suit. The greatcoat and socks will help, but only a fool goes traipsing out in winter weather alone. There's not a farmhouse within twenty miles in that direction."

Vasili didn't speak, reserving his energy for the path ahead, but his thoughts would not turn off. What would he do if they did not find her? He could not bear the idea. She had to be safe. They would find her.

Mary slowed her pace, her breathing laboured. "This is hard work."

Vasili wanted to urge her to hurry. He thought only of his Katya, alone in this vast wilderness. He'd failed her once again. A few tears dripped onto his cheek and into his moustache.

They trudged in silence for a while, following the snowshoe tracks. The sun was out, a cold sun in a cold sky. But at least they weren't stumbling along in the dark as Katya must have done.

An hour passed. George was now a black stick on the horizon. Vasili glanced back to the house, shrunk in the distance. The only sounds were their joint laborious panting and Mary's moccasins whomping on the snow.

She stopped, puffing. "Have to rest for a minute."

Vasili offered his arm. "Okay, but not too long."

Mary leaned on him for a moment. "You're right. Best to not stay still. My toes are getting numb in these moccasins."

Vasili tried wiggling his toes and couldn't feel them.

Then, a single shot of gunfire cracked the air. The piercing sound torpedoed Vasili's ears. He saw George on a knoll ahead, the gun hoisted above his shoulders. Vasili sprinted forward.

As he ran, George grew larger. He could barely breathe, but continued to run, as if his legs had taken control of his brain, his long, thin ancient legs launched into a marathon. He stopped two feet away from George.

Katya, his little bird, lay on her back in the snow, eyes closed, coat unbuttoned and thrown open, her face the whitest white, blue fingers clasped together on her chest.

George stood there clutching his gun, expressionless. "She's gone, Vasili. I'm sorry."

Vasili dropped to his knees beside his daughter.

Mary came up behind him. "Is she?"

"She has no pulse. She's not breathing," George said.

"It might be hard to get a pulse on her wrist." Mary bent and laid her fingers on either side of Katya's windpipe and held them there for several minutes. Then she Ḧopped on the ground next to Katya, opened the two coats she was wearing, and pulled the younger woman into an embrace. "She's not dead. The blasted cold has slowed her heart."

Looking up sternly, Mary barked orders. "George, you get back and bring the toboggan and a big pile of blankets. Vasili, you get on the other side of her. Open your parka and snuggle in —we need to warm her up, but not too quickly. Too fast and she might have a heart attack."

So, Vasili laid in the snow up against his daughter, willing the heat out of his body and into hers. He could not allow her to die. He'd die himself before he let that happen. A crow circled overhead.

Epilogue

The damp cold of late February in New York seeps through the bandages and into bones of my fingers, even those bones of the four fingers that now only exist in my mind. The spirit of Niccolò Paganini no longer inhabits these hands. Ghosts shy away from deformity.

Yes, we are in New York. When Papa sets out to do something, he makes sure it happens, even if it means smuggling a half-crazed daughter out of her chloroform-ridden hospital room.

Sergei Rachmaninoff, Papa's friend, found us a place to live and signed up students for Papa straight away. Our apartment looks out onto a bustling street. Black umbrellas float on the sidewalk below. The doorbell chimes and I hear Papa greet one of his pupils. Some days I go into the music room and watch from the corner chair. Today I'll stay in my bedroom. The metronome begins its tick, tick, tick, and unpracticed fingers plunk a few awkward notes before Papa's gentle voice interrupts. He hums the tune and says, "You see?" and I can't help but smile.

My violin sits on display atop my bureau cushioned by a thick embroidered cloth that's prettified with red and purple patterns. I keep the instrument out of the case to look at, and the sight of it makes me stronger every day. I'm not yet able to touch it. In a week the doctor removes these bandage mittens from my hands.

It will take practice, but I will play again. I must perform again. If Niccolò Paganini could enchant his audience using a single string, I can surely do as well or better, impaired only by two lost fingers on each hand. By next year I should be prepared. I'll be on stage at the Metropolitan Opera House. Here, in the city, they call it the Met.

Sergei tells us Antonio has returned to Moscow. I'm now convinced he was never the spirit of Niccolò Paganini. That was simply a figment of my imagination—one of my apparitions. Even the spectre of Niccolò would never abandon his music like that. I'm glad Antonio left. Now, nothing will distract me from my plans. Sergei said he lasted only two months at the Met, 'A little problem with the drink.' Papa says not to worry about Antonio. He'll stay safe in Russia because he wasn't bourgeois born.

I glance down the street to the intersection and see a crow perched on a lamppost. These creatures are not sorcerous or special in New York. They are simply birds.

Acknowledgements

This book has travelled a long rocky road—from the futon I slept on in the dining room at Linda Wright and Chase Harris's place in 2001, to Green College at UBC during Booming Ground the following year. There, under the eye of Gail Anderson Dargatz, plus fellow pupils, Ann Birch, Annette Yourke, and Caroline Gleeson, it morphed and changed. Next it slumbered in the bottom drawer and underwent a page-curling operation. More recently, Lara Sleath and Nancy Baye treated the reworked novel to a keen editorial probe.

To first readers, Elizabeth Boyd, and Jackie Bateman—thank you. My gratitude pours out to everyone who has nudged this novel along on its journey.

I must also thank my late grandmother, Etta May Hislop. Spry to the age of 101, she loved to talk, and regaled us with her many and detailed stories of life on the Saskatchewan prairie in the 1920s.

While plenty of books helped me to understand music, mental illness, and the link between creativity and the mind, four of them proved invaluable. An antiquated hardcover entitled, "Music" by C.C. Spencer assisted with terminology. Two fabulous publications by Kay Redfield Jamison, "Touched with Fire" and "An Unquiet Mind," rescued me countless times. Intimate chronicles in Patty Duke's "A Brilliant Madness," offered a rare and unique perspective on psychological issues.

As always, thanks to my husband, Karl, for his infinite patience.

About the Author

Laurel Mae Hislop

Laurel lives and writes in Vancouver, British Columbia, Canada. Her collection of short stories, Chitchat was short-listed by the Whistler Independent Book Awards in 2016. This is her first novel.

Visit Laurel's website @ https://mannamarkbooks.com